LITTLE BOXES

LITTLE BOXES

ROBERT COBURN

The New Atlantian Library

THE NEW ATLANTIAN LIBRARY
is an imprint of
ABSOLUTELY AMAZING eBOOKS

Published by Whiz Bang LLC, 926 Truman Avenue, Key West, Florida 33040, USA.

For information contact:
Publisher@AbsolutelyAmazingEbooks.com

ISBN-13: 978-0692327180
ISBN-10: 0692327185

Other Books by Robert Coburn

A Loose Knot (A Jack Hunter Mystery)
A Deadly Decption
The Pink Gun (A Jack Hunter Mystery)

A word of appreciation to my wife for her help in making this book possible. She initially suggested that I write the story. And kept me on track throughout. She is my first reader and demanding editor. Thank you, Laura.

And thanks to my publisher, Shirrel Rhoades, who gave the go ahead on this project.

LITTLE BOXES

AUTHOR'S NOTE

Passover Lane runs for one long block along the southwest side of Key West Cemetery, separated from the cemetery by a tall wrought-iron fence. Immediately on the other side of that fence lies an unbroken row of 43 sad little graves--children who all died within seven years of each other, from early 1963 through 1970. Twenty-nine lived less than 24 hours, others lived only a few weeks or months. In one year alone--1965--thirteen infants died, though there was no epidemic or natural disaster, such as a hurricane, at the time. The row also includes nine undated small graves.

These are facts. The story that follows is strictly fictional and is not meant to suggest the true reason for these untimely deaths.

1965

The coffin was twenty-four inches long. Blue in color and adorned with lace. It weighed about thirty pounds. An unbelievably heavy load for any man to carry.

Nonetheless, Stephen Reynolds bore the little box containing the body of his newborn son from the hearse across the grassy expanse of the cemetery. Family members waited silently at the gravesite next to Passover Lane.

The child had died suddenly on the day following his birth. His name was Charles.

Charles had been born at home, the birth assisted by a midwife. The local doctor had looked in on the mother and infant the next day, at which time the baby began suffering spontaneous hemorrhaging. The physician was unable to save his life.

Stephen arrived at the gathering, where the funeral director took the coffin from him and placed it by the grave. Martha Reynolds, the mother of Charles, screamed and fainted. She was helped back to their car, which was parked inside the cemetery. The service, now even briefer, continued to its end.

Sprays of flowers, some fresher than others, covered adjacent graves. Before too long, though, an even greater profusion of grave flowers would line that stretch of Passover Lane.

1937

The telephone rang just as she was about to reach a climax, its intrusive jangle causing an involuntary thrust of her pelvis against her partner's. She cried out in pleasure. Her partner came.

"Don't answer it," she gasped.

"I have to."

Dr. Claude Ranzoa rolled off of his wife and reached for the telephone sitting on the bedside table.

"Yes?" he said, breathing heavily into the receiver. "Okay, I'll be there as soon as I can."

He replaced the phone onto its cradle and sat up on the side of the bed.

"There's an emergency at the clinic," he explained. "I've got to dress."

He leaned down and kissed his wife.

"I'm sorry," he said and smiled.

"That's all right, Claude."

Victoria Ranzoa pulled the covers up to her chin and returned the smile.

"Do you think you'll be very long?" she asked.

"I don't know. I'll call you from there."

He went to the bathroom and then proceeded to get dressed.

~~~

The Ranzoa house was an elaborate classical residence that had been built in the late 1800s by Ernest Ternant Ranzoa, a prominent attorney. Ernest had two children, Samuel and Claude. The boys' mother died in

1908 of unknown causes and they were raised by their father and a series of nannies.

Samuel, the oldest, followed his father into law. Claude became interested in medicine.

Samuel married into an old Key West family and the couple produced three children, a daughter, Louise, and two sons, Samuel, Jr. and Robert Ternant. Claude was to come to marriage later in life.

After graduating from medical school in Atlanta, Claude returned to Key West and set up a practice on William Street. He moved back to the family home on Caroline. His father died two years later. At the probating of the will, Claude was left only the now-empty house in its entirety. The rest of the estate, including several other properties, went to Samuel.

The successful but still single doctor eventually met Victoria Tabor, a vivacious young woman fifteen years his junior, at a party given by one of the survivors of the 1935 hurricane. Victoria's family was from West Virginia. They'd come to Florida to work on the railroad. Claude and Victoria married in 1936.

~~~

"Robert!" Claude said in surprise, seeing his nephew standing at the front door just as he opened it to leave for the clinic.

"Uncle Claude!" Robert grinned. "I was just in the neighborhood. Thought I'd drop in and say hello to you and Aunt Victoria. But I see you're on the way out."

"Ah, yes, have an emergency call at the clinic. But you go on in. Victoria will like the company, poor little thing. I won't be too long."

Claude turned and shouted. "Victoria! Robert's here. Come down if you're decent."

"I wouldn't want to impose," Robert said.

"Nothing of the sort. You can keep her company while I'm away."

"Be down in a minute," Victoria called from upstairs.

She hastily dabbed on some lipstick and sprayed a poof of cologne on her neck. Then she wrapped herself in a robe and came downstairs.

"Robert," she greeted. "So nice of you to come by. Go into the parlor. I'll make us some tea."

Victoria bussed her husband on the cheek and closed the door after him.

Robert was in his twenties and already a man-about-town in Key West. The reputation included that of being a ladies man as well.

Victoria liked Robert. While she was devoted to Claude, it was fun to occasionally be with someone more her age. Claude realized this and was happy to have Robert there.

"Claude said that you might be going up to Tallahassee next week," Victoria chirped as she entered the parlor. "Will you be as naughty there as I hear you are in our little town?"

She leaned over to place the tea service on a table in front of the sofa where Robert sat. Her robe fell open, exposing her nude body.

He reached up, cupping her breast, and with the other hand pulled her to him.

Claude returned from the clinic later that evening. Victoria was already in bed. He quietly looked in, and seeing that she was asleep, went downstairs to do some work.

Nine months later Victoria gave birth to twins, a boy and a girl.

CHAPTER 1

"You see, Jack, you know who's in trouble when you talk to the delivery truck."

"Uh-huh, and that's why we should make an offer on this Vesuvius joint. Because the truck touted it?"

"You're missing the point about the joint, hee-hee."

Billy Bean got up from the table to make a fresh pot of coffee. Jack Hunter had gotten into town the night before and was still on West Coast time. He and Billy were partners in the Inedible Café. Jack had flown in from LA and had gone straight from the airport to his house on Ashe Street in hope of getting a good night's sleep, but his mind had busied itself with worry nearly until dawn.

"What might that point be?" Jack yawned.

"Here's how it works, Jack," Billy said from over by the coffeemaker. "I know most of the fellows that service the restaurants in Key West. I mean the guys who drive the semis. When a restaurant starts cutting back on its orders or buying cheaper stuff, it means business is falling off. But they still got to make the overhead. So they don't buy top of the line anymore. Choice cuts, fresh produce. Things like that. Drop it down a level or two. Still charge their customers the same price as before. People get on to that. Start noticing they're spending big only it's not as good as it used to be. "

Billy returned to the table and refilled Jack's cup. The restaurant was empty, the last breakfast customers having cleared out.

"Hell, Jack, I know when a place is going down before the owner does, hee-hee."

"Okay, Billy, it's just I never thought about expanding the Inedible Café. I mean, well, adding the bar was a great idea and all. And it's working out fine. But what? Take on another restaurant? I'd like to think a little more about that."

"Take all the time you need, Jack. But leave enough for us to do something."

~ ~ ~

Jack decided to walk back home from the restaurant. The distance took up a good piece of the two-by-four mile island that was Key West. It was still early enough to beat the humidity. Best time of day, hands down.

He'd taken Olivia Street to Windsor Lane. The cemetery lay ahead. Oddly, there were fond memories for him here. Long ago, when he'd first arrived in Key West, a different man in a different place, he had found solace in this peaceful venue. He turned left on Windsor Lane and headed toward the main entrance on Passover Lane.

His wandering on the grounds led him to a row of tiny graves. He read the inscriptions on some of the headstones. They were all children. Infants even. And so many. A sudden sadness fell over him and he hurried across the cemetery to the Frances Street gate.

Back at his house, and now strangely tired, he fell asleep on the sofa. Unsettling dreams floated through the shadows of his mind, whispers in unfamiliar rooms came from behind locked doors.

He awoke feeling chilled and his body clammy. It was early afternoon and getting hot. He'd been asleep for nearly three hours. Distant thunder rumbled in the Gulf.

~~~

Key West Bight looked the same as he'd left it. But with one small difference. Astrid Kelly's sailboat, *Justice*, was no longer in port. Astrid had sailed south right before Jack, himself, had flown back to Los Angeles.

Actually, Astrid being gone made a *big* difference to Jack. Once, he'd considered her a friend and had hopes of their relationship turning into something deeper. What it did turn out to be was one of duplicity on Astrid's part and toxic for him.

Old flames were fanned anew, however, when she'd shown up unexpectedly on opening night at the Undrinkable Bar. Flames soon to be doused, however.

Jack had walked from Ashe Street over to and down Grinnell, dead-ending at the Bight. It felt good to be in the sun after his disturbing dreams. A breeze kicked up and the sky darkened, offering slight relief from the humidity.

Thunder cracked after a bolt of lightning struck the horizon. A sudden pelting rain cleared the boardwalk, everybody crowding into the nearest bar.

Jack had been beside Schooner Wharf when the storm hit and he ducked inside. He was lucky enough to grab an empty stool at the bar before the place filled up. He ordered a beer.

The rain drummed loudly on the canvas roof, then began to die off and, in a wink, the sun was out again. But not before Front Street had been flooded to the sidewalk.

Jack nursed his beer, his thoughts returning to the cemetery and the children's graves. Something was wrong there. He didn't know what but he intended to find out. But where would he start? He took out his cellphone. The phone rested in a stainless steel case. A similar case had once saved his life. He dialed Alice Devereux, a private detective he'd worked with before, after her sex-change operation who owned the Conch Detective Agency.

"You back in town, honey?" Alice answered.

"How'd you know it was me?"

"Modern times, baby. Caller ID."

Jack had always been hopelessly naive about technology. He actually still owned a fountain pen.

"Look, Alice, I was wondering if we could have dinner tonight? Something I'd like to run past you."

"Sure thing, Jack. Where did you have in mind?"

"There's a place Billy told me about. The Vesuvius. You know where it is?"

"Yeah, but maybe you might want to give that another think."

"That so? Well, I like to try it anyway. Around eight?"

"See you there."

~~~

The Vesuvius was located on upper Duval Street in what was once an old Key West home. Probably the nicest thing about it was the back deck, which offered an unobstructed view of the sky and a million stars on a clear night.

"How'd you like the pasta?" Alice asked Jack, one eyebrow cocked.

"Overdone," Jack answered. "The shrimp were dry, what there were of them, and they must've cooked them in burnt motor oil."

"Didn't I say?" Alice smirked.

"Yeah, well, I'll write it off. Look, what I wanted to talk with you about is going to sound kind of crazy."

"I love it when you talk crazy, honey," Alice laughed.

"I'm serious," Jack said somberly. "It has to do with something I saw at the cemetery. You ever been there?"

"Not lately," Alice told him. "I hear it's pretty dead."

"Right, and everybody's dying to get in, too. I know all the old jokes, Alice. This is about something else, okay?"

"I'm sorry, Jack. Go ahead."

Jack refilled Alice's wine glass and topped off his own. There were no other diners. They had the place to themselves. Even traffic was slow outside on Duval.

"There is a children's section. It's to the right when you enter the main gate on Passover Lane. It runs along the fence all the way up to the intersection at Windsor Lane."

"That's so sad," Alice said quietly. "Children's sections. I've never liked those places. Always have some kind of angelic name. Like it was a damn nursery."

"A lot of the graves are in poor condition. A few are even unmarked. But here's the thing. It seems like an inordinate number of them died over a short period of time. I'm talking about a couple of years. One year in particular. Something's not right."

"Hold it a moment, Jack. Go back to why you were at the cemetery in the first place."

"I sometimes go to the cemetery just to clear my head, you know? It's peaceful and kind of interesting to read the old headstones. I got on to it the first time I was in Key West. Anyway I was there yesterday and kind of stumbled onto the children's part. But here's my question. Why so many infant deaths?"

"I can't answer that, Jack. Maybe there was some kind of epidemic. When did you say this happened?"

"The most occurred in 1965. I haven't counted them yet. Think I'll go back and do that tomorrow. Epidemic, huh? Wonder how I could find out?"

"Check with the health department. Or maybe the library. It'd have a history of the island."

"Good idea. You wouldn't be interested in nosing around, would you?"

"I don't think so, Jack. Tell you why. I believe you're going to find that there's nothing sinister going on. There'll be a perfectly good reason why those poor kids passed so early. And if it turns out not to be, well, that would be a something for the cops. The other reason is that I'm going to be out of town for awhile."

"Too bad," Jack said. "Think I could use your help."

He looked around for the waiter to bring the check and, seeing no one in sight, got up and went inside to get it himself. Add indifferent service to the list.

CHAPTER 2

The present Key West cemetery came into being in 1847. The original, located in the southern part of the island, had been washed away by a hurricane the previous year. Graves of the wealthy and prominent were marked by impressive monuments that were shipped here. Locally-made markers were generally brick or cement. Symbols on the headstones have meaning, and provide insight into that resident's life. An anchor would mean hope. Oak leaves suggested strength. A lamb or a cherub signified the death of a child.

Jack had gotten up with the chickens, which in Key West isn't a difficult thing to do. The birds seldom sleep. The house next door to him harbored a particularly vocal rooster that upstaged the sunrise every morning.

A rosy dawn brightened into a sky as clear as a martini. After a quick shower and a cup of coffee, Jack threw on a t-shirt and a pair of shorts. And was out of the house and into the cool freshness of the beginning day.

The cemetery opened at 7:00 and Jack was at the gates as they were unlocked by one of the staff.

"Good morning," he greeted the man. "Looks like it's going to be another beautiful day in you know where."

"Going to be hotter'n hell, if you ask me," the man told him.

Jack walked to the children's section.

Today he'd brought a notepad and pen with him and, starting with the first child's grave, a cement box standing above the ground and about three feet wide by four feet wide with a slab on top, wrote down the child's name and dates of birth and death. He continued recording each tiny grave until he'd reached the last site at the cemetery's First Avenue.

He had counted fifty-six marked and inscribed graves along the row that lined the fence. There were also a number of other stones that bore no words.

The sun climbed to a higher position and drew a bead on Jack. The man at the gate had been right. It was going to be hotter'n Hell.

Jack left the cemetery and continued walking down Margaret Street toward the Key West Bight. He didn't know what he would do with the information he'd gathered.

Rather than continuing to the Bight, he changed his mind mid-course and turned left at Southard Street toward the Key West Library, which was on the corner at Elizabeth. Perhaps their research department could help him.

The air conditioning enfolded him in a chilling embrace as soon as he walked through the door. A welcome relief from the increasing heat outside.

"I was wondering if you have any records of Key West during the 'sixties?" he asked the librarian.

"Would that be the 1960s or the 1860s?" a young woman said with a small smile.

"The 1960s," Jack smiled back.

"And what is it that you're looking for?"

"I'm not sure," Jack said. "Actually, I guess I want to know if there was any kind of epidemic or something around then."

"Well, I'm not familiar with anything like that happening, but you might check with our historian. His office is back by the rear entrance. Oh, I forgot. He's on vacation."

"Don't suppose there's anyone else, is there?" Jack said disappointedly.

"Let me think a minute," the girl said, glancing around the room. "Ah, yes, Leon is here. He knows everything. Nice man. Kind of our unofficial historian. Come with me. I'll introduce you."

She motioned for Jack to follow.

"Leon, how are you this morning?" she greeted an older man seated at a reading table. "This gentleman is looking for some information about Key West. I wonder if you could give him a few minutes?"

Leon looked up and smiled.

"Be glad to," he said.

"I'm Jack Hunter."

"Leon Frankel. Have a seat. What can I do for you?"

"The lady mentioned that you might be able to answer a question I have. What I want to know is, was there an epidemic or a hurricane or something that took place around the mid-nineteen sixties in Key West?"

"No, nothing like that. I think we probably had a few storms but nothing too serious. Why do you ask?"

"Well, this is probably silly but I was at the Key West cemetery recently and I noticed all these children's graves where they were buried during that time. I wondered what could have happened to them. The yellow fever thing was over by then, right?"

Leon leaned back in his chair.

"Lot of history in the cemetery," he said. "That's my hobby, Key West history. I'm sort of an informal historian. Funny, I go to the cemetery often but I've never paid that much attention to the children's section. Yes, to answer your question, yellow fever was finished long before the 1960s. I can't say that anything like an epidemic has occurred here since. One thing, our population was much larger at that time due to the military build-up during the Cuban crisis. Normally, we are around twenty-five thousand. Then, it was more like fifty-thousand. All those young Navy wives with time on their hands got pregnant and had babies, I guess."

"Well, that would keep them busy," Jack laughed. "The infants that died, you're saying they were from military families. Were they all buried there?"

"I don't know. People who were temporarily assigned to duty in Key West wouldn't have had family plots in the cemetery. That's why the children's area runs along beside the fence, I suppose. But I wouldn't be surprised that some families suffering the loss of a child would have had that little body sent home to be buried there."

"Then, there also could be more children's graves from that period of time in family plots, is that right?"

"Well, certainly there could be. You would have to check with the sexton at the cemetery. He might have a record of that. Otherwise, look into the Monroe County registry."

"Yeah, that's a good idea. You know, I counted thirteen graves from 1965 alone along that fence. All infants. Don't you think that's a lot of early deaths for one year? I mean, especially if you're saying that number doesn't even include those that might be buried elsewhere around the cemetery or the country."

"You asked if there had been an epidemic," Leon sighed. "There wasn't." Then added reluctantly, "Of course, there are always rumors."

"Rumors?" Jack repeated. "What kind of rumors?"

"Ask around, my friend. This is Key West. Everybody's got a story with a different answer for everything. Sorry I couldn't be of more help."

Jack thanked Leon for his time, and leaving the coolness of the library, he made his way to the coffee house on Southard.

~~~

The coffee shop was just off Duval. A comfortable little place that served good pastries and coffee anyway you wanted it. It also served up the latest gossip.

Jack ordered a latte and took a seat on one of the sofas. He was the only customer there. Someone had left a copy of the *Key West Citizen* on the table. He picked it up. Nothing of too much interest inside. His latte was ready and he got up to get it. Returning to the sofa, he spotted a bulletin board and stopped to read the notices pinned to it. One caught his attention. *Historic Key West Cemetery Stroll*. It was scheduled for tomorrow morning. The piece further stated that there would be presenters at different gravesites to give the history of those buried there.

Perhaps they could shed some light on the children's site, Jack thought to himself.

He headed back to his house on Ashe Street.

~~~

It was late afternoon before Jack had completed listing the children's graves in chronological order. The large number of burials started in 1963 and continued until 1972, but one year – 1965 – stood out starkly. Thirteen infants died and were buried that year. Again, he'd wondered if there could possibly be more little souls laid to rest elsewhere in the Key West cemetery. And what of those buried out of state? There was that possibility to consider as well. His mind ever more burdened with each new discovery.

He'd also taken care of another worrisome piece of business. He had called his oncologist, Dr. Jessica Skye, at the UCLA Medical Center. During a routine physical exam, a blood test had revealed that Jack had a very low platelet count. These were small cells involved in clotting. The low count could mean anything. Including cancer. Dr. Skye had told Jack not to worry about it. They'd run some more tests to find out what was going on. But it was a smoking gun, she had warned.

The test he'd called about today was an important one, the last of a series the doctor had ordered. He was anxious to know what they'd found out. But there would be no joy, or otherwise, for him today. The lab hadn't returned the results to the doctor. And even more deviling, it was now the weekend and he would have to wait until Monday. Smoking gun. But don't worry. Yeah.

CHAPTER 3

"Got a nice quiche on the bar menu, Jack. Don't see quiche served in most bars, hee-hee."

Jack occupied a stool at the Undrinkable Bar. Billy stood next to him. It was early and the bar was empty. One couple sat at a table in the dining area.

"Not too hungry tonight, Billy. Maybe later. I'll stick with the wine for now."

Billy had poured Jack a glass of Cakebread Cabernet Sauvigon from the Napa Valley. Billy was partial to California wines though he wouldn't turn down certain French labels.

"I think you're right about Vesuvius," Jack said. "They're in trouble."

"Didn't I say?" Billy chuckled. "Start cutting back and it's just a matter of time."

"Yeah, well, Alice and I had two over-cooked entrees for ninety-five bucks plus another forty-five for a bottle of cheap-chuck red. Service was nothing to write home about, either."

"Pretty place, though, ain't it, Jack?"

"The backyard is great."

Another couple entered the restaurant and Billy turned his attention toward them.

"Gotta run, Jack. Customers waiting. Give 'em something to write home about, hee-hee."

"Sure. Later on I'd like to talk with you about another subject, okay?"

"Right, we going to have to make a decision soon about that Vesuvius. Glad you on board with it."

Jack waved him off. On board? He hadn't given the restaurant a second thought. He took a sip of wine. It was pleasant. Billy did know his stuff.

Unanswerable questions and serious concerns weighed heavily on Jack's mind. The children in the cemetery, puzzle pieces dumped out on a table to be put together without a picture to go by. And now a reason for a worrying question closer to home, and depending on the answer, one of greater concern. His test results being delayed. The smoking gun continued to loom.

The bartender showed up.

"Hey, Jack," she greeted. "Billy took care of you, I see. Sorry I was late. Damn car had a dead battery. Seems I left the headlights on. So mad I could spit."

Jean Thornton had started tending bar at the Undrinkable Bar right after it'd opened at the Inedible Café. She was a personable lady and an attractive one.

"Seems on time to me," Jack said. "Key West time is any time as long as it's good. Car okay now?"

"Yeah, guys down at Larry's, that's where I get my car serviced, well, they're the sweetest bunch you'd ever want to know. They came right over and jump-started my old wreck. And I was on my way in no time. Isn't that just so nice? You playing tonight?"

"No, left my sax at home," Jack smiled.

"Too bad, I love your music," she said, refilling Jack's glass.

"Thanks," Jack said. "Let me ask you something. You've lived in Key West for awhile. You ever hear of anything strange about some babies buried at the cemetery?"

"Oh, you must mean the story about the monster doctors," Jean laughed. "It's nothing. Good for telling at Halloween."

"Monster doctors? What's that have to do with those kids?"

"I don't know if it really happened but there was supposed to have been these two doctors that treated all those kids buried out there that died. It's probably another Key West rumor thing. There's all kinds of crazy stuff people talk about down here. Made up mostly and the nuttier the better."

"Yeah, you're right about that," Jack laughed. "I've heard a few of them."

"You going to eat, Jack?" Jean asked, wiping down the bar.

"No, think I'll finish this and maybe head home. Make it an early night. Still on West Coast time. The walk will get me ready for bed."

~~~

Even the best of intentions occasionally fall short. Jack made it as far as Duval Street before hailing a taxi.

"Pier House, please," he told the driver.

"You want the Duval tour?" the man asked. "Or should I cut over to Simonton and save some time."

"Might as well do Duval," Jack said. "The night's young."

Duval Street was unusually quiet and they didn't catch a traffic light until Eaton. Then it began to crawl.

"Drop me at Green Street and you can pick up those folks," Jack said. He'd spotted a couple standing in front of Sloppy Joe's signaling for a cab.

"You got it, bud," the cabbie said, pulling over smoothly.

Jack got out of the taxi and joined the Lower Duval promenade. In no time he was in the Chart Room.

The floor was covered with peanut shells dropped there by the last drinking shift. Jack went over to the barrel standing by the popcorn machine and filled a bowl with nuts for himself.

"Bud Lite," he told the bartender. "Kind of quiet tonight. Been that way long?"

"Place emptied about twenty minutes ago. Pick up later."

Jack nodded. His eyes fell on the small placards in the edge of the bar. Each little brass plate held the name of the person whose ashes had been placed in a hole drilled there. A mausoleum of sorts. Jack had seen them before. He'd thought being interred in a bar was a great idea. Always around for happy hour, he'd joked. At the moment, however, he wasn't much in the mood for jokes.

He slapped down a fiver on the bar, scooped out the remaining peanuts from the bowl and left. Cutting through the Pier House parking lot, he picked up Simonton and took it up to Angela and then to where Windsor Lane doglegged into Passover Lane and the Key West Cemetery. He paused by the cemetery fence. The children lay on the other side.

He was unaware of how long he'd lingered on the sidewalk staring at graves beyond, until a passing chill brought him back to the moment and he continued on Ashe Street and home.

CHAPTER 4

Sunlight had filled the bedroom when Jack awakened with a start, a disturbing dream silently closing the door and slipping out the back of his mind. He sat up quickly and saw it was past eight o'clock. He'd either slept through the rooster's wakeup call or, better yet, something had happened to the damn bird. Now he had to hurry.

He showered, dressed, wolfed down a slice of cold pizza from the refrigerator and was out of the house in thirty minutes flat.

People were already gathering at the cemetery when he arrived. A number of bicycles lined the fence at the main gate. And inside he could see a small group standing in front of the U.S.S. Maine Monument. A lady was setting up an information booth at the entrance. He approached her.

"Good morning," he greeted.

"Hi," she said. "Are you here for the tour?"

"No, I'm just going to wander around. But maybe you could help me with a question. It's about all those children's graves."

Jack motioned toward the fence to the right of the entrance.

"I noticed a lot of them died during one year in particular," he continued. "Was there something special that happened back in the 1960s?"

"Well, it is sad, isn't it," the woman nodded. "I'm not familiar with all the dates. But there was no disease that I ever heard about taking place then. Children got sick. The island was sort of isolated. Medical treatment wasn't as good as it is now. Could be anything, I guess."

"Still, that's kind of hard to believe. All those children. I mean, somebody should have known something, don't you think?"

Another group of visitors stopped at the booth.

"Excuse me," the woman said to Jack. "I've got to take care of these folks."

She gave each person a pamphlet and directed them to another woman who'd be their escort during the tour.

"Well, there is one story," she said, returning to Jack. "Some people say the children were treated by a couple of doctors. And that they were either incompetent or Lord knows what. I certainly don't know. That was before my time."

"That's incredible," Jack said quietly. "Were the doctors ever charged?"

"I don't believe so. I understand they eventually moved away."

"Amazing. Do you know their names?"

"Armand and Ardell Ranzoa. They were twins from an old Key West family. In fact, some of the family still live here."

"No kidding? And nobody ever tried to do anything about it? The doctors, I mean. Prosecute them, that kind of thing."

"Like I said, it was just a rumor," the woman told him. "And a very nasty one. The Ranzoas were, and still are today, a respectable family."

"What about the doctors?" Jack asked. "Are they still alive?"

"That I wouldn't know," the woman said impatiently, now anxious to get off the subject. "Here come some more guests. I really have to attend to them."

"Thank you," Jack smiled.

He left the woman and wandered over to the children's graves. Another person was there. A middle-aged man. He was squatted down at one small slab and had placed a bouquet of flowers on top of it. He stood as Jack came up.

"Beautiful day for the cemetery tour," Jack said.

"Yeah, the Preservation Society got lucky," the man laughed. "Last time was a downpour."

"Are you part of the tour?" Jack asked.

"No, just paying my respects."

"Oh, I'm sorry," Jack said, gesturing to the tiny grave. "Didn't mean to intrude. Is this a relative?"

"She was my baby sister."

"That must be tough," Jack said. "I never had a sister or a brother."

"Well, I never got to know her. None of us did. As you can see, she only lived for a couple of days."

"I've noticed a number of graves here where the children died within days or weeks of their births," Jack commented. "Wonder what went wrong?"

"There's a story. I've never been able to find out whether or not it has any substance. Mostly rumors. Concerns a couple of doctors. Again, I don't put any stock in what some folks say happened. I was pretty young at the time myself."

"Would those doctors be the Ranzoas?" Jack asked. "The lady at the tent over there mentioned that name."

The man looked down at the grave and let out a heavy breath.

"Like I said, I was young when Grace died. That was my little sister's name. Grace. I'm Henry Overmeyer, by the way."

"Glad to meet you, Henry," Jack said, sticking out his hand. "Jack Hunter."

"That sounds familiar. You in politics or something?"

"No, nothing like that," Jack smiled.

"Well, as I was about to say," Henry began anew, "she was having difficulty breathing. Apparently, she'd been born with premature lungs. So my parents took her to the doctor's office. There were two doctors. And you're right, they were the Ranzoas. Armand and Ardell. Brother and sister. Had taken over their dad's practice. Funny how both became doctors. Anyway, Armand was the one who saw her. While she was there, Grace went into cardiac arrest. Doctor Armand couldn't revive her."

"My God," Jack said incredulously. "A heart attack? She was just a little thing."

"That's what my folks thought. But there it was. What can you say?"

"Would an autopsy have shown what happened?" Jack wondered aloud.

"There was no autopsy," Henry Overmeyer said firmly. "How could you have an autopsy done on such a tiny child. It wouldn't have been right."

"No, I supposed it wouldn't have."

"I heard that the two doctors left town," Jack said. "Does anyone know where they went?"

"I wouldn't know about that," Henry said. "Doubt if anyone does. The family is very private."

A flight of ibises that had been resting on the power lines strung above Passover Lane glided down to the cemetery, landing just beyond where the two men stood. They immediately went to work flushing out insects hidden in the grass.

Jack wished Henry Overmyer a good day and left him with his little sister. He wandered over the cemetery's Fourth Avenue, passing several groups of visitors along the way. Soon he was alone in a quieter section. A few feet ahead of him a large iguana lizard, who'd been enjoying a moment in the sun, ducked into its burrow beneath a broken concrete slab.

He had hoped to discover more children's graves in the family plots but it was becoming a daunting task as the sun rose higher and the humidity increased. He would save that for another day. One less crowded, too. The cemetery was filling up with the living as more people joined the tours.

Jack exited the cemetery through the Frances Street gate. He passed a group of artists busily painting in plein aire on the corner of Angela. He stopped for a moment. The subject of their work was the cute little house standing across the street from them. He wouldn't have minded owning the painting one of them was doing but couldn't figure out how to ask without insulting the others. He moved on.

This business with the cemetery was verging on obsession. He had to either do something about it or forget the entire thing. Well, he wasn't going to forget it, so what *was* he going to do?

He continued down Frances, passing by stunningly beautiful houses – some with their front doors open and inviting a glance inside – but Jack paid them no mind. His attention was now centered on making a plan of action.

He'd already listed the children's graves by date and age of the deceased. By luck, he had spoken with a relative of one, Henry Overmyer. Perhaps he could find other kin. There were also the family plots to investigate further. He'd get on that tomorrow morning. Then there were the two doctors. The Ranzoas.

And then what?

What was the point here? After he had gathered all of this information, what would he do with it? No one had asked him to stick his nose into what had happened to those children. They had simply died and were buried, as far as he knew. Certainly, the number of deaths over a short period of time was unusual. But did that mean foul play was involved? Something sinister? Any sane person could see right away that the only thing behind these graves was coincidence. Statistically, if he even bothered to consider factual evidence, the number of infant deaths to population would probably point to a reasonable figure. Of course, that wouldn't hold a candle to rumor. No, rumor is a much juicier thing. And two mysterious doctors? Who could resist that?

Obsessed? Possessed would better describe his present state of mind.

Still, something inside urged him to continue. Perhaps it was a sense of misguided duty. He didn't care. Whatever it was that drove him, he would stay the course. He would take this thing as far as he could.

He had walked to the Key West Bight without even realizing it.

CHAPTER 5

Detective Earl Gleason's morning was being spent in sweltering heat on Stock Island. He was investigating an ADW. Mr. Randy Price had been charged with having committed the assault with a deadly weapon on Mr. Gordon Stunt. Mr. Price apparently possessed a keen proficiency with box-cutters and had considerably sliced up Mr. Stunt. There'd been witnesses to the incident and Gleason had come to interview them.

"He pulled out this funny knife thing and cut him across the neck," one witness said. "Blood all over the place."

"Yeah, and don't forget where he stabbed him in the chest," the other told the detective, indicating a spot on his own chest below the left clavicle.

The two witnesses, a man and a woman, lived near the marina but not close enough to benefit from any ocean breeze. The crime had taken place in Key West, however, which is why Gleason was involved rather than the Sheriffs Department. Key West was Gleason's turf.

"All of you were together at the Baba Room on North Roosevelt," Gleason stated. "Did you know the people involved? There were three. Two men and a woman."

"We'd seen them at the bar before," the man said. "But we weren't exactly friends or anything like that. Just happened to be there when they were."

"So tell me what happened," Gleason said. "Was there an argument?

"Well, it seemed the one who got cut was kissing the woman that'd come with them and the other fellow didn't like it, I guess," he recounted.

"And what happened next? Did he tell the man to stop kissing her?"

"He just all of a sudden started stabbing this guy," the woman laughed nervously. "Didn't say a word. I mean we were right beside them at the bar. We could've been cut ourselves."

"Who called 911?" Gleason asked.

"The bartender," the man told him. "We jumped back to get out of the way and by the time we'd figured out what was going on, the fellow that stabbed him had run out the door. Is the other guy going to be all right?"

"He's at the hospital."

Gleason thanked the couple and returned to his car. He looked over his notes before driving away. The ADW would be bumped up to attempted murder. He didn't think Florida's stand-your-ground-law would be a viable defense on this one.

Crossing the bridge into Key West, he hung a right turn onto Roosevelt and drove to the scene of the crime. One more look around wouldn't hurt.

The detective often revisited the scene during his investigations. It had become sort of second nature. He rarely found any new physical evidence but that wasn't the main reason for coming back. It put him in character.

Gleason, who had a passion for the theater, likened a criminal investigation to a play with three acts. The acts being defined by elements such as action, climax and resolution. The acts create the plot. Most of the play is made up of complications. So here was Gleason's play at the Baba Room in three acts:

Act I. Two men and a woman enter the bar together. They apparently know each other. But something's up with them.

Act II. Suddenly one man violently attacks the other.

Act III. The plot unfolds in the investigation, the denouement. The resolution.

In this particular crime, jealousy would appear to be the motive. The inciting incident was the man kissing the woman. Now another complication enters. Jealousy over whom? A fuse had obviously been lit before they ever came to the bar where Mr. Price decided to cut the shit out of Mr. Stunt.

There'd been nothing more for Gleason to learn at the Baba Room. But for now he had all he needed. He returned to the police station to finish up Act III.

~~~

The deck canon's report from the schooner echoed across the water dislodging memories long hidden. A sniper had placed a .50 caliber round into the adobe wall which the insurgents had ducked behind. A rocket-propelled grenade wouldn't have been deadlier. The wall had blown out on the opposite side, carrying fragments of lead and masonry with destructive force. Jack's squad cautiously approached.

Two enemy dead lay sprawled on the ground. Along with the body of a child.

The little boy, who had apparently been outside the house when the firefight started, had also taken refuge behind the wall.

It was declared to be collateral damage. Sad, but unavoidable.

True, but Jack had never seen a dead child before. It had affected him mightily.

The memory faded as quickly as it had come and a line of yachts berthed across the Bight came once more into focus. Jack took another sip of espresso. It had grown cold as he sat on a stool in front of the small shops along the boardwalk, his mind elsewhere.

That morning's stroll through the cemetery had left him in a quandary. What next? He had many unanswered questions that gave rise only to more suspicions. And that was about it. He tossed the remainder of his espresso into the trashcan and headed home.

~~~

"I'm winding up the Randy the Ripper case, Lieutenant," Gleason said. "Talked to the wits this morning. It's pretty cut and dried, no pun intended."

"Yeah, well, congrats. Usually the easy day was yesterday, or so they say," Jay Halderman grinned. "You're lucky. Think you can get it to the DA this afternoon?"

"No problem. You know, there was a funny thing about this. Price attacked Stunt because he was smooching with the lady, so you'd think she was Price's squeeze. Not at all. Price had the hots for Stunt. They'd dated a couple of times and he had hopes of it becoming a steady thing. However, Stunt was jerking Price's chain by getting it on with the woman. Pisses off Price, so he goes and cuts the hell out of his boyfriend with a goddamn box-cutter. Isn't that something?"

"Takes all kinds," Halderman nodded sagely. "By the way, our old friend Jack Hunter is back in town. Fonze told me."

Fonze was a nickname for Alphonse – Alphonse Devereau, who'd been a cop with Halderman when both were in the Jacksonville PD. Fonze, however, was now Alice the private investigator, after having undergone gender reassignment surgery.

"Why that's just peachy. Is the mayor having a parade for him?"

"Wouldn't be surprised," Halderman chuckled. "You ever hear from that female detective in Los Angeles?"

"Laura Dalton," Gleason said. "We had dinner once when she was here during the Lovewell murder investigation. But nothing came of it, really. Have a feeling that she and Hunter might be a little tight. Too bad, she seems like a pretty decent sort."

"Smart and good-looking to boot, as I remember," Halderman added with a wink. "She and your pal Hunter saved the KWPD's butt on that homicide and drug case."

"That how you see it, Lieutenant?" Gleason asked indignantly. "Personally, I don't recall their being so damn important. More of a nuisance, if you ask me."

"Ah, lighten up, my boy," Halderman smiled. "Everybody contributed then. You okay with that?"

"Suppose I'll have to be, won't I?"

"Good job on the Baba Room case, Detective," Halderman said, all businesslike. "Try to get the paperwork over to the district attorney today."

CHAPTER 6

Jack stopped in Five Brothers and got a sandwich to go. What was left of the cold pizza at home would be better put to use as roof shingles. He trudged up Southard to Ashe and turned right toward his house.

The little couch house had been unaffected by the merciless heat of the day and was invitingly cool inside when he opened the door. After striping down to his shorts, lunch was the next piece of business. He grabbed a beer from the refrigerator and took it and the sandwich to a small parlor-like room he used as an office. It was a cozy place, windowed on three walls. A desk faced the back yard. On the desk sat a laptop computer.

Jack fired up the computer, which was an accomplishment in itself for him. He'd never been much of a geek because there'd never been a real need for him to become one. His situation, having changed drastically twice over the past couple of years, now called for a basic proficiency at minimum with the damn machines. Consequently, he had taken a computer course at a junior college back in LA.

The computer up and running, he went to the web and typed in 'children's deaths'. Not too much came up in that category. Next, he tried 'baby deaths'. Same outcome. 'Infant mortalities' paid off. The screen immediately filled with a surprisingly large number of sources. He began at the top.

By the time he had read and printed out those of which seemed most pertinent, he had amassed quite a stack. Infant mortality, he had learned, was the death of a baby before his or her first birthday. Further, the *infant mortality rate* is an estimate of the number of infant deaths for every 1,000 live births. Statistically, it works out to six infants. This was something.

He ate the rest of his sandwich while he thought about that number. In a single year, 1965, he'd counted thirteen graves. Seven of those were neonatal, infants who'd died within 27 days of their births. The other six were post neonatal, 28 days to 364. Taking those thirteen deaths together for one year, statistically, you needed two thousand babies to have been born in Key West in 1965. That had never happened. Statistically, the local ratio of deaths to births was off the charts.

What had happened to those poor children? No history of a devastating plague. No record of a monstrous storm having swept over the island. What then? Aliens from outer space?

There were complications, of course, that were often responsible for many deaths. Birth defects, maternal health conditions, problems during labor and delivery, improper care or lack of any care.

Taking all of this into consideration, he still had to ask "But so many?" What had gone wrong with all those children buried in the Key West cemetery?

The doctors had to figure in somehow, he thought. The ones the woman at the cemetery had told him about. Of course, they had treated these children! What were their names? He looked through his notes he'd jotted down.

There it was. Ranzoa. Henry Overmeyer had said that the doctors had moved out of town long ago. But the family still lived in Key West. He'd look them up.

Armand and Ardell

Victoria was two weeks past due when she gave birth to twins. A boy and a girl. Her husband, Dr. Claude Ranzoa, delivered the infants with the assistance of a nurse at his clinic on William Street.

The children were born puzzlingly different. Although to look at them, other than their gender, you would think they were normal. Two healthy little babies.

As they grew, Armand became the quieter one, a follower rather than a leader. However, he was quick to join in the play. In his early school days, he was often reprimanded for disturbing the class. The teachers considered his behavior that of a hyperactive child, something he would grow out of and certainly not a cause for concern.

Ardell had an outgoing personality, was forward and showed great determination in whatever she undertook. She excelled in studies and was more athletic than her brother. Everyone called her a tomboy, a rough girl.

Both sister and brother were smart and began to share mutual interests. Especially in science. The Ranzoas tried to satisfy and nurture their children's academic interests and curiosities but soon found these efforts to be somewhat limited locally. Also, a veil of unhappiness had fallen over the two children. Armand and Ardell were *eventually sent away to a private school in the Northeast. And while their parents were saddened by the children's absence, they were also relieved. As if a weight had been lifted.*

Rumors and hurtful talk regarding the twins had become a Key West staple. The fact that there was some truth to the hearsay, a physical condition known only by the parents, pained even more other members of the Ranzoa family. Cousins avoided the twins out of ignorance. Embarrassment portended a family disgrace and eventually split the bond between Claude and his brother, Samuel.

Claude and Victoria were quite accepting of the abnormality their daughter had been born with. But even as a medical doctor, Claude Ranzoa had never come across this particular condition. Especially in twins that seemed almost identical, save for their sex. In his mind it was a fascinating study.

Others had also been fascinated by the twins but not for any scientific reasons. Some of their early playmates, and later even more during the short time they'd been in local schools, had noticed something different about Ardell, and were confused, to say the least, by exactly what was she supposed to be. Teasing did not fall lightly on the twins.

This became a bigger problem for Armand than for Ardell. He was angered by the whispering and smirky finger pointing and felt that he had to defend his sister against the schoolyard taunts. Violence was not in his makeup and fighting did not come easily, but nonetheless he attacked the tormentors with vigor. And the scraps resulted in many trips to the principal's office. Notes were sent home.

But always to Armand and Ardell everything about themselves was normal. And to their mother, as she often and lovingly told them, they were her beautiful threesome.

The children excelled in studies at the private schools and later in college, graduating in three years instead of the usual four. Both were accepted to medical school and were awarded their degrees in 1960.

After an internship and residency at a hospital in Virginia, they joined their father's practice in Key West. The year was 1962.

CHAPTER 8

There were only two Ranzoas listed in the telephone directory with residential addresses, Jack had discovered. There was also a Ranzoa law firm. He chose the lawyers.

"Ranzoa and Partners," the receptionist answered.

"Hello, my name is Jack Hunter. May I speak with Mr. Ranzoa?"

"Which Mr. Ranzoa, may I ask?"

"How many are there?"

"What is the purpose of your call, sir?"

"Yes, I'm a writer – television producer, actually – and I'm researching a possible story on old Key West families."

This had come to Jack right out of the blue.

"Well, we are a law office. I'm not certain how we could help you. What was your name again?"

"Hunter. Jack Hunter."

"Mr. Hunter, if you will leave your number, I will pass on this information to Mr. Ranzoa."

"Thank you very much. And which Ranzoa, may I ask?"

"One or the other," she replied humorlessly.

That went over well, Jack thought to himself after ending the call. Although he did like the research angle about Key West families. He'd have to work on that.

Anxiety demanded his attention again. He still hadn't heard from Dr. Skye's office. The results from the blood work should certainly be there by now. So what was the holdup? He'd wait a little longer before calling them.

~~~

Earl Gleason couldn't understand why he had awakened in such a foul mood. His divorce was final today. He should've been clicking his heels or something, he figured. To celebrate, he'd even bought a ticket for the new play that was opening tonight at the Red Barn.

Now he was sitting at his desk and still feeling pissed off. He couldn't put his finger on it. The box cutter case was with the DA. Nothing else pending. He went to get a cup of coffee from the machine.

Back at his desk, he read a report that had been taken about a tourist going missing. Man had walked out on his wife at the hotel where they'd been staying. Hadn't returned. Jeez, how many times did that happen in Key West?

Still, the guy had been gone two days. Wife said he hadn't taken their car either. He pushed the report aside just as the Lieutenant walked over.

"See you got that missing hubby report," Jay Halderman said.

"Yeah, you want me on it?"

"Looks like you're clear."

"Okay," Gleason sighed. "I'll call the man's wife. The asshole husband has probably crawled back by now."

"You all right?" Halderman said. You don't look so hot."

"I'm fine. My divorce is final today."

"No shit?"

~~~

"That Vesuvius turning out kind of interesting, hee-hee. Think we ought to be making an offer soon, Jack. How 'bout you? You ready to expand the empire?"

Jack had ridden his bicycle to the Inedible Café and was having a coffee with Billy. It was a completely red bike that Billy had presented him with soon after they'd met. Jack had named it Whizzer.

"I don't know," he mused. "You've seen their books? I haven't. Like to know how deep they're in before we start talking money."

"Told you I talked to the delivery man," Billy bristled. "Don't need to see no damn books. Deliveryman knows what the hell's going on in this damn town. Better make an offer before somebody beats us to the punch. That's what I think."

"How about this then?" Jack compromised. "Let's say to them that we might be interested in making an offer. See how they feel about selling."

"Okay, that sounds like a start anyway," Billy nodded. "When do you want to do it? Make an offer?"

"Don't want to make an offer yet. Just find out if they're interested. You get in touch with them, Billy. See what they say. Now I have something I want to ask you about."

"Sure, Jack, nothing serious I hope, hee-hee."

Jack remained silent for a moment. No one else was in the restaurant. Even the street was quiet.

"Have you ever been over to the cemetery?"

"Cemetery's a sad place, Jack. Not where I want to spend time until I have to."

"Well, that's kind of what I want to talk about," Jack smiled. "There's something very sad in the cemetery."

Jack recounted his visits to the children's section of the cemetery and what he'd learned so far, including the rumors about the Ranzoas. Billy listened without saying a word until he'd finished.

"Why would anybody want to do something like you think they did to those little babies?" Billy asked incredulously. "Baby did nothing wrong. Just got born, that's all. 'Sposed to love that baby, not kill him. All those little baby graves, you said? My, my."

"I don't know the answer," Jack said. "But something's not right. I do know that. Something happened that wasn't natural."

"Well, how are you going to find out? Nobody's going to tell you if they did a bad thing to those babies. Person who done it might even be dead himself now."

"That's the problem all right," Jack sighed. "Guess I'll just keep asking around until I find somebody who knows something. I've called one of the Ranzoas. He's a lawyer. Haven't heard back yet."

"Ranzoas pretty powerful folks around here, Jack. Better be careful before you go messing around."

"That so? Good, I'll keep it in mind. Thanks."

"Well, you might want to talk with Davy Jones," Billy then suggested. "He was a mate of mine when we were young fellows. Worked at Twombley's Mortuary back around the time you're talking about. He might've even buried some of those children."

"That's outstanding, Billy," Jack said excitedly. "Could you call him for me? See if he remembers anything?"

"Sure, Jack, I'll do that. What about your friend, Alice? Could she help you out?"

"I don't know, Billy. I could certainly use some help but I'm not sure Alice wants to get involved in this."

"Yeah, well, Alice is a smart lady, hee-hee."

Jack's cellphone rang. He saw it was a 305 area code number. He was going to take the call but a slight commotion outside drew his attention. He let it go to message.

CHAPTER 9

Jack bicycled over Olivia Street to Ashe, passing the cemetery along the way. He considered cutting down Windsor Lane to the main entrance but decided that he'd had enough for the day.

Once home, he grabbed a beer from the refrigerator and took it out on the front porch. The sun, now settling in comfortably to the west and promising another spectacular show for Mallory Square, cast a radiant glow on all of Ashe Street. Jack rested his feet on the porch rail and took a long drink from the cold bottle, letting it slide slowly down his throat. It felt good.

He checked his messages.

"This is Bob Ranzoa," a stranger's voice announced. "I'm returning your call."

Jack's feet hit the floor. He checked his watch, saw that maybe somebody was still at Ranzoa's office, and dialed the number.

Same voice answered.

"Bob Ranzoa."

"Mr. Ranzoa? This is Jack Hunter. Sorry to have missed you."

"Ah, yes, you're the gentleman who's writing a story about Key West, I understand. How can I help you?"

Jack squeezed his brain, frantically trying to come up with a quick answer.

"Living history," he said at last.

"I beg your pardon?"

"I'm thinking about the old families," Jack explained. "Those who still live and work here."

"Well, I guess that would include us," Bob Ranzoa laughed. "But I'm not sure what you mean."

Jack scrambled to build on his idea.

"Each generation," he explained. "How they were affected by events of the time. Any skeletons in the closet, that sort of thing. Black sheep. You see what I'm talking about?"

"Sounds interesting," Ranzoa chuckled. "Let me ask you this. You say you're writing this history. Are you an author? I mean, should I know you?"

"No, sir, this is a first for me," Jack admitted truthfully. "I have worked in television production, however, so I might consider making the story a docu-fiction film. Sort of an interpretation of the facts."

Docu-fiction. Jack had used the bullshit term first coined by the scumbag who'd murdered his wife, Pamela. He had no idea why it had popped into his mind.

"Interpretation of the facts," Ranzoa laughed. "Sounds like the law business. You say you worked in television. Where was that?"

"Gaysome Hoigh in Los Angeles," Jack told him, stretching the truth to its limit. It was his old advertising agency.

"One of those independent movie companies, huh?" Bob Ranzoa said. "I would like to know more about your project. Why don't we get together, say, day after tomorrow? Around three-ish okay with you? Just come to our office. We're over by the courthouse on Whitehead."

"Thanks," Jack said eagerly. "I have the address. See you at three."

~~~

The sun had begun its disappearing act, to the delight of the crowds at Mallory Square, when Detective Gleason pulled into the parking lot at the Ebb Tide Hotel on South Street. He'd earlier called the manager to arrange for a private area where he could interview Virginia Hayes, the woman whose husband had gone missing. In today's atmosphere, it wouldn't have been wise to have conducted it in her room with just the two of them.

"I'm Detective Gleason," he informed the person behind the desk, a young lady dressed in a trim blouse and skirt. "Here to see Virginia Hayes."

"Yes, sir, pleased to meet you. I'm Yolanda Grant. Mr. Olsen, our manager, has everything ready. I'll ring him that you're here."

"How about Mrs. Hayes?" Gleason asked.

"She's with Mr. Olsen."

John Olsen approached Gleason with his hand stretched out.

"Good afternoon, Detective," he greeted. "If you'll follow me, I'll take you to our guest, Mrs. Hayes. She's waiting for us."

The two men walked toward a patio area set off from the small lobby of the hotel.

"Terrible thing about Mr. Hayes," Olsen grimaced. "Probably nothing serious, though. I've seen it before down here. Of course, I'd never mention that to Mrs. Hayes."

Virginia Hayes started to get to her feet as they approached.

"Please don't get up, Mrs. Hayes," Gleason motioned, and then to Olsen, "If you could just make sure we aren't disturbed, that would be great."

Olsen bowed out and Gleason sat in a chair across from where Virginia Hayes was seated.

Gleason noted that she was a woman of medium height, probably in her late thirties, had big hair, should exercise more and was a smoker. A pack of Marlboros rested on the glass-top table. He also noticed some bruising on her upper right arm as if it had been grabbed. Hard.

"Perhaps we could begin with the last time you saw your husband," he said.

"I already told the policeman that," Mrs. Hayes answered sharply.

"Yes, ma'am, but why don't you tell me, if you wouldn't mind."

"All right, we got down here two nights ago. Clarence went out right after we checked in. Said he wanted a beer. I haven't seen him since."

"He didn't ask you to come with him?"

"Nope, said he wanted to take a little walk. See the sights. We'd driven down from Alva."

"Alva. Where is that, Mrs. Hayes?"

"It's outside Ft. Myers."

"Well, that'd be a good long drive for one day, I guess."

"That's what Clarence said."

"Now, I have to ask you this. Is there any reason you can think of for your husband to have gone off? I mean, alone?"

"If you hinting that were we having trouble, the answer is no! We'd gotten married not all that long ago."

"How about friends? Did your husband have any people here in Key West that he knew? Possibly he's with them. Happens often. Buddies get to partying, forget about the time."

"We've never been here before. So there's nobody we'd know, is there?"

John Olsen cruised slowly past in the hall. Gleason shot him a glaring look and he quickly disappeared.

"Uh-huh, so as far as you are concerned, there was nothing unusual about Clarence going for a beer by himself and staying out all night, even though you'd just gotten in town," Gleason said. "When did you first become worried?"

"The next day when he hadn't come back. See, he'd do that at home every now and then. Go out for something and let time get away from him. Clarence had an car accident some while back and I think it kind of affected his thinking a little."

"You're saying he has a history of disappearing?"

"No, I'm just saying he's stayed out late once or twice."

Gleason had his own suspicions about that. Guy was a strayer.

"I see, but you didn't report him missing until yesterday. Why was that?"

"Well, I went to bed right after he went out the night we got here. I figured he didn't want to wake me when he came back. Probably because it was so late. Then he must've left the next morning before I got up."

"You didn't awaken when he came to bed?"

"I'm a sound sleeper."

"And he never returned on the next day, either?"

"Nope. Okay if I smoke?"

Virginia Hayes pulled a cigarette out of the pack and lit it without waiting for an answer.

"Didn't you think that was strange?" Gleason asked. "Your husband not returning?"

"Well, hell yes I did, that''s why I called you all. We're supposed to be leaving here tomorrow morning."

Gleason paused and looked at her for a couple of seconds, then bit his lip and nodded.

"All right, Mrs. Hayes, I guess that about covers everything. Do you have a picture of your husband that I could have? We'll want to put out a bulletin. Maybe run it in the newspaper, too."

"Got one here in my billfold you can have. Clarence is kind of a short fellow. Wiry, though."

Virginia Hayes dug around in her purse for the wallet. She pulled the photo out from behind her driver's license and handed it to Gleason.

"Thank you, ma'am. I'm very sorry about your husband, of course, but we'll find where he is. It would be better if you could remain in Key West until he shows up."

"I'll have to call my boss and tell him. I'm supposed to be back at work day after tomorrow."

"I'm sure he'll understand. Where do you work?"

"Bruno's Grocery. I'm a checker. Haven't been there for too long so I don't want to mess up."

"How about Clarence, he work there, too?"

"He works at the marina at Fort Myers Shores."

Gleason left Virginia Hayes on the patio. She lit up another cigarette as soon as he walked away. He stopped at the front desk. Yolanda Grant was still on duty.

"Miss Grant," he said quietly, leaning across the counter. "Could you tell me where Mrs. Hayes' car is parked? And do you have the license number?"

"It's in number 27," she read from a registration form. "Silver Honda Accord. Florida license 683 5GH. In the back of the lot over to the side next to the wall. There's a lot of shrubbery so you might miss it. Just turn left out the door and follow the building around."

Gleason had no trouble finding the Honda. He walked over to it and peered in through the windows. Maybe Clarence Hayes was sleeping in the car. Worth a shot.

Couple of empty paper coffee cups, candy wrappers, old newspaper, nothing of interest. He circled the vehicle. At the rear, however, he discovered something of great interest. What appeared to be a small blood smear on the trunk lid. He quickly returned to the hotel.

"Mrs. Hayes, I was wondering if you could come to the parking lot and open the trunk of your car for me," Gleason asked. He'd found Virginia Hayes still sitting on the patio. She lit another cigarette.

"Why would you want me to do that?" she asked, after exhaling a long stream of smoke.

"I found what I believe to be blood on the trunk lid," Gleason said seriously. "It could have something to do with your husband."

"Probably fish blood is all you saw," Virginia Hayes scoffed. "Clarence went fishing the day before we left."

"All the same, ma'am, I'd like to look inside the trunk."

"Well, you can't because I'm not going to unlock it!"

Gleason had called in for assistance before returning to the hotel. He'd had an uneasy feeling about the car trunk. Two uniformed cops entered. He waved them over.

"Officer, I need you to stand by a Honda Accord parked in the hotel lot until we can get a court order to impound it," he said, turning to one of the policemen and handing him a piece of paper. "It's in space number 27. A silver 4-door sedan."

"Wait a minute, you can't do that!" the Hayes woman said angrily and jumping to her feet. "I've got to leave this damn place tomorrow or I'll lose my fucking job!"

"Mrs. Hayes," Gleason said, returning his attention to the irate woman. "I'm going to need you to go with this other officer to the Key West police station. "I will meet you there to take a statement. Thank you."

"What about my car?" she yelled.

"Your car will be impounded until we can test the bloodstain," Gleason told her. "That is, unless you agree to open the trunk now."

"I told you it was fish blood!" Virginia Hayes snapped. "Don't need to put up with your harassment."

"Very well, then," Gleason nodded and motioned to the cop. "Officer?"

The uniform cop led Virginia Hayes to the waiting patrol car. Gleason stopped off at the front desk.

"Please do not let the maid clean Virginia Hayes' room," he said to the desk clerk. "I'll need a court order to examine it. Should have it by morning."

"What if Mrs. Hayes wants to go in?"

"Husband paid for it. She has the right to use it. Just no maid service."

~~~

By the time Gleason had finished interviewing Virginia Hayes, it was past ten that evening. He had an officer call a taxi for Mrs. Hayes. On her way out of the police station, she promised that they'd be hearing from her lawyer.

The requisition for an impoundment order had been faxed to the court and a judge had expedited its approval. The vehicle was towed to the secured yard. The tech guys would be on it first thing in the morning. He was wrapped up for the night. It had been a long day.

Gleason sat at his desk, mentally reviewing where he stood in the investigation so far. As a three-act play it went something like this: Act I: Woman reports her husband missing. Act II: Woman interviewed. Spotty story, seems in a hurry to leave town. Blood smear found on car trunk lid. Woman refuses to open trunk. Etc, etc. Act III: Stay tuned.

He momentarily drummed his fingers on the desktop and then got up. As he removed his jacket from the back of his chair, his ticket for opening night at the Red Barn fell from the vest pocket. Shit! He picked it up, shook his head and tossed it in the wastebasket. And the damn play had been completely sold out for its entire run!

It was too late to eat and he hadn't much of an appetite anyway. He decided to stop by Vino's for a glass of wine.

CHAPTER 10

Cuba lay some ninety miles across the Florida Straits from where Jack Hunter now stood at Southernmost Point. The night moonless with only the stars separating sky from sea. A thousand insects swarmed around the street light above the brightly painted marker.

His thoughts drifted to another time when he'd stood at this very spot, the black horizon an imperceptible demarcation in the faint hint of dawn while he waited to leave the island.

Sparrow Lovewell had come to his rescue back then. Had driven him to Miami. To the beginning of a new life, in fact. Yes, it was possible to go home again, he'd discovered.

So much had happened since he'd remade himself. He'd come from being a fugitive to attaining a fortune. And because of that, he'd made a promise to himself. Do some good.

Was that what he was doing? Sticking his nose into another's painful past? Obsessing over rumors? Perhaps digging up things better left buried? Buried, yes. Children gone but with disturbing questions concerning them left behind and, in his mind, demanding to be answered. And that was it, wasn't it? Questions that he would somehow find the answers to. Answers that hopefully would serve some good.

He checked his watch. Nearly ten. It had been a couple of hours since he'd left the house on Ashe Street. Wandering aimlessly, he had strolled along White Street, passing the former Port au Prince Gallery where Bashford Wills had died from an overdose. Continuing to South Street and to Vernon and then checking Louie's Backyard where he found most of the diners had left the restaurant. Finally, he had wound up here at Southernmost Point. He had been surprised at the distance he'd covered. Hardly aware, his mind on the Ranzoas the entire time.

After the phone call, he had Googled them. Not much to learn there. An old family law firm founded by Samuel Ternant Ranzoa and handed down to Robert Ternant Ranzoa, first, second and third. He'd always wondered about people who did that sort of number thing with succeeding generations – I, II, III – other than kings and popes.

He took another look toward Cuba and started walking to Duval Street. Pedestrian traffic was light until he passed Truman. Coming to Olivia, where he'd normally turn for home, he decided to continue down Duval. Vino's was right up ahead. The idea of a glass of wine suddenly appealed.

He climbed the short flight of steps up to the porch. All the chairs were taken. Inside, one stool was free at the bar. He sidled into it and glanced over to the guy sitting next to him.

"Jesus! It's you again." Earl Gleason said in surprise, turning to see who'd sat down.

"No," Jack grinned, "it's not Him, it's only me. But don't feel bad. It happens all the time. How're you doing, Detective?"

"All right until now," Gleason said, dour-faced. "What brings you to town?"

"Just business," Jack answered. "Billy's thinking of buying another place."

Gleason arched his eyebrows and took a sip of wine from his glass. For several different reasons, Jack was not his favorite person. A couple more people came in and joined a group at a table over to the side of the room. Everyone made a big fuss at their arrival.

"What are you drinking?" Jack asked.

"I don't know. Val Chelley recommended it. She owns the joint. I'm not a wine connoisseur."

"I'll have the same," Jack said to the bartender, pointing at Gleason's glass.

"How's Laura doing?" Gleason asked. "You two still seeing each other?"

Jack felt a little taken aback by the detective's question. Still seeing each other? What business was it of his if they were. He changed the subject.

"Look, I want to ask you something. Have you ever been to the Key West cemetery?"

Now it was Gleason's turn to look puzzled.

"Sure, I've been there. Not a place I make a regular habit of visiting. Why?"

"Well, it's this," Jack said, turning in his seat to face the man. "There are these children's graves. Something about them is funny."

"Funny. What? Have their graves been vandalized?"

"No, no, nothing like that. A lot of them died in 1965. That's what."

"It happens to everyone, children included. What makes the year so important?

"Couple of things," Jack said. "First, there are too many graves. It doesn't make sense that all those kids died in one year. The second thing is, there's a rumor that they were all treated by the same doctor. You never heard of anything happening back then, huh?"

"If you mean unsolved kiddy serial killer cases, no. Look, Hunter, what you're talking about was over fifty years ago. If anything suspicious took place, it would've been investigated. Rumors live forever in this town."

Jack smiled and motioned to the bartender.

"I'll settle up," he said to the man. "Put his on the tab, too."

Jack left Gleason at the bar and headed toward Southard. The street was quiet and suited his mood. He ought to go home, he knew. There was nothing to gain by walking the night away on Duval Street. But he was too wired.

The feeling was a familiar one. Flashback to what seemed to have been a thousand years ago, yet still as vivid as yesterday. Far down-range, hidden in rubble that was once a village, awake for twenty-four hours with another night to go. Eyes wide open for any movement, ears sharply tuned for an enemy's voice. Wired.

Duval Street had taken him to where the water began. Where the sirens tempted the unwary to come, come across to Sunset Key, to Wisteria Island and beyond to the Gulf of Mexico.

CHAPTER 11

Jack opened his eyes to find that he was fully dressed and sitting in his living room. His legs ached. Small wonder, since the night before he'd tramped over most of the island. He must've been so tired that he hadn't even made it to the bedroom.

A cup of instant coffee – two heaping spoonfuls – did the trick. Then a quick shower to seal the deal. Fully awake now, he slipped on a pair of shorts, pulled a t-shirt over his head and stepped into a pair of flip-flops. From in the chair to out-the-door hadn't taken more than twenty minutes. He headed for the Key West library.

~~~

Across town at the police station, Detective Earl Gleason was on the phone with the technicians at the impound yard. "Pop the fucking trunk," he ordered. "I'll be right there."

~~~

"Jameson about puked when we opened it," Gabe Hodges said. "Can't say I blame him. It was enough to gag a maggot."

Hodges was speaking to Gleason in an office at the impound yard. The Honda sat out in the main shop, its trunk lid standing open.

"Tell me again what made you think someone was inside," Gleason asked.

"We heard him break wind," Hodges coughed a laugh. "I know it's not funny, detective, but the guy actually farted."

Gleason couldn't help but smile at that himself.

"Well, I guess that's part of the decomposition process," he said. "Gases build up, all that good stuff going on, something's got to give."

"Yeah, well, it must've had something awful to give because it stank up the entire shop."

"Is the medical examiner on his way?" Gleason asked.

"I suppose so."

Gleason entered the shop and walked over to the car. The body, an adult male, lay curled on his side in the trunk. Buried in his left temple up to the sole was a woman's red shoe with a stiletto heel.

The victim was Clarence Hayes. Gleason had no doubt. Same person in the picture his wife had given him, the one *The Citizen* had run this morning. He would run his prints, etcetera, etcetera.

Gleason's cellphone rang.

"Yeah?" he answered.

It was a call from the police station. Two people had phoned in that they'd seen the missing man.

"Set up an appointment at the station for them, okay? Also, put out to all departments a person-of-interest call on Virginia Hayes. Pick her up on sight. Yeah, her hubby's no longer missing."

Dr. J. L. Small, the medical examiner, arrived.

"What've we got today, detective?" he asked, smearing a dab of Vicks on his upper lip. Gleason had done the same thing to mask the putrid odor.

"DB in a car trunk," Gleason said, his eyes still on the body.

"Well, that's a kick in the head," Small said dryly, noticing the woman's shoe.

"Yeah, I'd be interested in your take on that, doctor. Was it a kick or a smack upside the head?"

"Either way, it did the job. Instant death, I'd say. Know who he was?"

"Lost husband," Gleason said. "And now is found. Wife reported him missing. Paper ran his picture this morning. All along he was in the fucking trunk of their car."

"Well, if you've seen enough, detective, I'll have him moved to the morgue. Maybe get started on an autopsy tomorrow. No promises."

"Sure," Gleason nodded, "I've got all I need. Photographer's been and gone. Forensics will sweep the trunk after you've finished."

"Great performance last night at the Red Barn," Small said, stepping back from the Honda. "*The Cherry Orchard* was done about as well as it could've been. Wouldn't you agree?"

"Afraid I missed it."

Gleason left the ME at the car. Walking to the parking lot he called The Ebb Tide Hotel. Yolanda Grant was on duty and picked up.

"Miss Grant, this is Detective Gleason. Have you seen Mrs. Hayes this morning?"

"No, she wasn't at breakfast but I can ring her room."

After seven rings, Yolanda Grant came back on line to Gleason.

"I'm sorry, sir, but Mrs. Hayes seems to be out."

"Thank you."

Gleason was just getting into his car when his cellphone rang.

"Gleason," he answered.

"Detective Gleason, this is Yolanda Grant at the Ebb Tide Hotel. I just spoke with the maid and she said that Mrs. Hayes' room was empty! All of their things are gone. She never even checked out! The woman just stiffed us!"

"Thanks you, Miss Grant. Tell the maid not to clean the room, if she hasn't already. I'll be there as quickly as I can."

~~~

Leon Frankel was at his usual table in the library when Jack approached him, carrying a paper bag. Inside were two cups of Cuban coffee he'd bought at Five Brothers.

"Good morning, Leon," he said quietly. "Got time for a coffee?"

Leon looked up and smiled. "Against the law. No food or drink in the library."

"What say we go to the little park next door?"

Finding a vacant bench was no problem since the park had just opened for the day. The two men seated themselves. Jack handed Leon one of the cups.

"Careful," he cautioned. "Eddie makes it *muy caliente*."

"*Sí, y muy bueno*," Leon said.

"The last time we spoke," Jack began, "it was about the children buried in the cemetery. I'd asked if there'd been some sort of epidemic since so many seemed to have died in one year. You said, no, there wasn't any disease or

70

anything like that but there were rumors. Could you tell me what you meant?"

"That would just be spreading more gossip, Jack. No one ever proved there was anything to it."

"Well, humor me, then," Jack laughed. "I mean, there's usually something behind a rumor, right?"

"If you consider hearsay."

"Well, rumor has it that there's a connection between those dead children and a couple of doctors who've apparently vanished," Jack said. "Does the name Ranzoa mean anything?"

"An old Key West family. Very powerful at one time, I might add. Maybe still are. I know what tree you're barking up, Jack, and I advise you end it right there."

"So you're saying any hearsay about the Ranzoas might have something to it, huh?"

"What I'm saying is don't stick your nose where it doesn't belong."

"Thank you. I'll keep that in mind. You see, I have an appointment with one of them this afternoon. I'd earlier called their law firm and spoke with one of the partners."

Leon took a sip from his cup.

"Stuff's still too hot to drink," he commented. Then after a long pause, said, "Probably with Robert, right? The old man wouldn't have even given you the wrong time of the day. He can be a mean bastard, if he takes of a mind."

"Yes, it was Robert," Jack answered. "He called me and I called him back. Said I wanted to interview him. Told him that I'm doing a film about old families here."

"Sounds like a crock," Leon laughed. "I'm surprised he bought it. They're a private bunch. Wily, too."

"So, what *is* their story, Leon?"

~~~

Yolanda Grant unlocked the door of Room 122 and stepped inside. Gleason followed. Behind him trailed a technical officer. He'd called for one to meet him at the hotel to document any evidence they might find. He saw that housekeeping had left the room untouched, as requested.

"Maid hasn't cleaned, I see," Gleason said. "Thanks."

"No problem," Yolanda said. "Mrs. Hayes requested no maid service. Some guests are like that, want a little more privacy, I suppose."

"Probably so," Gleason said. "I'll close the door after I'm finished."

"Take all the time you need, detective. By the way, we're reporting her skipping out on us."

"Sure," Gleason smiled and the woman turned and left.

He stood and took in the room to get the feel of the scene before proceeding. Nothing seemed out of place. Just another empty hotel room waiting for the maid to arrive.

Apparently, Virginia Hayes had pulled up the sheet and bedspread and tucked them in. He wondered if she did that at home rather than make the bed. Gleason yanked them back. Nothing there. Such as a bloodstain. Also, he saw that the mattress was indented on only one side, one pillow had been used, the other still plumped. She must have noticed that. Yet the Hayes woman had offered that her husband must've returned that first night and then had gotten up and was gone again before she'd awakened.

He opened the closet and ran his hand over the top shelf. Empty. Same for the medicine cabinet in the bathroom. Back at the bed, he got down on his hands and knees for a look underneath. Not even a dust bunny there. Chalk one up for good maids.

The detective stepped through the sliding glass door and out onto the patio. It was a ground-level room. Shrubbery offered some privacy from any passerby and also from the parking lot but you could've heard anyone talking on the adjoining patios of the rooms on either side. He made a mental note to ask the desk if those rooms had been occupied. He stepped back inside.

Then he turned and looked back at the door to the patio. He remembered it hadn't been locked when he went outside. She could have left the hotel that way.

Returning to the patio, he saw that some of the foliage and plantings surrounding it were broken. A short, and now easily visible, path led away. He and the tech officer followed it out to the hotel parking lot.

And there, in a recessed area at the back, stood a trash dumpster.

~~~

The hotel readily gave their permission to search the dumpster. Gleason borrowed a ladder from maintenance and climbed up for a look inside. Fortunately, the bin wasn't too large and even so was only a quarter full. And, as far as his nose could tell, contained nothing disgusting. He threw his leg over the edge and eased himself down.

His attention was immediately drawn to a bright object in one corner. He bent down for a closer look.

"Well, what do you know," he whistled and called out to the tech, "Better get in here and grab a shot of this."

The tech officer joined Gleason in the dumpster and began taking pictures of the find. After he'd finished, Gleason bagged the subject of interest, a woman's red shoe, hardly worn and possessing an extraordinarily high heel.

CHAPTER 12

Jack had dressed to the nines for the occasion. Tan lightweight worsted wool trousers sharply creased, smartly tailored black blazer, crisp cotton white shirt worn with an open collar, and an expensive pair of Italian brown loafers. He looked like he had stepped right out of a fashion ad. He'd taken a taxi to keep it looking that way, too.

The cab dropped him off in front of an old Victorian house on Whitehead Street. A bronze plaque next to the front door read Ranzoa Law Firm. Jack knocked and then went inside.

"Yes, sir, may I help you?" a young lady possessed of smiting beauty and sitting at a desk in the foyer asked.

"Good afternoon, my name is Jack Hunter. I have an appointment with Mr. Robert Ranzoa. I believe he's the younger one?"

"Please have a seat and I'll ring him," she said through perfect teeth.

Jack grinned back and sat on a small antique sofa that wasn't all that uncomfortable. He took in the surroundings.

An oriental carpet covered a floor that was of oak and looked old. Could even be the original wood, Jack suspected. A tall window stood next to the entrance, green draperies hanging almost to the floor. On the wall behind the sofa hung an oval mirror with a gilded frame.

Pocket doors closed off the parlor next to the foyer. A staircase behind the reception area led to the second floor. Robert Ranzoa came down the steps.

"Mr. Hunter," he beamed. "Bob Ranzoa."

Ranzoa was a man about Jack's age and height. Black wavy hair and sad hound-dog eyes. He wore an off-the-rack blue suit and looked like he should spend a little time at the gym.

"Nice of you to come," he said, taking Jack's hand in a firm grip. "We can talk in the parlor. Would you like anything? Water? Coffee? A drink?"

"No, thanks," Jack smiled. "I'm fine."

Ranzoa slid open the pocket doors and motioned Jack to enter.

The parlor was an airy little room with windows on three sides. A cast-iron fireplace set in a slate mantle stood in one corner. In the center of the ceiling hung a small crystal chandelier. Another oriental rug covered the floor. On it sat a round conference table with four chairs. Ranzoa pulled out one for Jack.

"So you're in the movie business?" he said, seating himself in the opposite chair.

"Actually, I was in the advertising agency business," Jack corrected.

"Oh, I must've misunderstood," Ranzoa said, puzzled. "Then is it advertising you wanted to talk to us about? Because if it is, we really don't do much."

"No, no," Jack laughed. "I was a producer at an ad agency. Worked with a lot of film companies. I'm on my own now and I'm considering making a documentary."

"I see," Ranzoa nodded. "Isn't that expensive? I mean, you hear about these movies costing millions to produce."

"Not what I have in mind. Although money wouldn't be a problem."

Ranzoa gave a little bewildered laugh.

"Really?" he said. "That's hard to believe."

"Key West isn't Hollywood," Jack explained. "No actors. Just real people. No union problems. I'll hire locally, do the camera work myself. I think a story about the old families of Key West would be great. Never been done, as far as I know."

"Why would anyone care? I mean, a movie about my family? Sure, we've been here for more than a hundred years. But so what? The Ranzoa law firm? Real estate? Some politicians? Doesn't sound like, what do you call it in the biz? Oh, yeah, box office material."

"You just mentioned lawyers and politicians," Jack pointed out. "Right there is a combination crying for a story. I've also heard there were doctors in the Ranzoa family. What about them?"

"A great uncle or something," Ranzoa answered, smiling. "Don't remember anything outstanding about him. Our family has grown kind of small since then. Actually, just my dad and myself now."

"But weren't there a couple more Ranzoas who were doctors?" Jack asked. "Brother and sister. Little more recently?"

"I'm not sure," Ranzoa answered, this time somewhat hesitantly. "I'd have to ask dad. He's more up on the family history than I am."

"But you see what I mean, don't you?" Jack persisted. "The old families were the movers and the shakers. They built Key West."

"I've always felt the fishermen, cigar makers, carpenters and the like built the town," Bob Ranzoa said wryly.

"Of course they did," Jack agreed. "But it's the *founding* fathers that I'm interested in. I'm also going to talk with other families here. Yours is the first."

"Okay," Ranzoa nodded. "Like I said, my dad's better on that subject. Let me talk to him."

"That'd be perfect," Jack smiled. "Think he'd be willing to get together?"

"Have to ask him. So, how long are you in town?"

"For a while. Hey, I just have to ask this. What's the deal with your receptionist? She's really something. Is she married?"

"Her name's Lydia Blackwell. I don't think she's your type, Jack. Know what I mean?"

"Too bad," Jack said. "I was going to offer her a job in Hollywood."

Bob Ranzoa laughed.

"My wife's up in Tallahassee working, so I'm free for the night. Want to grab a couple of beers? The Green Parrot's right up the street."

~~~

The Green Parrot, anchored on the corner of Southard and Whitehead since the beginning of time, was an open-windowed bar that'd once been called the center of the universe. Published drinking hours were during the a.m.'s. – 10 a.m. to 4 a.m.

The late afternoon shift commanded the bar and conversation was running smoothly when Jack and Bob Ranzoa slide onto a couple of barstools.

"Been here before, Jack?" Bob asked.

"A few times. Get some great bands every now and then."

The bartender placed two cold Buds in front of them.

"Want glasses?" she asked.

"Bottles' fine," Jack told her.

"So, how 'bout you, Jack?" Ranzoa asked. "You married?"

"No, my wife and I split up."

Jack didn't include that she'd also been murdered and he'd been considered a suspect for awhile.

"Happens, I guess. Too bad. Any kids?"

"Nope."

"We don't, either," Bob Ranzoa said wistfully. "Well, at present we don't. We're planning to. A boy would be nice. Can't wait too long, otherwise it's the end of the line."

"I'm sorry?" Jack said, turning to him.

"There won't be a Robert Ternant Ranzoa, the Fourth, to take over the firm unless I get busy."

He laughed at his own joke and continued, " Karen, that's my wife, isn't against having children. But she has her career for now. And to be fair, so do I. She's an aide for a congressman. Actually, the one for this district. But my dad just can't handle the idea of having to wait around for a grandchild. Really got him fucked up. Doesn't know who to blame. Me or Karen."

"Aren't there others?" Jack asked. "I mean, do you have any brothers or sisters?"

"I'm an only child," Ranzoa answered. "Spoiled rotten. Privileged. All the vices."

"What about cousins, that sort of thing."

"Not too many of those. Some on my dad's side were killed in the war. I don't know which war. Had an aunt who moved to Cuba ages ago. Heck, we're the only ones still around."

Another pair of Buds appeared in front of them.

"Those cousins who were doctors, Armand and Ardell? That's their names, right? You know if they're still around?"

"You seem to know more about my family than I do, Jack. Yeah, I might've heard some mention of them but they would have been before my time. Don't know anything more."

Jack took a big pull from his beer.

"They had some kind of clinic here in town," he said, refusing to let go of the subject. "So they must've been an important part of the community, wouldn't you think? I heard that they moved. You wouldn't know where?"

"Maybe they moved," Ranzoa nodded. "I don't know anything about them."

"You should go to the cemetery," Jack said seriously.

"Do I look that bad?" Ranzoa laughed.

"No," Jack smiled. "I've visited it a couple of times. Interesting place, actually. One thing I noticed was all these children's graves. Seemed like they all died around the same time. That's why I was curious about the doctors. People said they might've delivered them. Maybe they knew what'd happened. Nobody else seems to."

Bob Ranzoa chugged his beer and stuck up two fingers for the bartender to see.

"I wouldn't know anything about that," he said. "You know, you look familiar. I can't place my finger on it but I'm sure I've seen you somewhere before."

Jack shrugged. He noticed a pool table standing in the back of the room. It was vacant.

"Shoot a game?" he asked, nodding toward the table. "Nine ball, okay?"

Bob Ranzoa shrugged a yes.

"Five bucks a game?" Jack grinned. He'd once been a hot stick in pool.

"Illegal to gamble here," Ranzoa said. "Sure. Five bucks."

"I'll rack, you break," he said to Jack.

Jack chalked his cue stick and placed it between his fingers, while standing at the head of the table. He stroked hard and cue ball smashed into the tightly racked balls, sending them scattering. The four-ball went into a side pocket. Jack had position on the one-ball. An easy shot and he stepped around the table to line up on number 3. He miscued, rolling the cue ball about six inches.

Bob Ranzoa chalked up and sank the three. Then the five, six, seven and eight.

"Nine in the corner," he announced. Game over.

Jack racked the balls without saying a word.

Ranzoa broke and then proceeded to run the table.

"Nine in the side."

"Jesus," Jack said. "I didn't know I was playing a pro."

"You're not," Ranzoa smiled. "I was the number three ranked *amateur* while in college."

"I thought amateurs weren't paid," he said, handing him a ten-spot.

"World's changed, Jack."

Returning to the bar, Ranzoa ordered another round.

"So, let's lay down our cards," he said, swiping his mouth. "Are you bullshitting me with this movie thing?"

"I'm serious about talking with you and anyone else about your family history. Why would I bullshit you? It could turn out to be big."

"I don't know, man," Ranzoa laughed, chugging half his beer. "Fucking movie. I just can't see it happening."

~~~

Carl Fischer was Detective Gleason's first witness. Fischer had made the appointment for 5 o'clock. He was a man in his early twenties and worked for one of the jet-ski rentals. The two of them sat in an interview room.

"So this is what it looks like, huh?" Fischer commented, taking in the small windowless room. "Like in that TV show."

"Thought we'd have a little more privacy in here," Gleason smiled. "Don't worry, though, we'll make you look good on the tape."

Fischer's eyes darted about looking for a hidden camera, then he laughed.

"That's a joke, right? I mean, seriously, you really aren't taping this."

"No, no cameras," Gleason said. "Those are for the bad guys. I am recording our conversation, but no video. Just relax and tell me what you saw, Mr. Fischer."

"Well, I was at Lateda having a drink."

"This was inside or outside?" Gleason interrupted.

"At the outside bar. This couple walked up. Stumbled up, at least the woman did. I thought she'd already had a few. Then I saw these ridiculous high heels she was wearing. Lucky she didn't break an ankle."

"What were they like?" Gleason asked. "The shoes."

"Man, you could nail yourself to the floor with those things. Vulgar looking red things. She was bitching about her feet hurting. Wonder why, huh?"

Gleason chuckled.

"She was pissed off at the dude she was with, too. And he wasn't fucking liking it."

"How do you know that?"

"Because he grabbed her by the arm right here." Fischer indicated on his own bicep. "Hard, too. She said for him to stop it. Said he was hurting her."

"Could you hear what the argument was about?"

"Not really. I mean, they weren't yelling at each other. Just speaking low and mean."

"What happened next?"

"The bartender told them to leave, said he wasn't serving them anything."

"And did they leave?"

"Sure. They weren't going to get a drink there."

"Did you notice which way they went after leaving Lateda?"

"They walked toward United Street."

Gleason removed two copies of photographs from a folder he'd placed on the table. He showed the first one to Fischer.

"Do you recognize this person?" he asked.

Fischer studied the picture.

"That's the dude who was in the paper, right?"

"And is he the one you saw at Lateda three nights ago?"

"I think so, yeah, although it's a little dark at the outside bar. Besides he wasn't smiling then like he is here."

Gleason paused for a moment and looked at Carl Fischer.

"You're saying now that you aren't certain?"

Fischer sighed. "I'm ninety percent certain, okay? Yeah, all right then, one hundred percent. That's him. What'd he do?"

Gleason ignored the question and picked up the next photograph.

"What about this woman?" he asked. "Do you recognize her?"

Fischer laughed. "Must be from a drivers license, huh?"

In fact, it was. Gleason had gotten it from the state motor vehicles office.

"I don't know, maybe. She looked better than that. And, like I said, it was dark. Still, yeah, I'd say that was the one."

Gleason put the photos back in the folder and stood up.

"Thank you, Mr. Fischer," he said, holding out his hand. "I appreciate your coming in."

The detective led Carl Fischer out. His next witness was due at six. He hoped to have better luck with him.

Right now, all he had was a so-so ID on Clarence Hayes and a maybe one on his wife. Virginia Hayes had said that her husband had gone out alone for a drink that night. Carl Fischer was unable to positively identify her as the woman who was with Clarence Hayes at Lateda. That person could easily have been someone Clarence Hayes picked up. The district attorney would recognize that in a minute, as would any defense lawyer.

His phone rang. It was the desk officer. His next witness had arrived.

Darlene Capps, like many others before her, had come to Key West on vacation and simply never left. That was eight years ago. It had been the water and perfect weather that'd stolen her heart. She was originally from Akron, Ohio.

"Please have a seat, Miss Capps," Gleason said, leading her into the interview room. "It is 'Miss', am I right?"

"It wasn't always but it is now," Darlene Capps smiled.

She had a broad, disarming smile, one that demanded a return in kind. A petite woman with blonde hair in a pixie cut. It suited her well.

"Where do you work, Miss Capps?"

"At the Key West Butterfly and Nature Conservatory. I'm a tour guide."

"Really? I've never been there."

"You should go. We have over sixty different species of butterflies."

"Well, I will certainly keep that in mind. Now, you said that you recognized the missing man whose picture was posted in the newspaper. Where was it that you saw him, Miss Capps? By the way, I'm taping our talk, just so I'll remember everything. That okay?"

"It's fine. I don't mind. Let's see, it was on South Street that I saw the man. I'd had dinner at Louie's Backyard and was walking home. I live on Amelia."

Louie's was located at the corner of Vernon and Waddell by Dog Beach.

"And what time was that?" Gleason asked.

"I don't know exactly," Darlene Capps answered, placing a finger to her cheek and smiling. "Maybe ten or so?"

"Alright, we'll say ten," Gleason smiled back. It was contagious. "And were you alone?"

"Yes, I'd had dinner with a girlfriend. She lives up near the Casa Marina. We met at Louie's. The man you're talking about passed by me heading up that way."

"What made you notice him?"

"Well, that's the strangest thing. He was with a woman. But he was walking in front of her. When they got closer, they looked like they'd been arguing. I mean, that's what drew my attention. He had this real angry expression on his face. That's why I remembered him. And she was glaring at him like she could've killed him. And here's the funny part. The woman was carrying her shoes. I could understand why, though. They were these super high heels. No wonder her feet were killing her. Actually, I remember the shoes more than I do her, bright red and shiny. Isn't that something?"

Gleason coughed a little laugh and sat up straight in his chair.

"Could you identify the shoes if you saw them again?"

"Oh, yes, you don't see many stilettos like those ones around here."

Gleason nodded and now, with a wolfish grin, opened the folder containing the photographs. He'd also included a shot of the shoe he'd found in the dumpster.

CHAPTER 13

Twombley Mortuary was a brick single-story building with a long, sheltered carport on one side, where a grey Cadillac hearse stood waiting. Two windows with shades drawn flanked the front door. Jack opened it and stepped inside.

The room, surprisingly small, was empty. Across from the entrance was another door with a sign on the wall next to a buzzer. The sign read 'press for service'. Jack pressed the button.

A moment later, a man opened the door.

"How may I help you?" he asked.

Jack, somewhat startled, said, "Are you Davy Jones?"

"No, I'm Mo-rel. Davy doesn't work here anymore. Hasn't for some time now."

Mo-rel was an older man, slightly stooped, and spoke with dramatic inflection.

Jack looked beyond the man, for only an instant, into the next room. Of what he expected to see, he had no idea.

"That's our chapel," Mo-rel enlightened him. "The room where we conduct our other business is behind it."

Jack made a grim face and said, "My name is Jack Hunter. Billy Bean, at the Inedible Café, mentioned a friend of his, Davy Jones, worked here and he might be able to help me with some research I'm doing."

"I know Billy Bean," Mo-rel grinned slowly. "Yes, he and Davy used to be great pals. You say you're doing some research with Davy? He's in the real-estate business now."

"Well, not exactly with him," Jack explained. "I was curious about some children's graves in the cemetery and Billy told me to ask Davy."

"What was it you wanted to know about those graves?" Mo-rel intoned, an air of suspicion now in his voice.

Jack let out a breath and said, "In 1965, more than a dozen children, infants actually, died and were buried there. What the hell happened?"

~~~

"I've checked every means of leaving the island," Gleason told Jay Halderman. "Taxis, limos, car rentals, airport, buses, ferry. If it flies, rolls or floats, we're on it. And no one has any record of her. And we have her damn car."

They were in Halderman's office at the police station. Gleason had had the audio tapes of the two witness interviews transcribed. He just finished going through Darlene Capps'.

"So where do you think she is?" Halderman asked.

"I don't know," Gleason answered, shaking his head. "She could be at a guest house. Or chancing the street. Fuck, she could've stolen a bicycle and rode it out of town. Maybe she has someone she knows down here?"

"Well, we'll find her," Halderman said. "Patrol has her picture. There's a BOLO out for her as a person of interest in a homicide to Monroe County Sheriffs. We'll run her drivers license picture in the local paper. I've also notified all the county departments in south Florida to be on the lookout. They're keeping an eye on the Hayes house in Alva. Already talked with a neighbor of theirs, Tom Williams. He and his wife live next door. So we've got a handle on it."

"You know this thing's still circumstantial," Gleason said. "I mean, that's what the DA's going to say. The woman whose other shoe belongs to the one we've got in the evidence room could've been someone the vic met in a bar. If Virginia Hayes goes to trial, her defense lawyer's going to be all over that."

"Why do you think she did it that way?" Halderman asked. "Killed her husband, dumped his body in the trunk of their car, and then reported him missing? Weird shit, if you ask me."

"I think she panicked when she realized what she'd done," Gleason speculated. "Decided to hide the body until she could figure out what to do next."

"Yeah, but why the missing report?"

"Alibi. She thinks if the cops believe he's run off, then it's no big deal. After that, she leaves town and dumps Clarence Hayes somewhere on the way back home."

"That could work," Halderman agreed. "Why'd it happen in the parking lot? Pretty convenient. Car right there."

"Maybe they wanted to get something out of the trunk. Started arguing again. They'd already been at it according to our witness. Things start getting out of hand and Virginia Hayes pops her hubby upside the head with a shoe you could use for an icepick. He wasn't a big guy. She could've easily put him in the trunk. Especially if she didn't have to drag him far."

~~~

No giant shark fin cutting through the water. Jack peered through the binoculars again, pulling the Atlantic Ocean closer.

"Let me try the damn things," Billy said, reaching for the glasses.

The two of them stood at the end of the tiny pier jutting out from Duval. A great white shark, whose position had been reported daily in the papers ever since it'd been spotted off the coast at Jupiter, was due to cruise past Key West today. Everyone on the island had followed its progress. Bets were being placed on whether or not Carcharodon carcharias would even show. Pools were started in several bars on the exact time it would cross Duval Street. The fish, originally having been reported to be 16 feet long, had suddenly grown to 23 feet – two-man sub size – now that it was closing in on Key West waters.

Billy squinted into the eyepieces.

"Shark's a night swimmer," he pronounced knowingly. "Won't see him in day time."

"What say we head back to the restaurant?" Jack suggested, thinking to himself that he'd never heard anything about sharks' swimming habits. Nocturnal or whatever.

Billy agreed and Jack put the binoculars back in their case.

"Don't know about those folks who own the building that the Vesuvius is in," Billy said, as they turned onto Whitehead Street. "Might not be wanting to rent it out for another restaurant."

"They might not, Jack, but I think we ought to go talk directly with them. Drive up to Miami. Only take a day. How 'bout it?"

Jack remembered the last time he and Billy drove to Miami and were nearly caught in a swamp fire.

"I'm not sure that's a good idea," he said.

"That's 'cause your head's so wrapped up in those dead babies," Billy snapped. "Don't have time to spare for anything else. Friends, business, nothing!"

Jack fell silent. They'd crossed Truman before he spoke again.

"Moe over at Twombley's had quite a story to tell about those dead babies."

"Who?" Billy asked.

"Moe Wrell," Jack said. "The old guy that works there."

"You must be talking about Mo-rel, hee-hee."

Jack gave Billy an odd look.

"Guess it's all in how you say it," he said. "Anyway, some of the things he told me sounded like there should've been an investigation."

"What makes you think there wasn't, Jack?"

"Didn't sound like there'd been much done. At least as far as the cops went. Business as usual is what I get out of it."

"The cops didn't do anything because there wasn't anything for them to do," Billy said. "Those poor babies died because sometimes babies just die. You talk with Davy Jones before the next time you go poking around Twombley's. Leave that crazy old Mo-rel to himself."

~~~

William Street

The clinic was an ordinary two-story structure, put up in the late 1800s and owing its longevity to the generous use of Dade county pine throughout, a densely grained wood so hard as to occasionally defy a driven nail and considered hopeless as a meal by termites. The building had been through several transformations. Built originally for a seafarer's family, over the course of time it had seen use as a cigar maker's shop, a brothel, a grocery store and lastly, as the clinic of the Doctors Ranzoa.

The house had long ago shed its porch in favor of a closed-in front extending out to the sidewalk. Inside, a cramped waiting room faced William Street. A long hallway ran off it to the rear. Two large examination rooms were set across the hallway opposite from each other. A small laboratory followed, occupying one side in the back with a kitchen taking up the space on other side. The staircase for the second floor and a bathroom finished off the ground floor. Upstairs was basically unused, save for filing cabinets, odds and ends, and worn-out furniture.

Oddly, a musty gloom seemed to have settled over the entire place at one time and had refused to leave. It was not a happy house.

Mrs. Sharon Gibbs sat in the waiting room with her three-month old son, Ned. This was her fourth visit to the clinic with her child and she was worried.

"He just seems so puny," she said to the receptionist, Joanne Futrel, a woman her own age. "He nurses, but I'm not sure how much he's getting. Do you think it has to do with his mouth?"

Little Ned had been born with a cleft lip.

"Doesn't seem like it would," Joanne smiled. "The doctor will know, though."

"Which one is seeing us?" Sharon asked.

"You get both of them today," Joanne answered, and added with a laugh, "Two for the price of one."

Her intercom buzzed and she got up from her desk.

"I'll take you back," she said. "They're ready."

Joanne knocked on the door and entered. The walls were painted in a glossy cold white. White linoleum tiles covered the floor. A large light hung from the ceiling illuminating an examination table which stood in the center of the room. Both Armand and Ardell Ranzoa waited by the table. On top of a pedestal tray, positioned by the table, were a stethoscope, several vials of clear liquid and a hypodermic syringe. Against the wall, a tall medicine cabinet with glass doors displayed a frightening array of surgical instruments.

It was chilly in the room and Sharon hugged Ned closer to her breast.

Armand and Ardell greeted Sharon and Ned with broad smiles.

"How's our little fellow feeling today?" Armand said, taking Ned from his mom's arms and sitting him on the table.

Ned began to fret.

Ardell picked him up and held him close while gently patting his back.

"There, there," she cooed. "You're a big boy now."

"He hasn't been nursing as well," Sharon said, anxiously.

"Have you tried solid food?" Armand asked.

"I gave him some strained peas but he didn't like it too much. I'm just so worried."

Ned began to fret again.

"Sharon, I know you're concerned. I would be, too. But I think you might be upsetting little Ned," Ardell said. "Why don't you step out into the waiting room until he calms down. Dr. Armand and I will take care of him."

Sharon hesitated. Instinctively, she didn't want to leave her child, whether upsetting him or not.

"Could I just wait outside the door?" she asked.

"That'd be fine," Ardell smiled.

Sharon stood in the hall by the examination room and listened through the closed door. Only silence came from within.

Dr. Ardell suddenly opened the door.

"He's okay," she said. "Probably just needs a little booster shot. I have to get it from the back."

"Can I come in now?" Sharon asked, looking past Ardell to where her child lay on the table.

"Why don't you wait here," Ardell told her, slowly closing the door. "We'll only be a few minutes longer."

And indeed, Ned was back in his mom's arms soon afterwards.

"He's sleepy," Armand Ranzoa said. "Sometimes the shot will do that. It'll wear off before you get home."

Little Boxes

Sharon thanked the doctors, said goodbye to Joanne as she left the office. Ten minutes later she rushed back.
"Something's wrong!" she cried.

CHAPTER 14

Virginia Hayes liked what she saw. The face staring back at her in the mirror seemed a little younger, drew attention to her high cheekbones now that the old bouffant of hair had been chopped. And the new platinum blonde color? Well, classy was the word that came to mind, wouldn't one say? And she did just that, said it to her reflection.

Yes, she hadn't lost her touch. She could probably get her job back as a stylist at Dollie's Beauty Salon. Hell, maybe she'd look into it. Get back up to Georgia where she belonged. Start life over again. Only this time she'd do it right. To think what she'd given up by rushing out and marrying that bastard. Well, she'd never been good with choosing men, had she?

First though, she had to get out of this damn place. But where to? Not back home, the police would be waiting for her to show up there. Well, that was no big deal. She'd never liked living there. Fucking Clarence's house, anyway. She'd miss her car, though.

She'd gone to the drugstore and bought the stuff she would need as soon as the taxi had dropped her off at the hotel. Hair dye, scissors and new makeup. She'd also picked up a couple of shorts, tops and a pair of flip-flops. Back in the room, she got down to work.

It had taken half the night to finish and then clean up. No use leaving anything that might give the cops ideas.

Afterwards, she'd rested a couple of hours before slipping out by the patio. She hadn't wanted the hotel people to see her. Too bad about the bill but they'd get over it. Besides, people are always fucking over hotels. They just make it up on the next person anyway.

She strolled along Duval, pulling her roller bag, as the street woke up to start a new day. Just like her. Imagine that! Yesterday was done and gone and there was nothing she could do to bring it back. She stopped by a trash bin next to a Seven-Eleven store. No one was around. She emptied the rest of her clothes into it from her roller bag, keeping only some clean panties and a favorite blouse which she put in the new cloth tote she'd bought, and left the old roller bag beside the bin.

That's when she spied the guesthouse. Up the little lane running off Duval. Not too big, so it wouldn't be full of nosy people. It looked perfect. And best of all, it had a vacancy sign out front.

Registering wasn't even the slightest problem. She'd kept her old Georgia drivers license when she'd gotten a new one in Florida. The photograph showed her years younger. And those pictures were always so terrible anyway. It had her maiden name on it, too. Virginia Tilly. The woman at the guesthouse never even noticed it was an expired license. Wasn't that lucky?

And thank goodness she'd kept her own bank account in Atlanta and not turned it over to Clarence. Even though he'd pestered her about it from the moment they'd both said 'I do'.

Maybe God had bigger things in mind for her after all. She wondered. Clarence had been a test. Of course! Why, just look at the facts. Theirs had been a whirlwind romance. More a week of furious fucking, to tell the truth. She'd known he had a mean streak and still she went ahead and married him. God had given her a choice then and she had made the wrong one. The Almighty was testing her and she'd flunked. Well, now He had given her another chance. This time she was going to pass it with a big, fat A.

She rubbed a little pomade in her hands and pooched up her spiky hair. Yeah, she liked the look. Tilly, the new girl in town. Maybe she'd go out for a small celebration.

~~~

"What do you mean, Dr. Skye is on sick leave?" Jack asked, somewhat irritated. "Who am I supposed to talk with about my tests? And where is Dr. Skye anyway?"

"I'll answer your questions in order, Mr. Hunter," a very calm voice assured him from two thousand miles away. "By the way, my name is Bev Oakes. I work with Dr. Skye."

Jack sighed and said, "Good. I'm sorry if I seemed a little excited. It's just I haven't heard anything since Dr. Skye ordered the tests. And she'd promised to get back to me."

"Certainly, I understand," Bev Oakes said. "First, Jessica had an attack of appendicitis. She was operated on and everything is all right. However, though she's still out of the office, I'm in touch with her every day."

"Appendicitis? Out of the blue like that? I just saw her not that long ago."

"Well, those things happen. Anyway, I have your tests back and I'll talk with you about the results. Okay?"

101

Jack gave a tight little laugh and readied himself for the verdict.

"What the test showed is that your platelet count is normal. Now about that normal. It would be on the low side based on, say, a bell curve. But taking everything in consideration, all the tests we ran, etcetera, etcetera, your bell curve is simply placed on the low side of normal. Which means simply that you're fine. Make sense?"

"So I'm not dying? That what you're saying?"

"You're not going to die. At least from what we were originally worried about."

"That's great! Is there anything I should do? You know, to improve the platelet count?"

Jack got up from the chair and walked out on his porch. He was at home on Ashe Street. He'd earlier left the restaurant to check his mail in the hope of finding something from Dr. Skye. The empty mailbox prompted him to call the UCLA Medical Center.

"Yes," Bev said cheerfully. "Dr. Skye recommends that you eat lots of spinach. Not cooked. But raw. There's something in raw spinach that helps build platelets."

"Raw spinach? But Popeye eats it out of the can."

"Eat it raw," Bev teased. "I bet you know how to do that."

Jack ended the call with a big grin across his face.

~~~

Virginia Hayes followed wherever her fancy took her along Duval Street. She had no idea where she'd end up. But then, she was in no hurry to get there. She simply drifted along in the slow, flowing clutches of tourists.

She could be any one of them, down in the keys for a couple of days, lazing around. A perfect blend in her new pink shorts with Key West blazed in white across the seat, a yellow tank top stating 'Hi Cutie', and comfortable flip-flops adorned with plastic flowers.

Just before Southard Street a display in a store window caught her attention. She stopped to look. Knives of every description and size fanned out before her. Her eye fell on one in particular. A pocket knife no more than three inches long, slim and fashioned from stainless steel with inlaid pearl on its handle. The card beside the small knife introduced it as 'The perfect lady's push-button auto'. It looked quick and mean.

Sometimes a girl needs a little protection, you know? She went inside.

~~~

This thing about spinach had put Jack in a swivet. He'd rushed over to the market on White Street right after getting off the phone. But how much of the stuff was he supposed to eat? There were only three bunches in the produce department. Would that be enough? And how long would they keep? What was here looked like they were on their last legs. He bought them all.

Back home he rinsed off the bunches in the kitchen sink, placed one in a large bowl, and removed its wrapper. The others he stuck in the refrigerator. Rummaging in the cabinet, he found an ancient bottle of olive oil. This he drenched on the leaves and gave them a final toss. Then he dug in.

He didn't care for it one bit. Something was rancid. And the leaves were still gritty. Yet he kept at it until at last the bowl was empty. He guessed his platelets were happy now.

Maybe Billy could help him out at the restaurant. Whip up something a little more palatable. He removed the remaining bunches from the refrigerator and tossed them in the garbage. A walk to town might be just the thing. Settle his stomach and perhaps have a drink or two for being such a good boy and following the doctor's orders.

~~~

Detective Earl Gleason was struggling with Act III in his investigation. He knew he was dead right about the events leading up to the murder of Clarence Hayes. Acts I and II. He had the murder weapon, probable motive, witnesses of a sort, and now a prime suspect, Virginia Hayes.

Hayes, however, may have affected a different appearance. The techs had found hair clippings and traces of dye in the bathroom at the hotel.

The stiletto heel had been driven into the victim's head with such force that the killer couldn't withdraw it. Score one for the good guys. No doubt about the weapon. And he'd found what he believed to be the matching shoe, which forensics will be able to ascertain and possibly extract DNA. Exactly why she'd killed her husband will hopefully come out in the interview. But from what his witnesses have told him, it was in probably the heat of the moment. That might be of some help to the Hayes woman's defense at her trial. Of course, one small drawback at the moment was that he hadn't a clue as to where she'd gone.

He needed a break, and he was taking one by heading toward the Smokin' Tuna for an order of boiled shrimp, a cold beer and an earful of good music. Crossing over Caroline Street, he'd just passed the Bull when he noticed a woman approaching him on the sidewalk. Another tourist from the way she was dressed, yet there was something familiar about her. Apparently she had the same feeling about him because as Virginia Hayes got within eyeshot of Gleason, she screamed. The effect on the detective was one of immediate recognition.

"POLICE!" Gleason shouted. "PUT UP YOUR HANDS!"

He was so intent on grabbing ahold of her that he didn't see the knife.

~~~

Jack Hunter, who'd also been southbound on Duval, had put a grin on his face when he'd first spotted Gleason about twenty feet ahead. He'd been thinking about asking the detective about the graves. Suddenly, he was caught up in a whirl of commotion.

~~~

The knife ripped through the fabric of Gleason's shirt on the left side just below his arm as he reached for Virginia Hayes, its blade slashing across his ribs on the backstroke as Virginia readied to lunge at him again.

Jack saw what was about to happen.

"KNIFE!" he yelled. "SHE'S GOT A KNIFE!"

Gleason was momentarily started.

Jack hurtled into Virginia Hayes at full tilt and sent her sprawling onto the sidewalk, the cruel little knife flying from her hand.

Then time slowed down.

Gleason bent over holding his side.

Virginia Hayes lay facedown on the pavement and out cold.

"Cuffs," Gleason gasped, removing his own from their case and handing them to Jack. "Cuff her good." It'd gotten real personal now. He'd prove those red shoes were hers, one way or the other.

The patrol car screeched to a stop at the curb, blue lights flashing.

CHAPTER 15

Jack made page one in *The Citizen*, although the paper's makeup man had placed the story at the bottom. The top of the page belonged to the superyacht that had run aground in a protected area and plowed a trench through a hundred feet of endangered coral. The continuing story on the inside page about the arrest featured Jack's picture with a cutline: Local Man Helps Nab Suspect.

"I don't know what it is with you, Hunter," Jay Halderman mused. "Like a shit storm follows you around."

"Lucky thing's the way I see it," Jack told the Lieutenant. "Although a shit storm pretty much describes what went on."

He was at the police station by request. After last evening's romp on Duval Street and Jack had been cleared by the cops at the scene, he'd called Halderman to find out how Gleason was doing. Jay had asked him to drop by in the morning.

"No, I think you have something to do with it," Halderman said. "Let me count the incidents since our first meeting. Muggings. Death by overdose. Street fights. Shootings. Car crashes. Earthquakes. Sunk islands. I'm about to run out of fingers, Hunter."

Jack chuckled.

"So when's Detective Gleason coming back to work?" he asked.

"I'm giving him a week's leave. Pretty nasty cut he got from that woman. Yeah, and I guess both Earl and myself do owe you a hefty thanks."

Jack smiled, a slight blush filling his face.

"Don't suppose I could have Gleason's phone number? I'd like to give him a call. See how he's doing."

Halderman raised his eyebrows.

"Can't do that, Hunter. But I'll pass on that you asked about him. He have your number?"

Jack was certain that Gleason did but he wrote it down for Halderman anyway. Then he left the police station and rode his bike to the restaurant.

~~~

"That's the guy I was telling you about, dad," Bob Ranzoa said, pointing out Jack's picture in the paper. "Pretty brave thing, he did, huh?"

Father and son were breakfasting together at Blue Heaven. They'd started making it a regular thing two years ago. It was a convenient place for the old man to rag on his son before going to the office where Lydia might overhear. The senior Robert had an eye out for her.

"Mr. Hollywood," the older man grunted. "Think I've seen this fellow before down here. Don't remember exactly where but it'll come to me."

"Yeah," Bob Ranzoa laughed. "He seems like a nice guy. What do you think of his idea? Could make you a star, dad."

"Google. You ever hear of that?"

"Yes, dad, of course I have," Bob said. "What's that have to do with what we're talking about?"

"I'll tell you, Bobby. Your Mr. Hollywood was involved in a murder case back in Los Angeles. You see, I Googled the s.o.b. Found out a lot of interesting stuff. But that's not where I remember him from."

"You're kidding? He's a murderer?"

"That's just for openers. Next thing, he doesn't work for any goddamn movie company. Real estate's what he does."

Robert II sipped from his coffee cup and made a face.

"Goddamn stuff's cold," he muttered. "Waiter!"

"Here's what I want you to do," he said after his cup had been refilled. "Next time Mr. Hollywood calls you, invite him over to the house. I'd like to meet him."

~~~

8:oo a.m. West Coast time. Jack figured it wasn't too early to call Detective Laura Dalton, what with the three-hour time difference between them. He caught her at the LAPD shooting range.

"How's everything going?" he said while pedaling along Truman Avenue.

"Qualification day," Dalton answered. "So what's up on sin island?"

"Hang on a moment," Jack said, pulling over to the sidewalk where he stopped to continue their conversation. "I was on my bike."

He told her about the cemetery. Discovering the children's graves, so many of them dying in one particular year. And how odd that had seemed to him. And at odds with national statistics, he added. He brought up the rumors about the doctors.

"Their name is Ranzoa," Jack said. "Apparently they're no longer around. At least not in Key West. I've met a guy from the family. He and his dad are lawyers. Didn't seem to know much, or else didn't want to talk about it."

"Look, Jack, do you think you should be getting involved in this?" Laura asked. "I mean, if there had been any kind of crime committed, there would have an investigation. Rumors don't mean a thing."

"Yeah, but that's just the thing," Jack countered. "You have people here saying nothing happened, just ugly talk and all. Then there are others believing the two doctors were behind it. When I consider the number of graves and everything else, I kind of lean toward the doctors. And a cover-up."

"Oh, now it's a cover-up, too?" Laura laughed. "Jack, you're in Key West. Conspiracy center, USA."

"Yeah, it is funny, Laura, and I'd laugh, too. Except the numbers don't add up. One guy I talked with tied the deaths to a big jump in population back then. Military increase, he attributed it to. They'd had to have been screwing like bunnies. No, something else happened, believe me."

"So what are you going to do about it?"

"I need some help," Jack said. "Alice is away. I'd like to hire her but she's seeing her mom or something. You wouldn't want to come and freelance a little investigative work, would you?"

"Can't do, Jack. I'd have to resign, you know that. Besides, I've got four homicides. Also, there's another seminar the new captain wants me to attend. What about the KWPD? Have you checked with them? I mean, if anything went on like you suspect, surely they'd know. Did you ask?"

"Not yet but I was thinking about getting Gleason in on it. Remember him?"

"Of course I do. Give him my love when you see him. Hey, I've got to run. I'm up on the line next. Bye."

Jack ended the call. He didn't tell her that he'd seen Gleason last night. And he wasn't about to give him her love either when he next did see him. He got back on his bike and continued on the restaurant.

The Inedible Café had cleared of the breakfast crowd by the time Jack arrived. He left the bike in the alley behind the building and went in through the kitchen. Billy was sitting at a table in the dining room engrossed in the newspaper.

Jack pulled out a chair and sat down. Billy raised his eyes over the paper, a concerned expression on his face.

"You keep this up and I might lose a partner," he said, pointing out the article on the arrest. "How's Gleason?"

"Just came from talking with his boss," Jack said. "He's okay. They gave him a week off to recuperate."

"Well, at least those fellows down there have got some sense," Billy grumped. "By the way, breakfast's over and done with."

"Even for a partner?"

"Hell, what do you want? Fix you some eggs?"

Billy started to get up and Jack held out his hand for him to sit.

"No, I'm fine, thanks. Just wanted to ask about that friend of yours at the funeral home."

"You mean that fool Mor-el? Told you to stay away from him."

"The other one," Jack said. "Maybe I will have a cup of coffee."

He walked over to the coffee urn.

"What was his name?" Jack said, returning and sitting back down. "Denny something?"

"Davy Jones," Billy corrected. "Used to run around together, me and him. Davy no longer works at Twombley. Got a real estate business now."

"Yeah, that's what whatshisname said. Wonder if you could get ahold of him. I'll buy him lunch if he'd like to come here. What do you think?"

Billy walked over to the wall phone next to the kitchen door to make the call.

"Davy can't make lunch," he said, returning to the table, "but don't worry none. Said he'd meet you in an hour for a drink at Lateda. So maybe you'd have time to drop by the Vesuvius for another look, hee-hee."

~~~

To please Billy, Jack stopped by the Vesuvius on his way to Duval Street. He spent a few minutes looking at the patio, which was the best thing about the place. A great name for it came to mind. *Stella by Starlight.* He liked that. Maybe it'd be worth taking a chance on buying the dump just so he could call it that.

A few people were sitting at the outside bar when he arrived at Lateda. He chose a vacant stool at one corner.

"What can I get you?" the bartender asked.

"Nothing right now," Jack said. "I'm meeting someone here. You wouldn't know a guy named Davy Jones, would you?"

"Yeah, he comes in once in awhile," the bartender said, then, "wait a minute, here he comes now."

A distinguished looking black man, dressed in an impeccable white suit with a shaved head and a ten-thousand dollar watch on his wrist, stuck out his hand and said, "You must be Jack."

"Davy Jones, I presume," Jack smiled, shaking his hand.

Both men laughed.

"Just a Coke, Andrew," Davy said to the bartender. "How 'bout you, Jack?"

"Same."

"Billy told me you wanted to know about Twombley's," Davy said. "How is that?"

Jack let out a breath.

"It's something I've gotten myself involved with," Jack began. "You're familiar with the cemetery, right?"

Jack then repeated much of the story he'd earlier told to Laura Dalton, including the rumors about the two doctors.

"You believe that?" Davy asked. "I mean the business about the doctors being responsible for those deaths?"

"I don't know what I believe, except that something isn't right. Maybe it boils down to a hiccup in statistics. Bad year to be a newborn. Who knows?"

"Well, there was this one little girl we readied when I was at Twombley's. I think about her sometimes. You want another Coke? Think I'll have a shot."

Davy ordered two shots of Chivas from Andrew.

"I'm no longer in the funeral business," Davy said, sipping the scotch. "Haven't been for years actually. Left there right after Mr. Roscoe passed. Roscoe Twombley. He owned the mortuary. I sell real estate. Key West is still the place to buy, if you're interested."

He handed a business card to Jack.

"Thanks, I'll let you know," Jack said, pocketing the card.

"Yeah, don't call me, I'll call you," Davy laughed. "Anyway, back to that little girl. She was only five or six months old. Now she was at the funeral home. Man!"

Davy took a breath. And another sip.

"Still bothers me to think about it, Jack. Here was the thing. Like I said, she was a beautiful baby. I mean, if you could call a baby an angel, she'd be it. You know what I mean? Even lying there no longer in this world, she was still pretty. Perfect."

Jack nodded and said, "So that was it? The fact that she was beautiful upset you?"

Davy Jones remained silent for a full minute.

"There was more to it than that, Jack," he said at last.

CHAPTER 16

"They gave me some dope for the pain," Gleason said. "I'm doing okay."

Jack had returned home from Lateda when the detective had called. It was late afternoon and a storm grumbled threats from the distance.

"What about the cut?" Jack asked.

"Minor shit," Gleason replied.

In truth, the little knife had done quite a bit of mischief. A one-inch deep gash requiring a number of sutures. The wound was as clean as if it'd been made by a scalpel.

"As much as I hate to say it, Hunter, thanks for the assist."

"You're welcome," Jack said.

"No, I mean it," Gleason continued. "I think if she'd gotten to take another swipe, I might've been in real trouble."

The sky darkened with a clap of thunder. Raindrops began to dance in the street.

"I was talking with Laura earlier," Jack said. "She says hello."

Says hello, mind you, not sends her love.

"Hey, thanks, she's a nice lady. Miss her. Tell her hello for me next time you all talk. Think she might come for a visit? Really like to see her."

Really, huh? Jack filed that one away.

"Can't say when she'll be here next. She has a pretty full plate right now."

"Well, I can understand how that goes."

"Look, Earl, I'm glad you called. There's something I want to run by you. Has to do with the cemetery. You ever go there?"

Gleason coughed a little laugh. Jack could almost see him wince.

"For a minute or so I thought Virginia Hayes might be sending me there," he said. "No, it's not high on my bucket list."

"Think you could dope up enough to meet me there tomorrow morning? Say around 8:30? I'll buy us breakfast at Harpoon Harry's afterwards."

"What the hell's so important at the damn cemetery?"

"Won't know until you see it."

~~~

Gleason stopped in front of the main entrance on Passover Lane right on time. Jack was waiting.

"There's a spot ahead on Margaret if you don't want to park in the cemetery," he told him, sticking his head in the side window.

"I'll pull in there by the office," he said.

When he got out of the car, Jack noticed a slight hitch in his step.

"How're you doing?"

"Little tender," Gleanson replied. "So don't make me laugh."

"I don't think that will be a problem here, Earl. Although there are some funny last words on some of the headstones. Let's take a walk."

The grass, still wet from last night's shower, glistened like glass shards.

They came to the first tiny grave in the long row running along the fence. Jack stopped for a moment and then continued on to the next. And the next after that. Little boxes buried by broken hearts.

No words were exchanged between the two men as they slowly passed each gravesite. A dirty vase on one held a faded plastic flower. On another a bedraggled stuffed toy. Some graves were unmarked. Unvisited.

The row ended at an asphalt-surfaced lane, First Avenue.

"What do you think?" Jack asked quietly.

"Let me walk back by myself," Gleason said quietly.

Jack stood in the warming sun as the detective slowly made his way between the headstones, stopping occasionally to jot down something.

When he returned, he bit his lip and hesitated before speaking.

"Looks like nineteen sixty-five was a banner year," he said.

"There are even more graves in the sixties," Jack said. "But '65 has the biggest concentration. Lady said that after they'd moved the cemetery to here, they made this area the children's section. Only spot big enough not spoken for. Don't know if that means anything."

"So what's your take on all of this?" Gleason asked.

"I think something happened to those kids that shouldn't have," Jack told him. "Rumors have a couple of doctors involved. A brother and sister named Ranzoa. I've tried to look into it but haven't found anything solid.

Doctors seem to have disappeared off the face of the earth. That's why I wanted you to come here. See for yourself. Tell me if I'm crazy or not."

Gleason just shook his head.

"I can ask Jay about those rumors, I guess. But a thing like you're talking about would've been big news."

Jack agreed, "Yeah, you're right. That is, if anyone ever bothered to look into it. You know how old rich families can shut things down. Why don't we go have that breakfast I promised? There are a couple more things you ought to know."

They didn't walk back through the children's area but instead went the other way past the U.S. Maine monument to the exit.

~~~

Gleason and Jack commandeered a booth in the back. It hadn't been a busy morning at Harpoon Harry's so there were plenty of seats available. The waitress brought them menus but they already knew what they wanted.

"Scrambled eggs hard and bacon crisp," Gleason said. Jack ordered the same.

"I met this one guy at the cemetery," Jack said when the waitress left. "He was visiting his sister's grave. She'd died shortly after birth, couple of days or so. The man had been a kid himself at the time. Anyway, I told him that I'd noticed all the graves and asked if he had any idea about what'd happened?"

The waitress returned with two cups of coffee. Smiled, and with a turn was gone.

"The man actually mentioned the doctors," Jack said, sipping his coffee and getting back to the story. "Said his mom had taken her daughter to them for some illness, I forget what, and the poor child had a heart attack right in the office and died."

"Autopsy confirm that?" Gleason asked. "Heart attack on a newborn?"

"Wasn't any autopsy done," Jack answered. "If fact, the guy became upset when I asked the same thing. Said it wouldn't have been right to have an autopsy done on a baby."

Gleason nodded in agreement.

"A lot of people feel that way," he said. "Autopsy's pretty gruesome thing."

"Yeah, I guess so," Jack sighed. "I never considered that. Especially when it's done to an infant. Poor guy."

Their eggs arrived. Gleason drenched his in hot sauce. Jack was more of a pepper abuser. The grits weren't spared, either.

"You boys need anything else?" the waitress asked.

"No, ma'am," Gleason mumbled.

She spun away.

"My partner at the restaurant, Billy Bean, you remember him, don't you?"

"Of course I do. He's the one who tried to put the make on the hold-up guy, right?"

"Screw you, Gleason," Jack laughed.

Gleason grinned and polished off the last of his eggs. He picked up a piece of toast and began slathering it with grape jelly.

"Billy has a pal who used to work at Twombley Mortuary," Jack said. "I talked with him and he told me a pretty interesting story."

Jack then related how Davy Jones had been at the mortuary when the body of an infant, a girl, was brought in. The child had been extraordinarily beautiful, Jones had said, which somehow to him made her brief life even sadder. But he had noticed something disturbing during the body's preparation. The eyes were bloodshot. He'd examined them more closely and saw tiny red pinpoints. What upset him in particular was that he'd seen the identical condition before. With his niece, also an infant, who had been suffocated by her mother having rolled over on her while they both slept in the same bed. It was a terrible tragedy and one not uncommon.

"Petechial," Gleason said. "Shows up in death by strangulation or smothering. Has to do with blood pressure. Tiny veins in the eyes leak. So what was the deal? Was the girl rolled on by her mom, too?"

"Jones said she'd died at the doctors' office. The Ranzoas'. That's another one."

Gleason let that settle for a moment.

"He have any idea what the death certificate stated as cause of death?" he asked.

"If he did, he didn't mention it."

"That'd be interesting to see," Gleason said. "What was the date?"

"Had to be in the sixties," Jack said. "Just guessing. I could call him and ask if he remembers."

"Do that," Gleason nodded. "Yeah, since this thing seems to have made a big impression on him, he might know the date. Ask if he remembers the kid's name, too."

"There was another fellow who works at Twombley's," Jack said. "Been there forever. Told me some interesting stories. Maybe you'd like to check him out."

"Uh, maybe and maybe not," Gleason said. "We don't know if a crime has been committed. Not only that, but this all happened a long time ago. I can't go barging in on people. There are the families to consider, too. I don't want to go rushing in like gangbusters. Let's see what develops."

"That's the whole point, isn't it?" Jack said heatedly. "Families of those children. Like that poor bastard I talked with whose little sister he never knew is dead and buried. I'm telling you there's something wrong about all those graves out there!"

"Hey, take it easy!" Gleason said. "I'm going to the station and finish up some paperwork. I'll ask around. Okay?"

CHAPTER 17

"Just tell me now," Robert Ranzoa said into the phone. "Don't send any emails. And burn everything you have when we're finished."

He was in his office at the firm on Whitehead' speaking with a private investigator in Miami that he used from time to time.

"No, no," Ranzoa said, lowering his voice. "I don't need any outside help. This is a family matter."

Ranzoa could call in any 'outside help' himself should it come to that, but he didn't mention it to the investigator.

The investigator gave his report while Ranzoa listened, tight-lipped and giving an occasional nod in silent confirmation. When it was over, he thanked him and ended the call. Then he punched in his son's extension.

"Bobby, ask your Mr. Hunter to drop by the house for cocktails this evening."

~~~

Key West basked happily under a tropical sun but Jack was in a dark and cheerless mood. He'd remained at the harbor after Gleason left, following the boardwalk around to Front Street and from there going on to Mallory Square.

Several nice yachts were outbound in the channel between Sunset Key and the Square and Jack stopped to watch them pass. He took out his cellphone and punched in a number.

"This is Davy Jones," the voice answered.

"Mr. Jones, Jack Hunter here."

"Decided on buying a house after all, huh?" Jones laughed.

"No, but that gives me an idea. I might need you as a buyer's agent. You up for the job?"

"You bet. Name the time and place."

Two cruise ships had docked earlier and passengers were still being pumped out like bilge water in a steady flow. A group of them chattered past.

"One other thing," Jack said. "You mentioned an infant when we last talked. Said how pretty she was. Do you remember her name?"

Davy Jones paused for a moment before answering.

"She was Samantha Adams," he sighed. "The death was in November of nineteen sixty-five."

"Thanks, Davy. I'll let you know about the other thing."

Jack next called the Key West police department and asked to speak with Detective Earl Gleason. Another officer answered.

"Gleason's on leave," he told Jack. "Is this police business?"

"I just had some information for him," Jack said. "I'll call back."

Jack ended the call and scrolled up Gleason's number. He'd captured it when the detective had first phoned him. He hadn't wanted him to know, that was all.

"What the fuck?" Gleason said when he answered. "How'd you get this number? Oh, shit. Of course, I called you."

"Sorry about that," Jack said. "I tried to get you at the office."

"Well, I'm not there am I? I'm supposed to be on a medical leave. Recuperating at home. All that good stuff. So what's up?"

"I have a name and date for the girl Davy Jones mentioned," Jack said. "The one with the bloodshot eyes? Maybe it'll help."

Gleason took down the information.

"Are there any records the police might have?" Jack asked. "For instance, where do they keep death certificates? Doctor has to sign them, right?"

"Look, Hunter, I'll do what I can, okay?" Gleason said sharply. "I mean, this thing isn't the crime of the century yet. If even a crime has been committed. Like I said, we don't know anything. There are a lot of questions."

Jack let out a breath.

"Yeah, we don't know," he said. "And no one will ever know unless somebody starts looking for answers and asking more questions. But there is one thing I already know. My gut tells me there's a problem with this whole damn mess. You've got the girl's name. Do what you can."

He didn't wait for a reply before hanging up.

People were still spilling out of the cruise ships. Jack took Front Street down to where he could cut over to Truman Annex. He entered the gated community and immediately was freed from the crowds.

The Annex isn't a bad place for a stroll. Perhaps a little too sanitized for some. It's kind of like being on a movie studio lot where they could shoot a very wealthy, up-dated version of Our Town. White picket fences running the length of the street. Manicured plantings surrounding each home. Mostly empty structures. Second and third homes. Seldom did you see anyone in them.

Once past the Little White House, he had the sidewalk practically to himself. Lizards scurried back and forth across his shadow, the sun having drifted westward. He came to Southard Street and turned left to leave the Annex. The restaurant wasn't all that far from Thomas Street. He headed there.

~~~

"Keep that water hot, boy!" Billy ordered. "Hot, hot, hot! And don't leave no sunk knives. Come back and run my hand around the sink to see if the water's hot and cut myself on a sunk knife, gonna get bad real fast, hee-hee."

Billy was teaching the ropes to the new hire, a young Hispanic man.

"When you finish here, come out front and see me. Give you something else to do. Have to stay busy if you're going to learn."

Jack entered the restaurant just as Billy was about to settle at a table with a cup of coffee and the morning paper.

"Hey, Jack," Billy called out brightly. "Have a seat. Let me get you a cup."

The dining room was empty, the lunch crowd having cleared out.

"So what you up to?" Billy asked, returning with a coffee pot.

"This and that," Jack told him. "Nothing big."

"Still driving yourself crazy over the babies?"

"It's under control. I had a thought about the Vesuvius."

Billy warmed his own cup.

"Wonder if we should just buy the whole shebang," Jack continued. "Building, business and all. The works. Not have to deal with the damn owners deciding what kind of business they want there."

Billy coughed.

"That's a lot of money you're talking about, Jack. People believe Duval Street is paved with gold. Besides, we don't even know if they want to sell. You think buying it kit and caboodle is a good idea?"

"Tell you the truth, Billy, I don't give a damn whether it's a good idea or bad idea. I really don't. I just want to move on."

Billy looked at Jack with a puzzled expression.

"You know what I think, Jack? We ought to just forget the whole thing for awhile. Let the dust settle. Vesuvius ain't going nowhere, at least not today."

A minute of silence passed between them.

"Forget the thing," Jack said quietly and more to himself than Billy. Good advice, he thought.

"Sure, Jack, we don't have to rush into any damn thing," Billy went on, a tinge of disappointment in his voice. "It was just an idea about us getting that new restaurant, that's all it was. Ideas come and go as they please. Got all the time in world, yes sir, all the time in the world. Don't have to do a damn thing."

Jack looked at his friend.

"I talked with Davy Jones," he said. "Think maybe he'd be a good person to represent us."

"Huh? Represent us for what?"

"I don't want to use my company in this deal," Jack continued. "Not that I don't have good people in Los Angeles, but we should keep things local. I'll get some figures worked up on what kind of offer we want to make and then you and I and Sparrow can meet with Jones. By the way, I have a great name for the new restaurant. Stella by Starlight. Pretty cool, huh?"

"But I thought we were forgetting about all that. Isn't that what you said?"

Jack's phone rang right then. It was Bob Ranzoa.

CHAPTER 18

Cocktail hour was 6:00 p.m. Dress was island casual. Jack had taken them at their word. He was wearing Bermuda shorts and a Hawaiian shirt. Flip-flops on both feet. How island casual was that?

The Ranzoa house stood on Fleming Street not all that far from where Jack lived. A fresh breeze had cooled the afternoon and he'd decided to walk there rather than take a taxi. Questions kept him company.

Who would be there? Bob Ranzoa hadn't been specific when he'd called with the invitation. Small gathering was what he'd said. This silly ruse of his, making a film about the family. Would he be able to pull it off? Embarrassing when he thought about it. And really, what the hell did he expect to gain? What? Ranzoa's going to admit to having a pair of serial killers in the old family tree? He ought to turn around and go back home. Call them up and express his regrets.

He came to the address.

The house projected a sense of self-importance, as if it were aware of its standing in the community. It had been beautifully kept up. Old moldings and architectural touches abounded, original and as fresh as the day the house was built. It rose three stories with a widow's walk on top. A wrought-iron fence backed by a perfectly trimmed hedge offered an ornate gate. Jack entered and continued up the brick walk to the front door.

"Jack, glad you could make it," Bob Ranzoa greeted, a drink in hand and wearing a pair of chinos and a yellow golf shirt under a blue blazer. No shoes. "Come on in."

He ushered Jack into the foyer. It was huge and grand.

"Dad's in the library," Bob said with a sweep of his hand.

Jack smiled. It seemed to him that Bob Ranzoa had gotten an early start on cocktail hour.

"This is quite a place," Jack remarked.

"Yeah, the old family home. Quite a place all right. C'mon, dad's waiting."

Robert Ternant Ranzoa II, dressed in a funereal black suit with a white shirt and dark blue tie, stood in the center of the room, hands clasped behind his back. Books filled two walls floor to ceiling. Another wall was wood paneled and featured a large fireplace. Comfortable chairs rested on an oriental rug.

"This is Jack Hunter, dad."

Jack walked up and offered his hand. Robert took it in a limp grip.

"Glad to meet you, sir," Jack smiled.

Robert simply nodded.

"Bobby, get our guest a drink, please. What's your pleasure, Mr. Hunter? I'm having a scotch."

"Scotch is fine," Jack said, looking around and realizing he was the only one there. "Looks like I'm early."

"No, you're right on time," Robert said.

"Just thought there'd be more people," Jack said uncomfortably.

"Bobby tends to exaggerate. Actually, I just wanted to have a little chat about your movie idea. It fascinates me."

"Here you go, Jack," Bob said, returning with two tumblers containing two inches of scotch in each. "It's neat. Hope that's okay."

"Only way to enjoy good whiskey," Robert stated, taking one of the glasses and raising it in a toast. "To the movies."

"I was just telling dad that I couldn't understand why anyone would be interested in a movie about our family," Bob grinned nervously, shooting a look at his father.

Robert showed a beatific smile.

"You might be surprised," Jack said. "I think people might be very interested in knowing more about you."

"Why don't you give us some examples of what they may want to know, Mr. Hunter?" Robert asked.

"Actually, I'm depending on you for that, sir. But for instance, I understand the Ranzoas have been in Key West for, well, how long, Bob?"

Bob Ranzoa, having left to refresh his drink, had just rejoined them.

"Oh my, we have great, greats going back forever," he said. "Not as many of us around now as there used to be, though."

Robert frowned.

"Yes, I understand there were a couple of famous doctors," Jack said. "Is that right?"

"Claude Ranzoa was a doctor," Robert answered quickly. "He was my father's brother. I didn't know him well."

"Claude. I'm not familiar with that name," Jack said. "I thought I'd heard of a brother and sister who were doctors. Twins even."

Robert paid Jack an appraising look.

"You already seem to know quite a bit about our family, Mr. Hunter," he remarked coolly. "I find that very interesting."

"Proving my point," Jack smiled. "I guess we tend to look at our own families as ordinary but often they are anything but. People love to know about other people, believe me."

"Well, actually I do know quite a bit about you, sir," Robert grinned.

"How is that, Mr. Ranzoa?"

Robert chuckled and called to his son, "Bobby, I think our guest needs a refill. Would you see to it?"

"I'm okay," Jack said to Bob and returned his attention to Robert. "You were about to say?"

"Have a seat, Mr. Hunter."

Robert Ranzoa motioned to two matching leather upholstered chairs facing each other in front of the fireplace. Jack took one and Robert settled into the other.

"You claim to be a movie producer in Los Angeles but there's no evidence of that," Robert told him. "At least not with any of the major studios or even independent film companies. What I did find out is that you once worked for an advertising agency in that city, but more interesting is that you were suspected of murdering your ex-wife."

"Right on the money so far," Jack said.

"Did you do that?" Robert asked, leaning forward in his chair. "Murder the woman?"

"You know the answer."

"I see, like O.J., huh?" Robert smirked.

Jack didn't comment. Bob had taken another a chair and remained silent. The light in the room had faded in the last of the day and Bob got up to switch on a lamp.

"I understand you have something to do with a restaurant here," Robert said. "Why here in Key West? I would've thought Los Angeles would better suit you."

"It's a long story," Jack said. "I'm surprised you're interested in that. I wouldn't think it would be of any concern to you."

"Oh, but I beg to differ," Robert laughed. "I'm beginning to think everything about you concerns me. You're a nosy person, Mr. Hunter. And I want to know what's your game?"

Jack had had enough of the cat and mouse.

"This isn't a game," he said. "It's serious."

Jack then told him about the children's section of the cemetery. How he'd become curious about the graves there, adding that he'd also discovered the graves of other infants who'd died during the same time. He mentioned the rumors naming the Ranzoa doctors, Armand and Ardell, as perhaps having something to do though certainly unintentionally, with the deaths. He also noted that he had visited the Ranzoa family plot and neither doctor was buried there, so he assumed them to be still living.

"So my question is are they still alive and, if so, where are they living? I want to talk with them, see if they can clear things up. I intend to find the answer whether you're willing to help me or not."

Robert's face had turned to stone.

"How dare you insult my family! You have no right prying into our affairs, no matter what your unfounded suspicions may be. I believe you are merely a trouble-maker, sir. I said to my son earlier that I had a feeling I'd seen you before. And now I remember. You were involved in that snafu involving Coco Key. And also with that dead boy who was found in the Bight. Seems like misfortune follows you, Mr. Hunter."

"On occasion it does, sir," Jack said. "But you'll also notice the misfortune is not mine but always falls on those deserving of it."

Robert Ranzoa narrowed his eyes.

"Our family has been here for more than a hundred and fifty years," Mr. Hunter.

"That's something," Jack said.

"I don't believe we have anything further to discuss," he said, getting to his feet. "Leave our family alone. Bobby, show Mr. Hunter out."

Bob Ranzoa obediently led Jack to the door. Neither said a word to the other. When he returned to the library, his father was still standing and facing the fireplace.

"Bobby, that man is bad for this family," he said without turning around. "Have nothing further to do with him."

CHAPTER 19

Detective Gleason's leave of absence wasn't helping much in his so-called recuperation. It would've been more restful if he'd remained on the job working a full shift.

After Jack's unexpected call, Gleason's newly ex-wife had phoned. She'd read the article in the paper about the arrest of Virginia Hayes and was concerned for him. He had assured her that his injury was nothing. Minor shit, his favorite words, he'd told her. Then, he'd suggested they have dinner together. Where the hell had that come from? He'd asked himself afterwards. Fortunately, she had shown better judgment and had declined.

Now he was back in the detectives' room at his desk waiting to hear from Tallahassee. He'd come in to email the department of records a request for the death certificate of Samantha Adams. Jack's earlier phone call had pricked his guilt.

"Gleason, if you don't need the time off, then give it back," Jay Halderman said, walking into the room. He stopped at the coffee maker and poured himself a cup.

"Jesus, can't anybody around here make a fresh pot?" he said aloud, dumping the sour-smelling coffee into the small sink.

"Hi, boss," Gleason greeted. "Just here for a moment. Be leaving soon."

Halderman pulled up a chair by the detective's desk and sat down.

"Our favorite homicide suspect is claiming police brutality," he said. "Just off the blower with the DA."

"You've got to be kidding," Gleason laughed.

"Gospel truth. Her lawyer's making a big stink about it in the papers."

"Well, a lawyer's got to do what a lawyer's got to do, I guess," Gleason said. "Suppose this little souvenir she left me on my side doesn't count."

"Actually, it does," Halderman smiled. "But we've got something better."

"Sure, that dumb shit Jack Hunter. Let him take the fall for brutality. He was the one who knocked her ass for a loop. To my everlasting gratitude, I'm not ashamed to admit."

"That's true, too. And the DA liked your report, by the way. No, Hayes's lawyer is blowing smoke, that's all. The better thing is, along with our friend Jack Hunter's eyewitness account we've also got moving pictures of the sorrowful act, son."

Halderman winked.

"What the hell are you talking about, Jay?"

"Tourist shot the whole incident with his cellphone. Brought it to the station today. Was going to post it on Facebook but then he thought it might be important for us to see it first."

"That's absolutely amazing," Gleason grinned. "Hey, while you're here let me ask you something. You ever been to the cemetery in town?"

~~~

Jack stood alone on Passover Lane, the children's graves at his feet on the other side of the iron fence ringing the cemetery. He'd walked there after his visit with the Ranzoas. It was still twilight.

That had been quite a meeting, he thought to himself. He couldn't say which had been more impressive, the old man's dominating personality or his son's absolute obedience. The poor guy seemed like a beaten dog around his father. There was certainly more to learn from this odd pair. But one thing was already clear. Robert Ranzoa was not a man to be taken lightly.

The senior Ranzoa was a son-of-a-bitch. And probably a powerful one as well. He had done his homework and had seen right through the movie ruse. Well, so much for that. Chalk it off as a dumb idea. Still, it got him a meeting, right? The kid had been the gullible one. Doubt if he ever hears anything more from Bob Ranzoa.

No question the old man knows what went on with those two doctors. Bastard. He was glad that he hadn't taken a drop of his lousy whiskey. Left it in the glass untouched. He also hadn't had anything to eat, had he? Michael's restaurant was just a block away.

~~~

Bob Ranzoa sat in his own living room. The television set providing the only light, the rest of the house dark and empty. A nature program was on. Crocodiles making hash out of wildebeests.

The missus hadn't returned from Tallahassee. Which was just as well with him. He wasn't sure how much longer the two of them could carry it off anyway. Being a couple. They might as well be on separate planets. The marriage

137

was so much split timber now, having hit the rocks long ago. The two of them still stuck to each other with political glue. Bob liked that phrase and repeated it aloud. He poured himself another big dollop of scotch.

He might never have married her had it not been for his dad. Her family was tight with those who mattered upstate. That's how it works in his dad's world. The way it's always been. What the fuck does love have to do with anything? Lions pulled down a zebra.

Jack Hunter. Now there was a guy for you. He liked him. Could've been friends even. Too bad old Jack was going to get fucked over royally.

CHAPTER 20

Gleason and Halderman cruised slowly down Passover Lane. A full moon presented the cemetery as an eerie canvas of bone-white stones and shadows.

"This whole stretch along here is the children's section," Gleason indicated with a nod. "I'm going to pull over and park."

Earlier the two cops had had dinner together and Gleason had continued to fill in his boss about the graves while they ate. The latest item being a copy of Samantha Adam's death certificate which had listed Dr. Armand Ranzoa as the certifying physician.

Both men exited the car. Gleason took along a flashlight.

"You can't see the dates from here," Gleason said, playing the light along the grave markers. "But I can tell you that in this bunch up ahead are five or six that died less than a couple of months apart."

"Maybe there was a plague or something," Halderman said. "Yellow fever was supposed to have been gone years ago but could've come back somehow and got them. Who knows?"

"Hunter was told the population explosion might've had something to do with it," Gleason put in. "But then said the percentages didn't add up."

"Population explosion? When was that?"

"Through the Sixties," Gleason said. "Had to do with all the military build-up after the Cuban missile crisis. Horny wives and lonely nights. Key West's own big bang theory."

They came to the main gate and then walked back to their car. Gleason continued to play the flashlight along the gravesites.

"Don't remember which one belongs to the Adams baby," Gleason said. "I'll find out tomorrow."

"Was there an autopsy done on her?" Halderman asked.

"Doubt so," Gleason said. "Parents weren't too keen on that. Only thing I got was they listed cause of death as SID."

"Sudden infant death's about the same as smothering," Halderman commented. "Autopsy could maybe have revealed if the death was intentional."

"Like I said, parents kind of resist having their kids cut up," Gleason said. "Then or now."

They came to the car.

"Look, Earl," Halderman said, "I don't know if anything other than rumor and suspicion is involved with these kids. Yeah, yeah, the Ranzoas. But that's all hearsay as far as a crime having been committed. You know that."

Gleason pulled away from the curb.

"I do know it, Jay," he said. "But your buddy Jack Hunter has a wild hair up his ass over this business. And to tell you the truth, I'm beginning to halfway believe him. One thing I'm going to do is get the death certificates on that whole row of graves. If Ranzoa signed them off, then I'm smelling a rat."

Halderman drew in a breath and slowly exhaled.

"Okay, I can't make it an official investigation," he said. "Can't bring in the department. This could be a fucking minefield. I mean, some of these families are still around. Don't want to go dredging up a bunch of sorrow, you know? And the damn Ranzoas? You don't want to even think about hitting that hornet's nest. Might not be many of them, but they're connected. And be careful with those death certificates in Tallahassee. Political jungle up there."

"So what are we going to do?" Gleason asked. "Let it ride?"

'Just can't make it official," Halderman smiled. "But if you want to birddog this thing on your own, I have no objections. You're on departmental leave, remember?"

Gleason grinned.

"Want to drop me back at the station so I can pick up my car?" Halderman asked. "My wife's going to be pissed off to hell for my staying out so late."

~~~

Gleason sat alone in his car, the only sound an occasional tick from the cooling engine. He'd dropped off the lieutenant twenty minutes ago and had now driven to his own place, a tiny apartment on Petronia Street.

He had the second floor, the back part of it. A couple shared the nicer, larger unit up front. But they were good neighbors and kept to themselves. They didn't know he was a cop.

He'd found the place through a buddy of his, another cop who'd had a friend that had lived there. The friend's friend had to split town suddenly and Gleason had let it be known on the sly that he might be looking for new quarters. The divorce was coming up fast. Things meshed and Earl got his bachelor's pad.

Actually, it was a comfortable little apartment. The problem was that Gleason missed his house. The one his new ex had gotten after the settlement and was presently living in. Well, tough shit was all he could say because he sure couldn't do anything about it now.

He looked at his watch. It wasn't that late. Vino's wasn't that far away either. He got out and locked the car.

~~~

Duval Street was taking a breather between rounds, the late night crowd having yet to begin the final crawl. Gleason mounted the steps to Vino's. A few regulars sat on the porch.

"Hi, there," greeted a blonde bartender he hadn't seen before.

"Hi, yourself," Gleason smiled, pulling out a stool to sit.

"Val not on tonight?"

"Nope, she's on vacation. I'm Glenda. Glenda McDowell. Like a dowel, only with two els instead of one."

"I'm Earl, one el."

"So what can I get you, Earl one el."

"Think I'd like a glass of merlot. Whatever you're pouring."

Glenda got his wine and rejoined a group at the end of the bar. Gleason offered a silent thanks for small blessings. He wasn't in the mood for conversation.

The room was empty save for Glenda's friends at the bar, who were now heavily engaged in hushed gossip broken by titters of laughter. He could just as well have been the only one there. Which was good because he had a lot to think about.

This business with the cemetery was getting to him. He couldn't put a finger on exactly why he'd become so affected. Seeing all those tiny graves in a row. Doesn't get much sadder. Sure, he'd seen worse. But this had to do with children. That made it different.

And that just might be his problem. He was looking at them as victims. But were they victims? Maybe they just died. Terrible thing to have happen to a child but nothing sinister about it. Cemetery was full of dead people. Naturally dead people.

Still, he couldn't ignore the evidence. Well, the evidence such as it was and even calling it that would be a stretch. What about the death certificate? Well, what about it? Sudden Infant Death. Yeah, there probably would've been petechial hemorrhage but nothing was noted. No need for there to have been. Guy that told Hunter about seeing the dead girl doesn't mean a thing. It'd be interesting if the same doctor's name showed up on the other death certificates. Or maybe not. Suppose the Ranzoas were the only docs in town? No getting around it, he had some digging to do. He grinned at his own pun.

"How you doing down there, Earl one el?" Glenda shouted.

Gleason realized he hadn't touched his wine.

CHAPTER 21

"**D**avy Jones coming by this morning," Billy announced as soon as Jack walked in. "Isn't that good news?"

Jack had ridden his bicycle to the restaurant and had come in through the kitchen. Billy had just stepped out from the pantry.

"I don't have any numbers for him," Jack said. "Haven't had the time."

"Davy don't need no numbers," Billy chirped. "Davy'll get this show on the road before somebody else comes along and snaps it up."

"Place isn't even on the market, Billy," Jack said. "No one's going to snap it up. Not anytime soon."

"Things happen quick in Key West, Jack," Billy said. "You know that better'n anyone."

Jack had no idea what his friend had meant but he let it go.

"Don't suppose you could fix me a spinach omelet?" he asked.

"Sure thing, Jack. Just go have a seat out front. Have that for you in a minute. Things happen quick around here, too, hee-hee."

True to his word, Billy delivered the omelet before Jack had finished his cup of coffee. It looked delicious. Even had a single leaf of raw spinach on top as a garnish.

"How's that, Jack? Put some extra spinach in it for you."

Jack took a bite and was about to answer when a man entered the front door and walked purposely toward them.

"Looking for who's in charge," he said brusquely.

"That'd be me, mister," Billy told him. "What can I do for you?"

The man pulled out an ID badge and said, "I'm with the health department. Need to see your kitchen."

Billy examined the identification card.

"Somebody from your place was here just a couple of days ago," he said. "Signed off on the inspection. Must be some kind of mistake you coming back."

"Nope, no mistake. Random call. Do them all the time. You want to show me your kitchen?"

Billy led the inspector back to the kitchen leaving Jack to enjoy his omelet. A few minutes later loud voices arose from within, followed by Billy storming into the dining room.

"Jack! That fool inspector says he found a damn mouse in the pantry!"

~~~

The health inspector had gone but not before taping a yellow closure notice on the restaurant's front door.

"This ain't right," Billy huffed. "Shut this place down for nothing. I was just inside that pantry and there was no mouse. Never been no problem with critters coming in here. Not when Cecil owned it and sure as hell not since you and me and Sparrow took over. Keep this restaurant shipshape all the time."

"I know you do," Jack sympathized. "Guy seemed like a tight-ass s.o.b. You ever see him before?"

"Wasn't the regular fellow," Billy said. "'Course they could've put somebody new on the job. Don't have to run it past me. Well, I better call the pest removal people. Have them send over their best mouse catcher. Don't suppose it'd be some ol' tomcat, do you? Hee-hee."

Jack laughed, too. For what it was worth.

~~~

Robert Ternant Ranzoa II breakfasted alone at Blue Heaven. His son, suffering a devastating hangover, had begged off having to attend their morning ritual. There'd been no new business to discuss. As far as Robert was concerned a message had been sent and things had been settled.

He cast an eye to a waiter and nodded at the empty coffee cup on his table. It was immediately refilled. He liked that. People jumped when he wanted something done. No matter what or where. Be it in a restaurant. Or at the board of health.

CHAPTER 22

Detective Gleason had been waiting at the cemetery for the gates to open. He'd then gone straight to the children's section and begun writing down the names and dates of death on the graves along the fence. Although he'd taken down some of them on his first visit, he made a complete list this time. Then he moved on to the others Jack had mentioned. Those buried in family plots.

It was late morning by the time he'd covered them all and now a thunderstorm was rumbling in fast. Fat raindrops began splattering against the headstones. He hurried toward the main gate, the list of names in his notebook weighing heavily in his pocket.

Once at the police station he sent a request to Tallahassee for the death certificate of each deceased child. Then he called Davy Jones.

~~~

Jones worked out of his office on Thomas Street. It was mainly a one-man outfit. A woman came in on weekends to help with the books. She was also a licensed realtor and worked with him during the season. This was off-season and a weekday. Davy was sitting at his desk when Gleason entered.

"Mr. Jones? I'm Detective Earl Gleason. Glad you could see me."

Davy got up from his desk and walked over to greet him.

"Yes sir, Mr. Gleason. Have a seat, please."

An abridged sofa with a small coffee table placed in front and two plastic patio chairs facing it served as a client area. Davy's desk was located farther back in the room. A potted palm separated the two sections. Gleason took one of the chairs and Davy sat in the other.

"As I said on the phone, I'm interested in anything more you could tell me about Samantha Adams," Gleason said.

"Well, I told Billy Bean's friend about all I know. And obviously you've talked with him. So I can't think of much more I can add."

Gleason smiled.

"Did you ever talk with the dead girl's mother?" he asked. "I mean afterwards."

Jones's face took on a sad expression.

"Mr. Twombley did. On several occasions. Poor woman. At the time, Twombley Mortuary served mostly the local community, so we always did everything we could to comfort the families because they were our neighbors, you see."

Gleason took out his notebook and flipped through a couple of pages.

"Jack Hunter, that's Billy's friend." Gleason said, looking up from his notes. "He mentioned your being particularly struck by the appearance of the Adams child. Could you describe for me what you'd noticed?"

Davy Jones inhaled deeply.

"Her eyes," he said. "The little girl had these red specks in them. I'd seen the same thing before with another child. She'd been accidentally smothered."

"Yes," Gleason nodded. "That condition you're talking about is called petechial hemorrhaging. Blood leaks from tiny capillaries in the eyes. Hard to spot. It can also be on the face. Even in the lungs. That would take an autopsy to find those, though. But back to Mr. Twombley, were you present when he spoke with Samatha's mother?"

Jones drew in another deep breath before answering.

"It was after the funeral. Mrs. Adams came to the mortuary. Said she'd been crying all day. Told Mr. Twombley she just couldn't stop thinking about her Samantha having died in that doctor's office right in front of her. Hard thing for me to even imagine. Seeing your child die."

Gleason leaned forward in his chair and said, "This happened in the Ranzoas' office? The Adams child died in their office, her mother said? You're sure of that? And in front of her? She saw that happen?"

"Yes, sir, all took place right in the office of the two doctors. Doctor Armando and Doctor Ardell."

He made a notation in his book. Davy Jones continued.

"Went on to tell how the one doctor was just holding the little girl up against his chest, like you hold a baby sometimes. Just holding her and rocking gently back and forth. Next thing you know, baby's not breathing. Just like that. Gone."

Gleason remained silent.

"I was over at the side of the room polishing some of the furniture, so I could hear what was being said. Terrible thing. Don't think I'll ever forget it myself."

"You said 'his chest'. That the doctor was holding the child against *his* chest. So it's Doctor Armando we're talking about, right?"

Jones's shook his head.

"Don't remember which one it was. If I said *his* it was just the way I was telling about it. Might have been *her*."

"Is Mrs. Adams still around?" Gleason asked. "I mean, does she live here in Key West now?"

"Yes, sir, I believe so. She was a young woman back then. I'm not aware of her having passed."

"No way you'd know if she still goes by Adams or has re-married?"

"We call her Sister Adams. Don't think she ever married again. Let me ask around for where she lives. Some church folks would know."

Gleason thanked Davy Jones for his time, handed him a business card and said that if he thought of anything else to please call him. Oh, and don't forget about the Adams woman, he added.

Back in his car, he reflected on what Jones had told him. Holding the baby tight against an adult chest. Tight enough to smother? Burking came to mind.

Long ago. The West Port Murders. Couple of body snatchers, William Burke and William Hare, killed their victims by the simultaneous smothering and compression of the torso. Quick and efficient. No visible injuries. Unmarked fresh corpses which they then sold to the local medical school.

Could that have happened to Samantha Adams? Held so tightly she couldn't breathe. The life literally squeezed out of her. Possible accident? Sure. Provable homicide? Not a chance.

He drove to the police station to see if there was any word on the death certificates.

~~~

Billy was right. The kitchen at the Inedible Café was spotless. Including the pantry.

Jack had removed every item in there himself, examined each shelf and had even gotten down on his hands and knees to check along the baseboard. No mouse door anywhere.

"If that guy found a mouse in here, he brought it with him," he said. "You'd expect to see droppings or something torn open and nibbled on."

"The health inspector is just setting us up, Jack. Thing I can't understand is why?"

"Me neither, Billy."

"Well, I called the exterminators," Billy said. "Can't get here before tomorrow. So we might as well lock up."

Billy turned off the lights.

CHAPTER 23

Gleason caught a call from Davy Jones just as he pulled into the police station parking lot. He had an address for Samantha's mother.

The detective ran the address to double-check and found that a Mrs. Brenda Adams was the sole resident. No other names were listed. Mrs. Adams answered the phone when he called. Yes, she confirmed, she was indeed Samantha's mother. And no, she wouldn't mind talking about what had happened to her daughter.

The house was on Thomas Street. A small wooden structure that looked as if it'd been there for awhile but had been loved and well kept. Gleason parked a few doors down.

"I appreciate your seeing me so quickly," he said, taking a seat in the living room.

The room was comfortably furnished. A maroon sofa and two matching easy chairs were situated around a coffee table. The television set stood in one corner and a small table holding a lamp and several photographs stood across the room. A framed print of Jesus Christ hung over the sofa and was reflected in the mirror on the opposite wall.

"Would you like some tea?" Mrs. Adams offered.

"No, thanks, ma'am. I'm good."

"Well, then, what can I tell you about Samantha?"

Brenda Adams was a petite woman in her late sixties with intelligent eyes and a quick wit. She wore her hair in a stylish cut and colored rooster red.

"This may be difficult but I'd like to hear from you what went on with Samantha at the doctors' office."

"They killed her." Brenda blurted out. "I've said so all along. Just nobody wanted to believe me."

Gleason was taken aback.

"Maybe I'm the one to believe you," he said.

Brenda dabbed away a tear.

"Samantha was only a little thing," she began. "I took her to see Dr. Ranzoa because there was this coughing sickness going around and I was afraid she might have caught it. Her poor body would just shake and shake when it came over her. But you know, that child never complained. Didn't fuss one bit."

"Which doctor saw her?" Gleason asked.

"Both of them. Doctor Armand held her while his sister, Ardell, examined her. Then they took her into another room to give her a shot."

"You didn't go with them?"

"No, it was just the next room. The door was open. Doctor Armand held her close to him and rocked back and forth like you'd do with a baby. I could see and Samantha was fine."

"Was Samantha fine when they returned?"

"She was asleep. It was four or five minutes until they were done with the shot and all. I thought it must been what they gave her that made her sleepy. But when I took her back in my arms, I knew something wasn't right."

Brenda Adams tightened her mouth.

"My baby was gone."

Neither spoke a word for a minute.

"Then all hell broke loose," she said.

"Did anyone call an ambulance?" Gleason asked.

"Wasn't much in the way of ambulances and hospitals back then, detective. We had a little clinic in town that another doctor ran and the Navy had their medical place. Besides, why would anybody need to call for anything? I was there with two doctors!"

"Yes," Gleason nodded. "And what about the doctors? What was their reaction when, as you said, all hell broke loose?"

"They reached to take back Samantha," Brenda said angrily. "And I wouldn't let them touch her. Then, of course, I had to give her to them. They tried to revive her. Shook her. Breathed into her mouth. And everything. But it was no use. I just cried and cried then. The tears just wouldn't stop coming."

"And you said they killed her? Why do you think that?"

"Because she was all right before. That cough was just a bad cough, wasn't a reason for her to die. Doctor Armand did something to my baby!"

"Yet nobody would believe you," Gleason said. "Who did you tell?"

Brenda dabbed at her eyes again.

"Anybody who stood still long enough to listen, at first," she said. "Neighbors, pastor at the church. Mr. Twombley, too. He's the one who buried her. Even talked with a policeman but nothing ever came of it. Pretty soon I was only talking to myself. Isn't that something?"

"Do you remember who it was you spoke with at the police department?"

"Man named Dan Berger. He was very nice. We stayed in touch for a long time. But it just seemed there was nothing anybody was going to do. Samantha was dead and buried and that was that. Like they say, the case was closed! Don't know if he still works there or not but his name was Dan Berger. Think he was a detective then, like you."

"How about your husband?" Gleason asked.

"Samantha's daddy had gotten himself into some trouble right before Samantha was born. He wasn't around to help when she died. And when he did come back he didn't stay here long. We never were married, you see. I took his name for Samantha's sake. And afterwards it was just easier to keep it. The truth is, I haven't seen him for years. Cleon Adams. Don't know if he's dead or alive."

~~~

Gleason requested a name and address for Dan Berger from the personnel department. He found that Berger had retired from KWPD twelve years earlier and was now living in Elizabeth City, North Carolina. He called the former detective.

Berger answered on the fourth ring. He sounded like a younger man than his obvious years would've indicated.

"I can see by your area code that you must be calling from the Conch Republic," he said. "Whatever it is you want, I don't have it."

"Detective Berger," Gleason laughed. "I'm Detective Earl Gleason with the KWPD. How are you doing, sir?"

"Up to now, I was fine. If this is about increasing my retirement pay, I'll be finer. Hold on a second."

Berger had put down the phone and Gleason could hear him speaking with someone else.

"Had to get those grandkids out of here," he said upon returning. "Got three of 'em and they can be a handful. My son and his wife both teach at the university. I take care of the children now and then. So what can I do for you, detective?"

Gleason explained how he'd become interested in the children's graves. That he was unofficially investigating the deaths. And that he'd spoken with Brenda Adams about her infant daughter.

"I can give you two pieces of advice, Detective. First, forget the whole damn thing. You won't find one iota of solid evidence. And as far as those doctors go? It's just another Key West conspiracy theory. All you'll do is drive yourself crazy like I did. But you probably won't drop the thing, so that brings me to the next piece of advice. Take up fishing and go out and buy yourself a Harley Davidson motorcycle. That'll keep you sane while you butt your head against that stone wall that doesn't get any softer. Believe me, son, I struggled over that case for years. It became a real jones. I refer to it a case because that was how I saw it. Nothing official was ever opened. But in my mind, it was and still is open."

"Did you look into any of them other than the Adams death?" Gleason asked.

"As best as I could at the time," Berger said. "Lack of evidence. No autopsies were asked for because no foul play was suspected. Couldn't go to a judge and request an order for exhumation without good cause. My hands were pretty much tied."

"But you believed there was a case for an investigation," Gleason said. "So what happened?"

"Politics, corruption, powerful people. Money. Take your pick. Any or all."

"That sounds pretty discouraging," Gleason said. "You're okay with that?"

"Hell no I'm not okay with any of it," Berger answered. "I was on my lonesome from the get-go. The department wouldn't or couldn't touch it. In the end I just ran out of time."

"Well, maybe I've got the time," Gleason said. "I believe Brenda Adams. I think somebody had something to do with Samantha's death."

"So do I, Earl," Berger said quietly. "Don't forget what I said about that Harley."

CHAPTER 24

Robert Ranzoa II sat at his desk, his hand lightly placed on the side of his face as if he'd just received a stinging slap. Actually, he was reliving a symbolic one that he had been given to both himself and his father nearly forty years ago by the cream of Key West society, the result of a regrettable incident involving the Ranzoas.

He'd gotten a telephone call from a friend at the time. A problem had arisen and needed to be settled. Immediately, quietly and completely. One that had to do with his niece and nephew and could possible affect the well being of the entire damn city. Could he and his father meet with some of the other prominent families to discuss what action to take?

The decision had already been made when they had arrived for the meeting. They were told that some people were getting nervous. Nasty talk was going around town. Suspicion was growing. What if there were an investigation, they'd asked? Not only by the local police which would certainly raise embarrassing questions if the papers got hold of it, but more. Suppose the state stepped in? Worse, the federal government? The scandal would cause God knows what kind of damage. Reputations would be hurt, some possibly beyond any hope of repair.

Didn't the two of them realize the goddamn economy was finally on a roll in this forsaken island? Investments finally were verging on big money to be made. Real estate, building projects, everywhere you looked the money trees were ripe and just begging to be shaken.

The elder Ranzoa was given his orders and they were carried out. Now an idiot named Jack Hunter has come along to stir things up.

Robert II dialed a Miami number.

~~~

Gleason had received eighteen death certificates from Tallahassee. There would be more to come. But all of these had been signed by either Armand or Ardell Ranzoa. Causes of deaths ranged from SDI to unexplained bleeding.

He wondered if there were other deaths he'd missed. Children who'd died in Key West but their remains had been sent to another state. If that were so, then an autopsy would have been performed. He could check again with the capitol. They'd have to have a record of the death. And also with the funeral homes who would've had to have done the autopsy. It was a long shot. And even if it turned out to be true, there would still be the problem of getting an exhumation order.

And then what? Have a child that's been buried for thirty years dug up to look for some specious evidence that probably no longer exists, if it ever did? Still, forensics have also come a long way in the past thirty years.

He called Twombley Mortuary.

~~~

Jack was passing by Pepe's on Caroline Street. The door off the sidewalk to the patio was open and offered an irresistible invitation to have a seat at the friendly little bar. Jack accepted.

"I'll just have a beer," Jack said, sliding onto a stool. It was the right thing to order because the temperature had edged into the low nineties.

"Make it the coldest one you've got," he added.

The electric fan clamped to the side of the fence just a few feet from where he sat swept the bar with a hot breeze. Adding more to the discomfort than relieving it.

"All the way from the bottom of the ice chest," the bartender said, placing the chilled bottle before him. "Been slow today. Think everybody's out on the water, if they can get there."

"I sure would be," Jack agreed, taking a long pull of the ice-cold beer.

He turned to face the inefficient fan and slipped his t-shirt up to expose his ribs and cool his mid-section. The bartender busied himself polishing glassware.

Jack's thoughts took up the subject of twins. He'd been the son of a twin, and that brought back the old painful taunts. Which twin had been his father and the other his uncle? There'd seemed to have been some disagreement according to the jokesters.

And then just to make the memory more unbearable, Howard, his designated dad, had had a heart attack and died while Jack was on deployment in Iraq. So what happened next? His mom married the surviving twin, Leslie. Without even a word about it to her son.

There had to be something weird and different about twins, Jack reasoned. Which brought him back to the present pair, Armand and Ardell.

His cellphone rang. It was Bob Ranzoa.

CHAPTER 25

Bob Ranzoa had made a date to meet Jack around eight that night at the Green Parrot. Said he had some information about the doctors. Jack had gone home to freshen up and was now occupying a seat at the bar. It was a slow night, the heat from the day sticking around as if waiting for a few cold beers itself before shoving off.

Jack checked out the bar. It was full but there was still plenty of standing room. A few people were shooting bull on the sidewalk. But no sign of Ranzoa anywhere. It was past nine.

His attention was drawn to a weird-o seated across from him at the bar and down toward its end. Buzzed haircut, tattoos running from his neck to his hands. He'd caught him giving him the stink eye and each time the jerk had looked away. Could mean nothing. The guy seemed to be alone. He was drinking a Coke.

Toward ten o'clock, Jack decided Ranzoa was going be a no-show. He might as well leave himself. He asked the bartender for his tab and stood up. The weird-o got to his feet, too.

"Twelve bucks," the bartender said.

Jack gave the man a twenty and told him to keep the change.

"One more thing," he said before the barkeep could get away. "You got any rolls of coins in the register? Anything will do."

"Think there might be some quarters. Just hope we don't need them later."

"Mind checking? I could use two if you can spare them."

The man brought Jack two rolls and he paid for them. Then he slipped the rolled-up quarters into his pocket and left the Parrot, walking up Southard.

He crossed Duval and noticed the weird-o had fallen in behind him. Continuing on to Simonton, he turned right to Angela toward the cemetery. The weird-o closed in and Jack was ready.

"Hey, Jack," the guy called out. Then nother, nearer and drawn out. "J-a-a-a-c-k."

Jack ducked and jumped to the side just as the man swung a length of pipe at his head, missing by inches. Pivoting, he delivered a quick right to the mid-section followed by a jarring left hook square on the jaw, staggering the man. A hard right cross put him down. Jack dropped the two rolls of quarters he'd had in his palms back into his pocket and grabbed up the guy by his shirt, hauling him to his feet.

"Tell me what this is about or I'm going to really kick the shit out of you," he growled.

"Fuck you," the man said.

Jack kneed him twice where it hurt the most and dropped him back on the pavement.

~~~

The young guy in the office of the small motel on South Street had been suspicious when Jack walked in alone with no reservation, no luggage, and wanting a room just for the night. But a cash offer with a little something extra for his trouble wiped away his concerns.

Now Jack lay stretched out fully dressed on the bed in room number 12, the last vacancy. The door double-locked. Curtains drawn. Lights out. No television on. His thoughts jumping all over the place.

Voices passed by outside, a man and woman. The door on the room next to his rattled open and quickly slammed shut. Muted laughter. A toilet flushed.

After the encounter with the weird-o, Jack had high-tailed it back to Simonton where he'd hailed a cab. Going home was too dangerous now. He had asked the driver if he knew of any place that might have a room available. Maybe somewhere off the main drag. The man said he'd earlier taken a fare to the Straits Motel. He'd remembered because of the vacancy sign being on, which was unusual for this time of the year.

His hands were still sore from the fight. Pennies would've been better to use. Dimes even more so. The quarter rolls were too fat. He couldn't make his fist as tight with them. Gripping a roll of coins had been an old fighter's trick. Like loaded gloves when boxing was really a dirty sport. It could turn a sissy punch into a sledgehammer.

One thing was certain. Somebody was definitely upset with him. It wasn't all that difficult to point a finger at the guilty party. Ranzoa. Had to be the old man. His son didn't come across as having the stomach for strong-arm stuff. Of course, young Bob had set him up. No big surprise there, he was under his dad's thumb. Poor bastard might not have even known what it was about. Still, he would keep an eye on him. His greater worry was Billy. He had to keep him out it. And how had they found out about his connection with the restaurant?

Sounds of lovemaking next door interrupted further thinking.

CHAPTER 26

Gleason sat in the lieutenant's office. Halderman was seated in his desk chair, his attention given to the window behind him. He spun around to face Gleason.

"You realize what you're asking for here, don't you?" he said.

"Yeah, an exhumation order."

Halderman sighed.

"Child's been buried for decades," he said. "Even if what you suspect is true, there might not be any evidence left. Bones, if even that."

"Hey, I know how it works, Jay. But this kid was embalmed. Body could still be preserved depending on how good a job the mortician did."

Gleason had discovered that one child had been prepared by Twombley and sent to Ohio where it was interred in the family site there. Dr. Armand Ranzoa had signed the death certificate. Cause of death had been listed as spontaneous hemorrhaging.

"Now here's a tidbit I found out," Gleason continued. "An anticoagulant by the name of heparin could cause something like that to happen. So I'm thinking, what if this stuff had been injected? Maybe a trace of it is still there. I mean, Twombley embalmed the body. If it is still intact and there's soft tissue, we could have an autopsy done. None was done at the time."

"Okay, first thing I want you to do is run this idea past forensics," Halderman said after a moment. "Tell them how long it has been and all. Then we'll talk about getting a goddamn court order. But don't count on it going anywhere."

Gleason grinned.

"One more thing, Earl. This is all still on the QT. I don't want the department involved. Don't want the chief to know. You're on sick leave as far as anyone's concerned. By the way, how's the cut?"

"Minor shit. No problem."

Halderman gave him a look.

"Okay, tough guy, like I said, play this thing close. What about your friend, Jack Hunter?"

"What about him?" Gleason shrugged.

"Work with the man."

~~~

Jack phoned Billy and told him to meet at the restaurant. He next called for a taxi to pick him up at the motel. The cab took him to Whitehead Street, then down to Olivia where he got out. He then cut through a few lanes eventually reaching the Inedible Café. The back door was open and he saw Billy in the kitchen.

"What the hell's going on?" Billy demanded as soon as Jack pushed through the door. "Davy Jones said the folks at the Vesuvius may not want to sell."

"I'm not surprised, Billy. Got any coffee?"

Billy put on a fresh pot while they talked.

"Got a shot of what's good in it, Jack. Think maybe we both could stand one."

Jack had explained why he felt that some of the recent events with the restaurant were connected with last night's episode.

"This goes beyond the bubba system," he said. "There you just have to pay your respects. Make sure the right people are hired. And support your local politician."

"So you're saying we should back off from buying another place? I was kind of getting to like Stella by Starlight, hee-hee."

"No, Billy, I'm saying *I* have to step away. From my involvement with the restaurant, with you and everyone else here until this thing is done."

Billy looked puzzled.

"You don't have to run away on my account," he said. "We're partners, Jack. What's that they say? Through thick and thin, hee-hee."

Jack had forgotten Billy's loyalty. It touched him deeply.

"Of course we're partners," he said, placing a hand on Billy's shoulder. "Of course, we are. Through thick and thin."

Jack's cellphone rang. He recognized the caller number.

"Yeah, what's up, Bob?"

"Hey, man, I tried to reach you last night," Bob Ranzoa said. "Had to do something for my dad and by the time I'd finished it was way too late. Sorry to have stood you up."

Jack laughed.

"You won't believe this but I had the same thing happen to me," he said. "Got all wrapped up in some business and forgot all about the time. Was just going to call you and apologize."

"No shit? Maybe we can get together tonight."

"Aw, can't make it. I'm leaving town today."

Jack ended the call after Bob Ranzoa said he hoped he'd call him the next time he was in town.

"Where you going, Jack?" Billy asked.

"I need a place to stay," Jack said seriously. " I can't go back to my house just yet."

Billy thought for a moment.

"Fellow I know has a boat over on Stock Island," he said. "Ain't much but it's got a bunk. I'll call him."

~~~

It was like a child's drawing of a sailboat. The perspective a little out of kilter and the dimensions somewhat skewed. Big where it should've been small. An aluminum mast, bereft of sail, stuck jauntily on the top of a tiny cabin like a finger making a point. Faded blue hull slightly off-key with the emerald green water. Basically, a most charming boat and just the ticket for him.

Jack paid the taxi driver, grabbed up his backpack and stepped aboard his new home. The little boat curtsied, dipping to one side as it accepted his weight. He slid open the hatch and stepped down into the cabin.

Inside was a different matter. Paneled in cherry wood and a niche for everything. A small galley with a propane burner on one side. Chart table with bench seats set ahead of it. Bunk with storage space below on the opposite side. The marine toilet shared the bow compartment along with the sails. In all, a very tidy cocoon.

After Billy had made arrangements for the boat with his friend, Jack had taken a taxi to the house on Ashe Street. He'd had it wait for him while he went inside to pack. Five minutes later he'd come out carrying a bag. If anyone had been watching they'd thought he was heading for the airport. And that was exactly what he'd wanted.

Taking no chances, he'd indeed had the driver take him to the airport and drop him at the entrance. Jack remained inside the terminal for a half an hour then exited in the middle of a large group and grabbed another cab to Stock Island. One thing he'd learned and learned well – Key West was a nosy little island always ready to pass along any tidbit about anyone or anything.

He set about to putting away his things.

~~~

To this day Stock Island continues to wrestle with an identity crisis. It all began years ago when life was much simpler and things were what their name implied. The island, just a long leap across the cut from Key West, had been home to live stock. It was Stock Island. No questions asked.

Then it became a commercial fishing center for the shrimpers and spongers. But the spongers eventually fished out, and while the shrimpers remained, the island turned its back on its barnyard heritage. Affordable housing, mainly in the prospect of trailer parks, meant working people could not only get by on what they earned but still have a little something left over. Stock Island was a thriving community.

Then things began to change again. Property values landed on the moon. Trailer parks disappeared. While not quite the Riviera, Stock Island was now on the way to being quite a tony place, albeit one where you could still almost afford to live. So far. And the shrimp boats were still in residence, although they now shared the basin with a new wealth of pleasure craft. How long its name would remain Stock Island would be any developer's guess.

"I'm at the Captain's Lounge," Jack told Gleason. "It's above the ships store. Just take Shrimp Road. You'll find it."

After getting squared away aboard his new home, Jack reconnoitered the area. To his surprise, also a little to his dismay, there was more activity going on than he'd hoped. Still, it would suit his needs until he could get this business with the Ranzoas settled.

"I'll fill you in when you get here," he said, ending the call.

Actually, he didn't know what he was going to do about the Ranzoas.

~~~

"The taxi took him to the airport," the man reported to Robert Ranzoa over the phone. "I saw him go inside the terminal."

"Did you see him actually get on the damn airplane?" Ranzoa queried.

"I didn't follow him inside. But he didn't come back out, either."

"Uh-huh, well, I guess that's about the best we can expect," Ranzoa said. "We're done. You can go back to Miami."

"What about my partner? He's in the hospital."

"Either go get him out and take him with you or he can catch the bus."

The man took in a deep breath.

"One more thing before you leave," Ranzoa said. "You know where his house is. Go over there and burn the goddamn thing to the ground."

"That's going to cost you extra," the man huffed.

"Don't tell me my damn business!"

CHAPTER 27

"Looks like you're on your way," Gleason quipped, pulling out a chair from the table. "Good."

"Not quite sure I know what you mean," Jack told him, sitting down himself.

"You're on Stock Island," Gleason smiled. "That's off Key West. Now you just keep on moving up the Keys."

"What would you like to drink?" Jack asked, ignoring the humor.

"Hell, I'll have a beer. Why not? Nice afternoon up here at the yacht club and all on millionaires' row."

Once their beers had come, Jack set about bringing the detective up to date. When he'd finished, Gleason fixed him with a look.

"Some asshole was taken to the hospital with a broken jaw and two busted ribs," he said. "Don't suppose you know anything about that?"

"Nothing," Jack deadpanned.

"I didn't think so."

Jack unconsciously brushed his hand against his pants pocket and felt the roll of dimes he'd earlier exchanged for the quarters.

"Word to the wise anyway," Gleason said. "Be careful out there."

"Hey, no need to dance around," Jack said. "That asshole in the hospital tried to jump me and he got what he deserved. Forget him. What the hell's being done about those kids is what I want to know? Are we in this thing together or what?"

"Settle down, will you?" Gleason said. "Fair enough questions. The lieutenant has ordered me to work with you. To tell you the truth, I'm not so sure that's a good idea. Yeah, you're a smart guy. And I appreciate what you did with that nutty woman who tried to kill me. But you're not a cop, Hunter. And it comes down to just that."

Jack leaned back in his chair and took a sip of his beer.

"I'm not trying to be a cop," he said. "That's your job. If you'll remember, that's why I showed you those graves. I was hoping you'd see the same thing I saw. And you did. And apparently, your lieutenant sees something, too. Otherwise, we wouldn't be sitting here together. And to that point, the reason I'm sitting here instead of at my house is because somebody is afraid."

Gleason picked up his beer and took a drink.

"I've done some research," he said. "Got the death certificates for those kids. Surprising thing. Most of them are signed by the Ranzoa docs."

"Now you're talking," Jack smiled.

"Yeah, it did raise a flag," Gleason continued. "Kid comes in sick. Leaves with a death certificate. One-stop shopping."

Jack didn't care much for the gallows humor but let it pass. He'd seen things himself in combat, however, and knew how it went.

"Now that's not hard and fast evidence of anything untowardly being committed, much less a criminal offense. But it might lead to a long shot and if that pays off then we could take it to the District Attorney."

He then explained about the child buried out-of-state who'd been embalmed.

"State law says if a body is to be shipped to another state, it must be embalmed. Nothing about an autopsy unless of course one is called for. Which, in this case, nobody seemed to have thought was necessary. Certainly not our doctor friends."

Jack was excited about this new development.

"So you're saying we might find real evidence with this child, providing there's anything left of it to autopsy?" Jack said. "Sounds gruesome."

"They usually are," Gleason said.

"Question," Jack said excitedly. "What is it that we hope to find?"

"Don't know for certain. The death certificate stated that the kid died from excessive bleeding. There's this drug called heparin. It's an anticoagulant. If the doctors shot up the deceased with heparin, then there could be traces of it still in the tissue. I went over all this with the Lieutenant."

"Wow, how did you come up with that?"

"I could say because I'm a big city detective but that wouldn't be entirely true. The fact is that it's been done before. A serial killer twenty or thirty years ago used it on some of her victims. They were children, too. Found it on the web."

Jack laughed.

"I won't tell if you won't," he said. "How else did she kill them besides causing them to bleed to death. You said it was a woman, right?"

"She smothered a couple," Gleason said. "I found that kind of interesting, too. Seems like she was following the Ranzoas' playbook."

"Jesus, you really think so?

"No, just kidding. She had nothing to do with the Ranzoas. They were in a world of their own."

"Back to the exhumation," Jack sad. "Suppose you dig up the body and find nothing out of the ordinary. I mean, what if after we've done everything possible to get to the bottom of this thing, we strike out? No proof of any crime ever being committed. Can you handle that? I'm not sure I can."

Gleason exhaled and sipped his beer.

"It wouldn't be the first time with me," he said. "It's exasperating. A kick in the head, man."

"Yeah, I can understand that," Jack said. "But how do you handle it?"

"You go back," Gleason told him. "Look at everything again. Try to find what you missed and where you went wrong."

"And even after that?"

"Then maybe the bad guy didn't do it."

~~~

They'd finished their conversation and Gleason had offered Jack a ride back to town but he'd refused, saying it'd be better for him to lie low on Stock Island.

Jack had discovered a tarpaulin stowed on board the sailboat and had stretched it over the boom to shade the deck where he now sat. The sun's business was about finished for the day and the western sky blazed in red, purple and gold.

Look at everything again, that was what Gleason had said. He walked in his mind back to the cemetery.

The rows of tiny graves. All children, some having lived for only one day. Not fully aware of this new world they'd entered. Still longing for the calm of a womb that'd been so brutally disrupted by their birth. A rain of discomfort they are unable to understand now falling upon them. Then, suddenly, something soothing. A familiar sound. The heartbeat hidden in their mother's breast. This incredible event from beginning to end in a single day.

He'd seen dead children. Still bodies that should have been up and alive, full of wonder. Casualties of the worst in us.

He thought of Henry Overmyer. The sad story of a sister he never knew. Perhaps Gleason should talk to him.

Those two doctors. Could they have been the victims of incredible bad luck? You had to consider that a possibility.

Leon Frankel had said the population in Key West had doubled during the time most of the deaths had occurred. Blamed it on the Cuban missile crisis for causing a military buildup. All those horny Navy wives, he'd chuckled. Then, of course, people smoked and drank during pregnancy. Not a healthy habit for the mother or her unborn child. And to cap it off, medical technology wasn't as good as it is now. Still, taking all that into consideration, it didn't add up. Too many dead babies. The number of graves in the cemetery was off the scale.

So was Key West some kind of outlier? That could explain the inordinate infant death count. But what else? Could it simply come down to the fact that the doctors were overwhelmed? Too much work. Missed a couple of things? Incompetent? It had been established that the island was short on medical facilities.

Maybe it was just a spate of sickly children being born and Nature running its course.

Robert Ternant Ranzoa II. Now there was a subject that bore further study.

CHAPTER 28

The police officer at the scene of the fire had recognized the address. There'd been a shooting at the location a while back. Also, the man who had lived in the house at the time had helped the KWPD in a drug bust. He wondered who lived here now.

No victim had been discovered inside after the fire was extinguished. The firemen figured an electrical short might be the cause. The cop wrote his report and word quickly got to Lt. Jay Halderman.

"Dammit, Earl," he said, "what the hell's going on?"

He'd called Gleason, told him what'd happened, and to get his butt down to the station.

"I stopped by his house on the way," Gleason said. "Firemen had gotten the fire under control before it got too bad."

"I know all that, Earl. I want to know what's going on with Jack Hunter?"

"He's staying over on Stock Island."

"Well, I guess that explains everything. Why's he living there instead of in his house? I realize he's a lucky bastard."

Gleason laid out the conversation he'd had with Jack, including the part about the guy in the hospital that Jack claimed having had nothing to do with. Then he added an interesting twist.

"The guy in the hospital who Hunter had nothing to do with checked himself out last night."

"Really."

"Nurse said this friend of his came in, another tough-looking character, and the two of them split. Said she heard one of them mention something about the job was done and they'd better get back to Miami. Makes me wonder now about that mysterious fire at Hunter's place."

"Does he know?" Halderman asked. "That his house burned down?"

"I'll break the news gently."

~~~

Jack was enjoying a late breakfast at a little restaurant on Stock Island. It was just off Highway 1 and he'd walked there from the marina.

"How's the omelet, sir?" the waitress asked.

"Perfect," Jack answered.

He'd ordered a spinach omelet and she'd told him that it was a good choice because they had just gotten in a fresh bunch. She'd reminded him of Barby, the waitress at the Inedible Café. And that had gotten him to thinking about the restaurant.

It was amazing how his involvement with the tiny graves in the cemetery had now affected others. Billy. Earl Gleason. Halderman. And not all of them in a favorable way. Indeed.

Obviously, he had placed himself in some degree of danger. The attempted assault by the thug proved that to be true. He should've known something was up when the mouse was found at the restaurant. But he'd never thought

184

it would have taken such a violent turn. All the more reason for him to drop out and for his friends to stay clear.

Gleason was a different animal, though. He was a cop, he could handle himself and, despite their differences, he respected his ability. He was glad to have him on his side.

He had considered calling Laura Dalton in Los Angeles. Update her and get her take on the deaths, maybe try again to bring her into the investigation. She was another police officer whose ability he respected. Among other attributes. She was tough, too. He admired that. But in the end, he had decided against calling her. The last time she'd been involved in one of his situations, he'd almost gotten them both killed. Now he was about to do the same thing, only in something becoming more and more dangerous? No, he'd asked enough of others.

He pulled out his cellphone to call Billy when the thing rang.

"Hunter, this is Gleason. Where are you?"

~~~

The little house on Ashe Street looked a mess. Yellow crime scene tape was strung across the front. A window smashed out on the porch. Scorch marks ran up one side of the building. Some of the plantings were crushed. Water still pooled in places.

Jack and Earl ducked under the tape.

"Right here is where the fire started," Gleason said, pointing to what was left of the circuit breaker box. "You can see how hot it was. Melted the wiring even."

"That was a new box," Jack said. "Brought in more power. Had the electrician check out the whole house while he was at it. New wiring and outlets. All new circuit breakers, by the way."

"Well, something wasn't right," Gleason said. "This looks like a bomb went off."

"I believe it was a bomb," Jack agreed. "I've seen this shit before."

"Yeah? Was that the time when you were a fire inspector?"

"This was a thermite grenade."

Jack explained to the detective how you could melt a canon with a thermite grenade and in fact he'd done that very thing himself more than once.

"I don't know where the hell you could get your hands on one," he said. "But I guess you can buy anything today. Get an arson investigator out here and have him take a look."

Gleason jotted down a note in his book.

"You want to go inside to see if there's anything you need?" he asked.

"Yeah, I'd like that if it's okay. Also, I'd just like to look around for a minute."

"Take your time. When you're through, let's go somewhere and have a pop."

The smoke damage was excessive. Fire had burned completely through one wall in the living room. Fortunately, the firemen had arrived before the blaze had gotten fully established. Otherwise he'd be walking through nothing but charred remains.

When was the last time he'd checked the smoke alarms? He couldn't remember, if ever.

Suppose he had been there when the fire broke out? With this much smoke, he wouldn't have had a chance. Alarms or not. Did whoever started this mess care if anyone was in the house? He doubted it.

So in essence this made two attempts on his life.

He wouldn't call the owner, Ruth LaVere, about the fire. It doesn't matter if she had insurance or not. He'd have the house put back in order himself. The woman that had built the bar at the restaurant did good work. He'd call her. What was her name? Oh, yeah, Melody Cooper. Pretty good singer, too, if he remembered right. She sat in one night when he was playing sax at the Undrinkable Bar.

Much of the furniture were antiques. He'd need someone to clean everything and possibly make repairs. Maybe Melody could recommend a good person.

He looked around the room again, then left the forlorn little house.

CHAPTER 29

Robert Ranzoa folded the newspaper and put it back on the table. He smiled to himself and looked to catch the waiter's eye.

"A little refill, if you don't mind," he called out, pointing to his coffee cup.

He was at Blue Heaven enjoying a late lunch. Again alone. Bobby was off to Miami with an envelope to be delivered.

The world was back in its groove. He wouldn't be hearing from Jack Hunter any time soon. Maybe Hunter could use the experience for one of his movies. He chuckled at that and continued with his rumination.

With power comes responsibility. He'd learned that from his father. It's all about getting things done the way you want them. The Ranzoas, along with a few others, have always gotten things done. This little island wouldn't be what it is today without the grit they'd shown. And look at the place now. All the result of their sacrifice and hard work. Every important family has a skeleton or two in its closet, that's a given. The idea is to keep them there. A careless moment from time past need not ruin the future. With power comes responsibility. A responsibility to keep that power.

Interesting that Mr. Hunter apparently has an investment in that pitiful restaurant. Well, he would buy them all out. Another talk with his friend at the health department would insure he'd get it at an attractive price, too.

His cell phone rang.

"Dad, I got a little problem," Bob Ranzoa slurred. "I got arrested for DUI."

~~~

Robert had rushed back to his office and phoned the jail where his son was being held. He'd found out that sonny boy had gone to a strip joint near Hialeah with one of the guys after delivering the payment. They'd both gotten sloshed and the cops had pulled them over on the 932 highway. Jesus Christ!

The officer had said Bobby would be released under his own recognizance but not for a few hours yet. He'd then gone on to explain how long it took for the blood alcohol level to drop to a sober number and that the man had been pretty drunk when tested. No, there hadn't been an accident involved and wasn't that a lucky thing? he'd chirped. Robert had thanked the officer and after hanging up had made the necessary call to the people in Miami.

It would be tomorrow before Bobby could get back down to Key West.

~~~

"What do you think I should do, Earl?" Jack asked the detective.

"Nothing," Gleason answered. "There's nothing you can do other than stay out of the way."

"Well, that's a little hard to swallow. I mean, I've been moused, attacked, burned out. Should I stay out of the way until they decide to get serious?"

They were at a little restaurant near Higgs Beach. Gleason was just finishing his lunch. Jack hadn't had much of an appetite. He was on his third cup of coffee.

"I think I should move back to town," he continued. "Maybe even back into my house. Fuck 'em. What do you say?"

"Why is it every time I think maybe you aren't as dumb as I thought, you disprove me?" Gleason said. "Listen or better yet, listen to what you just said. You were physically attacked, your house was nearly burnt down, and you were given a dead rodent. Seems like somebody's sending you a message and maybe you ought to start paying attention."

"I am paying attention. And I know who's behind this. That's what I'm talking about."

"I hear you," Gleason said, "but moving back to your house is a stupid idea. Stay on your yacht at Stock Island. We'll work from there."

"I don't know," Jack said. "I think I should confront the bastards."

"All in good time," Gleason smiled.

~~~

"Billy, tell Davy Jones to make another offer on the Vesuvius," Jack said on the phone from the deck of the little sailboat.

Gleason had driven him back to Stock Island. He'd agreed to give up the idea of moving into the house on Ashe Street. But hadn't made any promises about not getting into Ranzoa's face.

"I've had some of the guys in LA check out the property," he continued. "I know what it's worth and I would imagine Davy does, too. Tell him to use his judgment. If he feels we should bump up the fair market price, okay. But no more than five percent. We'll negotiate from there. But make sure he lets them know that it's an out-of-town buyer who wishes to remain anonymous. For now. "

"I thought we were going to wait awhile before we went jumping into that thing again, hee-hee."

"It's just an offer, Billy. They don't have to accept it."

Jack didn't really expect this would be of any interest to the Ranzoas but it was worth a try. He was certain they were behind the string of events that'd taken place so far. If they were aware of his involvement in the Inedible Café then they probably already knew about his interest in the Vesuvius. Key West being nosy again.

Jack's impression of Robert Ranzoa was that of a person who would crush anyone or anything that threatened to upset his little cart. And Ranzoa had shown he didn't mind raising the stakes. The question was, how far was he willing to go? Jack believed the answer was all the way.

He checked his watch. Too early for dinner. His new life as a sailor was becoming a big bore.

CHAPTER 30

"You're fired!" Robert spat out.

"Dad, you can't fire me," Bob said with a goofy laugh. "I'm a partner here, same as you. Besides, there're just the two of us. Don't be silly."

Bob had rolled in late that morning from Miami. He'd come straight to the office from jail.

"Goddamit, look at you!" Robert roared, jumping up from his desk. "Like some bum living down in the mangroves eating grits and grunts!"

Bob grinned and remained seated in the leather-covered chair stationed to the side. He stifled a burp.

"They released me early today," he said. "Took awhile to get the car out of impound. I didn't have time to change into my tuxedo."

Robert pressed his hands to his face and stood still.

"I'm a little hungry, Dad," Bob said. "Want to go to Blue Heaven for lunch?

~~~

Karen Ranzoa hung up the phone in her office near the new capitol building in Tallahassee. The call had come from one of her friends in records.

It wasn't so much that the information she gathered time to time from her different buddies meant anything important. Mostly it was worthless. But as someone once pointed out about a box of chocolates, you never know what you might get next.

What Karen had gotten this time had to do with a curious request for a number of old death certificates for children in Key West. The request had been made by a KWPD detective. And while the young congressman for the district hadn't even been born at the time of these poor unfortunate children's demise, perhaps he'd like to know about the detective's interest in them.

She knew damn well her father-in-law would. She composed an e-mail.

~~~

Bob Ranzoa had ordered breakfast for lunch but the eggs hadn't been quite up to the job. He'd decided to straighten out with a vodka and orange juice. In his estimation it had worked wonders. So he had ordered a second which he was now enjoying.

"You could be disbarred over that stunt in Miami," Robert hissed.

"So could you," Bob giggled. "Disbarred. Prison. Think I don't know what's going on?"

Robert glared at his son.

"Bobby, I don't know what you think. Nor do I care. Now finish your damn drink. I've got to get back."

Bob did as he was told.

"Give me your car keys," Robert ordered, "I'm calling you a taxi. Go home and go to bed."

Bob stood up and handed over his keys. Suddenly he didn't feel too steady. He turned and smiled to someone a few tables away and then collapsed.

~~~

The manager had called a taxi for the two men. Robert had accompanied his son to the house, with the driver threatening all the way that somebody was going to pay if the drunk got sick in his cab.

Now Robert was back at his office and slumped in the expensive swivel chair behind his desk. What a goddamn burden his Bobby was. Always had been, hadn't he? Weak sister. Momma's boy. Took after her side of the family. Well, good riddance for all of that crowd! Would he ever learn that he was also a Ranzoa and start acting like one? And finally, the last question always bound to come, why me? He closed his eyes.

His secretary interrupted him with a soft knock on the door.

"Sorry, sir," she said. "You have an e-mail from Karen. I printed it out."

That was a little presumptuous, he thought, printing out my mail. Bet she got an eyeful of the damn thing, too.

"I hope it isn't anything personal," he chided and motioned for her to leave it on the desk.

After she had left he picked up the piece of paper, yawned sleepily and read the message.

Fully awake now, he grabbed up the phone.

CHAPTER 31

"**J**ack, the exterminator left here awhile ago," Billy said over the phone. "Going to call that inspector fellow and tell him we're ready for him to come by."

Jack had walked over to the commercial pier at Stock Island and was watching a boat unload its catch.

"That's good," he said, "but before you call him I want you to do something. It'll only take a little time but do it right now."

Billy listened as Jack filled him in on what he had in mind. When he'd finished, Billy laughed and said that he would get right on it. Jack ended the call with a big grin. Two hours later Billy called back.

"Health fellow's done come and gone," he said. "Seemed to be in a big hurry. And you won't believe what he did and what I've got on that little camera. Can you get here?"

This was too good to pass up. Jack had to chance leaving his self-imposed exile on Stock Island. He called for a cab.

~~~

"See right there, Jack. We are walking into the pantry."

Jack and Billy were watching the movie that'd been recorded on the hidden camera. After Billy had phoned Jack about the exterminators, Jack had told him to buy one of the tiny action cameras. He'd said to have the salesman fit it with a remote switch and show him how to use it. Then for him to stick it somewhere in the pantry where it wouldn't be noticed but would have a good view.

"I told him to go ahead and check out the whole damn kitchen," Billy said proudly. "I'd be out front in the dining room."

"Smart of you, Billy."

"Look now what he's doing!" Billy said wide-eyed and pointing at the tiny camera screen. "Went straight into the pantry as soon as I left."

The picture showed the health inspector removing a dead mouse from his pocket and placing it on the floor behind some boxes.

"That's when he called me to come see what he'd found, hee-hee."

The camera picture filled with Billy entering the room. Billy took a quick peek over his shoulder at the camera. Fortunately, the other man's attention was being given to the box on the floor. Then he bent down and picked up the dead mouse.

"This is just too great," Jack said. "We've got him now. Call the little prick and tell him he'd better get his ass back over here."

~~~

"Gleason's on sick leave, Captain," Halderman said. "Nasty cut he got during that arrest."

"Well, apparently he's recovered enough to piss off somebody," John Gilbert said.

Gilbert had been with the Key West police department for twenty-two years, starting out on patrol. He'd been captain for the past three years. He was a fair man and a good cop. He was still married to the love of his life and they had a daughter in Florida State University.

"What the hell's with all these old death certificate requests from Tallahassee, Jay?"

Halderman had no choice. He told the whole story to his captain. When he'd finished, Gilbert just looked at him and shook his head in amazement.

"That rumor about those two doctors had been going around even before I joined the force, Jay. And you and Earl, and what's this other guy? Jack Hunter? Of course, I remember him now. He's the movie star who caused all that trouble with that drug bust. You all believe this shit is true? I'm surprised, really surprised, Jay."

Halderman blushed.

"I didn't want this to get to you, Captain," he said. "Didn't want to involve the department. Not that I'm trying to hide anything. Just I wanted to see if there was anything substantial here before bringing it to you. I'm under the impression that there might be."

"Impressions aren't facts, Lieutenant. These are facts. The chief gets a call from the councilman about one of our finest conducting a de facto investigation that's upsetting some citizens. Next he gets a call from the mayor who says the congressman wants to know what the hell is going on down here. The chief calls me on the carpet. Those are the facts. And you're saying you didn't want to involve the department?"

"I'll put Gleason back on duty, sir."

"Damn right you will."

~~~

Jimmy Mann from the city health department was beginning to sweat.

"You faked that shit," he said.

"You got it backwards, Jimmy," Jack laughed. "You did the faking by planting that dead mouse. Want to see it again?"

Jack ran the pictures from the pantry.

"Looks pretty real to me," Jack said. "I don't know who to give this to first. The newspaper or the district attorney. Both? What do you suggest, Jimmy?"

"I'll lose my job," Jimmy said.

"You'll find a new one in prison," Jack told him.

"Do you want money, is that it?," Jimmy asked. "I can give you some. How much?"

Jack winked at Billy.

"We don't want money, Jimmy. We want information."

Jimmy bit his lip.

"I don't know anything, man. My boss tells me what to do and I do it."

"Uh-huh, I think you're selling yourself short, Jimmy. I think you know a lot. Let's start with the name of your boss – the one who tells you want to do."

"Melvin Dillas," Jimmy said quietly. "But if he finds out I told you, I'm toast."

"Hey, it's like Las Vegas," Jack grinned. "Everything you say here stays here. What's with Dillas? Who's he tight with?"

"I don't know, maybe a councilman. I've heard him mention the guy before. Can't remember his name."

Jack continued grilling Jimmy Mann for another ten minutes. Then he told him to get the hell out. But not before he had him sign off on the health violation.

"So what do we do now, Jack?" Billy asked.

"Open up for tonight," Jack said.

"Hee-hee, sure we're going to do that but I meant about all this shady business going on with the health department? Jimmy Mann and the other fellow?"

"We're going to lay low for now, Billy. Hold on to everything we have until we need to use it. And that might come sooner than either one of us expects."

~~~

Jack had taken a taxi back to Stock Island and now sat on the tiny deck of the sailboat. He'd just ended a call to Laura Dalton in Los Angeles. The LAPD detective was moving. Her apartment building had been sold. And the new owners were planning to remodel and most likely raise the rent.

He'd called to tell her what had been going on with him but never got around to it. Better that he hadn't, he'd decided. She would've only been upset with him for once again sticking his nose where it didn't belong. And more so, concerned for his safety. Never mind that Detective Gleason was on the case. And God help them both if she learned about the fracas on Duval Street.

The good news was that she'd found a place in Encino, which was an easy commute to the Van Nuys division where she worked. Not only that, it was a single-family structure. No apartment building this time but instead a little guesthouse on a small estate. It had a bedroom, bath, kitchen, dining area and, get this, a swimming pool she could use. Yes, the cat could come with her.

He was glad for her. She had been his nemeses, savior, friend and perhaps one day might become more than just a friend. She deserved any break she could get.

Next, he called Gleason.

"Yeah?" the detective answered. He didn't sound happy.

"This is Jack, Where are you?"

"I'm fucking home getting ready to go to the office."

"Thought you were on some kind of indefinite sick leave."

"Someone upstate got wind of the death certificates I'd requested. Must've upset somebody important because the captain jumped on Halderman about it and he put me back on duty."

This wasn't good, Jack thought.

"So are you saying we aren't working together anymore?"

Gleason took in a breath and paused.

"Don't know, Hunter. It might be."

Jack considered telling him about the health inspector and what he'd learned. Then he decided he would save that for later.

"Do have some news for you," Gleason continued. "Arson inspector said your house had been deliberately set on fire. They're sending some of the residue around the fuse box to the lab. Guess they can tell if it was a thermite grenade. Hey, you're ex-Army, right? Did you do it? Torch you own place?"

"You have an odd sense of humor, Gleason. Anybody ever tell you that?"

Gleason laughed heartily over the phone.

"Look," he said after recovering, "the lieutenant has cut us some slack. He said what I did on my own time was mine to do. So, yeah, I'm still on the case with you."

Jack was relieved to hear this. He then told the detective about the health inspector.

"And you've got pictures of this asshole planting a dead mouse?" Gleason asked in disbelief. "Amazing!"

"Why don't we meet tonight after you're off?" Jack suggested. "There's this dive bar called Salty Dick's. You familiar with it?'

"Not sure but I'll find it."

"See you there around nine."

CHAPTER 32

Salty Dick's stood at the end of a short lane. Unless you knew exactly where you were going it would be easy to walk past without ever noticing, except on weekends when they had a band – then you couldn't miss it from a block away. Fortunately, the bar was a great venue for some really good musicians. You never knew who might show up.

This being a weeknight, however, only Jack was there waiting for Earl Gleason to arrive.

The detective came in and walked straight to where Jack was seated.

"You need a GPS to find this place," he said, pulling out a stool at the bar next to Jack.

"Want a beer?" Jack asked.

Before Gleason could answer the bartender placed a cold Bud in front of him.

"I'm a mind reader," he said.

Gleason gave him an odd look. Jack had earlier set up the gag with the bartender.

"Why don't we take 'em over to that table?" Jack suggested.

Another couple entered and went to the bar. The bartender turned on a satellite radio to a jazz station and the cool sound of Miles Davis began filling the room and providing a soft ambiance for conversation.

"I'm thinking of becoming a public figure again," Jack said once they'd settled at the table.

"What the hell does that mean?" Gleason asked.

"Just that I'm moving off the boat and back to town," Jack told him. "And this time I'm really going to do it."

"You're crazy."

"You're right," Jack agreed. "But look at it this way. Ranzoa thinks I've returned to LA. And why shouldn't he? He's tried to have me beaten up. Had the restaurant closed down. Set fire to my house. Any sane person would've split long ago. But what I'm thinking is that we should rattle his cage some more. And what better way than for me to show up in his face again? There's something else, too. Billy and I want to buy the Vesuvius restaurant. You familiar with it?"

"Yeah, don't eat there."

"My opinion exactly," Jack laughed. "I've checked out the place and I believe they're ready to sell. But a funny thing – apparently, I'm not the only one interested. Davy Jones found out that Robert Ranzoa is making an offer. I don't know how Jones knows it's Ranzoa but his being involved makes sense."

"I'm not sure I'm with you," Gleason said. "Help me out here."

"It's all part of Ranzoa's game plan to get me completely out of the picture. Even though he believes I've left town, he wants to make sure I don't have a reason to come back. Ever. That's why he got the Inedible Café shut down. Guess he found out about my involvement there."

"I think that's a stretch, Hunter. Yeah, somebody's sending you a message with all this other crap. And it probably *is* Ranzoa, although we can't prove it. But buying the Vesuvius just so you can't have it? Sounds like a couple of schoolyard kids fighting. You've slipped into paranoia, pal."

Jack laughed and took a drink of his beer.

"Possibly," he said. "That or maybe someone really is after me. But I did run a financial check on Ranzoa. He's not exactly rolling in money. Now, if I'm not being paranoid and he *is* trying to undercut me, I can dance with him there. Also, if he sees that none of his other threats has worked, then maybe we can flush him out."

Gleason cocked his head and looked at Jack.

"What do you mean flush him out?" he asked. "It's the damn doctors we're looking for. If they did commit a crime and Ranzoa knew about it and still helped them get out of town, then that would qualify for him being an accessory to murder after the fact. But the sad thing is if that's all true, then hell will freeze over before Ranzoa admits anything."

Jack sighed.

"You're right," he said. "All I want is some kind of justice for those children. Yes, if a crime was committed then there should be an accountability. As far as Ranzoa goes, he's a genuine bastard that needs to be brought down."

Gleason leaned back in his chair.

"Well, that's a problem, Hunter. You're now looking for vengeance. Me, I'm still trying to catch a killer."

Jack was taken aback by Gleason's assessment of him.

"I want to find the killers, too," he said. "We're both on the same page, Earl."

"I'm not blaming you for anything," Gleason said. "I understand. If I thought somebody had sent some creep to bash in my head and try to burn down my house, I'd be a little pissed, too. All I'm saying is that my focus is on a possible homicide. That's what I do."

"Okay," Jack nodded. "Point taken."

"I'm going to look into getting an exhumation order for that kid in Ohio. Don't know how successful I'll be."

"Just do what you do," Jack said.

CHAPTER 33

The two jet skis collided off South Beach. There were four people involved in the accident, two men and two women. One of the women was pulled dead from the water. The other three victims suffered various injuries ranging from broken bones to bruises. All four had been drinking, according to witnesses. The driver's BAL had tested above the limit.

"You'd think the ski rental people would be a little more careful," Halderman said to Gleason.

"They are," Gleason told him. "These jerks owned their jet skis. Trailered them down from Miami. I just wish someone had called 911 earlier. Maybe the water patrol could've broken up the party before they got into trouble."

Gleason had returned to work. The first case he'd caught was the jet ski accident. While it wasn't a homicide, it had involved a fatality. Since alcohol was involved, it became a police matter. The DA would determine what charges would be made once the investigation had been completed.

"Well, people come down here and forget to pack their brains," Halderman said. "By the way, welcome back."

"Thanks," Gleason said and then asked. "You know anybody in Miami SID?"

"No, can't say that I do. Why are you interested in their scientific investigation department? Don't think it'll be necessary to call them in on this jet ski accident, do you?"

"It concerns the exhumation we talked about. The one for the kid out of state."

Gleason explained that before he pursued requesting an exhumation order from the court in Ohio, he felt he should get a scientific opinion. Specifically, whether or not there would be anything remaining of the child to be tested. Bringing in the Miami forensic specialist could add some weight.

"I've given some thought on that exhumation," Halderman said. "You know, I'd mentioned that earlier. About the forensics. We have to be really careful with this thing, Earl. There's the family to consider. I'm not so sure I'd want to have my child dug up after thirty years. And if it turned out to be for nothing, well, you can see where that could lead. Yeah, call up Miami. See what you can get. But remember, it's on your time, not the department's. I don't need another talking to by the captain."

~~~

Gleason left the station early on a tiny fib. He'd signed out to interview a witness in the jet ski accident but instead went home. There he telephoned the Miami SID.

"You caught me at a good time, detective. I was just finishing my lunch."

Gleason had been put through to a Dr. Thomas Woo.

"Lunch?" Gleason laughed. "It's past four o'clock. You must work my hours."

"If they're long, I do," the doctor laughed back. "What can I do for you, detective?"

"I've got a couple of questions about decomposition times," Gleason said. "Good thing you've finished lunch, I guess."

"Ask away," the doctor said.

"I'm working on an old case and I might need to get an exhumation order," Gleason said. "The victim was a child, an infant actually. I suspect a drug might have been the cause of death, which could make it a possible homicide. The body was embalmed and interred in Ohio. Here's the thing. That was over thirty years ago. So my question is, do you think there would be enough left of the remains to find a trace of any drugs?"

"Thirty years ago, you say. And the child was buried in Ohio?"

"Yes, my concern is for the family. I'm sure they'd want to know what happened, especially if a crime had been committed. But if there's no chance of finding any evidence then I don't want to go through with the exhumation."

Dr. Woo took a moment before answering.

"There are several factors to consider, detective. Bodies last longer in a colder climate, so a person buried in Ohio might fare a little better than someone here in Florida. Be much better if he was buried in the tundra, as far as that goes. Then there's the matter of how complete the embalming procedure was and what medium was used. Embalming fluids are much more improved today than those used a few decades ago. Next thing would be the casket. Was it sealed? Placed in a water-tight vault?"

"I could try to find out all of this," Gleason said.

"I suppose you could," the doctor said, "but if you want my opinion, I'd say there's less than a twenty percent chance of your finding much of anything in that coffin. Even under the best of conditions I doubt there's any usable tissue left. I'm afraid the child is now body and soul with the angels."

"Twenty percent chance, huh?"

"More likely zero, detective, if you're a betting man."

Gleason thanked the doctor and ended the call. He had hoped to have heard differently. Halderman would never go for him getting a court order with zero chance odds. He decided to put the idea on hold for the time being.

There were still a few more people to interview. Maybe something solid would turn up with one of them. He suddenly felt a need to get out of his apartment. Just to be outside, no one particular place in mind.

He soon found himself on Olivia Street, having left crowded Duval behind. It was then that he knew where he was going. He continued to Windsor Lane and on down to the cemetery.

The children. Had they called? Unspoken voices heard by an unconscious ear? He didn't believe any of it. He was starting to spook himself.

He went inside and walked among them again. Names once strangers now familiar as his own. He came to an unmarked grave. Someone had placed a single rose on it.

Who could it have been, he wondered? A parent? Perhaps a distant relative? Or someone with a guilty conscience? Would there be a record of the grave in the sexton's office? He would check on that. He looked at his watch. The cemetery was about to close.

Now he stood outside the locked gates unwilling to leave. It was still light and he wandered down Angela along the cemetery fence on that side. Crossing Frances he came to Ashe Street where Jack Hunter had lived until the fire had burned him out. There was really no need for him to see the house but he went there anyway, hoping Jack hadn't moved back in.

A sad sight greeted him. Plywood sheets covered the broken windows. Trampled plants and broken shrubs littered the yard. He went up on the front porch. A new hasp with a padlock had been put on the door. Even the house had become a victim. He turned away and left.

~~~

Southard led back to lights and people. He felt a need to be among them. With the living and in the here and now.

Duval never looked so good. He spotted La Trattoria and headed for it.

The bar was full except for one seat at the end and next to the wall. Erin was on duty and busier than the proverbial one-arm paperhanger.

"Be right with you," she said over her shoulder.

"Take your time," Gleason answered with a smile. He was in no big hurry. Two women seated next to him were engaged in some serious talk. One had glanced up when he'd sat down. Now she gave him another quick look. He ignored her.

"Okay, what are you having, honey," Erin said.

"Vodka martini, straight up with a twist," Gleason told her. "Give me a glass of ice cubes on the side."

"Got it. You eating tonight?"

"Haven't decided yet."

His drink arrived and he plonked a couple of ice cubes in the glass and took a long sip. Fire and ice together and just the thing. A large group seated across the bar from him got up to go to their table. The empty space was quickly filled. Should he eat something? He reached for a menu.

So many choices. He put the menu back. That was where he now found himself, wasn't it? So many choices and where to go next. He was definitely getting nowhere with the children. It'd become a circular investigation, each death taking him back to the beginning. Doctor treats child. Child dies. Suspicious? Only if you want to make it so. There was no evidence of any crime having been committed. And he wouldn't find any. No matter if he dug up every grave in the cemetery and those in other states. He now fully understood the futility of pursuing that course of action. The forensic doctor in Miami was right. It had been too long. It was time to move the focus from the children. And focus on the doctors themselves.

He got a half order of spaghetti with olive oil and parmesan cheese.

CHAPTER 34

Jack had swabbed the decks, cleaned below, stowed what needed stowing and battened down the hatches. The little boat was as shipshape as it had been when he'd first come aboard and ready to set sail. But it wouldn't be sailing with him. He was leaving port in a taxicab.

From the back seat he glanced over his shoulder for a final look at what had been his home and safe haven. Billy's knowing about the boat had been a lucky break for him when he most needed one. It had removed him from the playing field. Given his opponent a false sense of victory, he had hoped. At any rate, he now knew what he was up against.

The taxi was taking Jack to his newly rented house on Center Street, which runs a short two blocks between Truman and Petronia. He'd called a vacation home agency late yesterday. They'd emailed him a picture of the house along with its particulars and he'd taken it for a month.

~~~

"Hello, Melody, this is Jack Hunter. You did some work for us at the Inedible Café, remember? You built the Undrinkable Bar."

Jack had settled into his new home. Two miniature bedrooms, small living room, tiny kitchen and one bath. A dollhouse but compared to his most recent quarters, it was a mansion.

"I have a new project you might be interested in doing," he continued. "I wonder if you could meet me there in about an hour?"

Jack gave her the address on Ashe Street. Next he walked to the scooter rental on Truman and picked out a bright red Vespa.

~~~

"It looks worse than it really is," Melody said. "The damage to the walls, both inside and the outer, needs to be repaired. But the joists aren't too bad. Replace a few and structurally I think we'd then be in business. What I'd do is pull off a little more of the inner wall so we can get a good look. Fortunately, nothing seems to have gone below the floor. Still, I'd check just to be on the safe side."

The two of them stood in the living room, a smokey odor permeating the entire house.

"I think the firemen probably did more harm than the fire," she continued. "Of course, if they hadn't put it out so quickly, we'd be up to our knees in cinders and you'd be looking at a complete rebuild."

"That's terrific," Jack said. "I didn't think I'd come off this lucky."

"Yeah, pretty amazing, isn't it? It's like the fire really concentrated on that one spot before it moved on. Weird."

Jack thought about his idea about the arsonist using a thermite grenade. He was certain that he'd been right.

"Tell you what," Melody said, "I'll put together an estimate including construction, electrician and painters. Also, I'll run down some cleaners to take care of the mess and get rid of the smoke damage. Have everything for you tomorrow. You said this wasn't an insurance job?"

"Nope, it's on my dime. And I'd like to get started right away, okay?"

"I'll get going as soon as the estimate is signed."

"One more thing, use the best people you have."

"Now you're being insulting. I'm surprised at you, Jack."

Jack blushed.

"I'm sorry," he said. "Just that I thought…"

"You think I'd use cheap labor to save you a couple of bucks? Usually it's the other way around. And really, would I be doing you a favor if I cheap-sided the job?"

"It crossed my mind. I just wanted to make sure, that's all."

Melody smiled.

"When you see the estimate, darling, you'll be absolutely certain that you are getting the very best."

~~~

"You look like some kid down here on spring break buzzing around, hee-hee."

Jack had ridden his scooter to the Inedible Café and was having a cup of coffee with Billy.

"Always wanted one," Jack said. "Like that red color? Hot!"

"Just make sure nobody has to pull you out from under a car," Billy said seriously. "Now, what's all this business about you leaving Stock Island?"

"Didn't have the stomach for it," Jack joked. "Kept waking up seasick."

"C'mon, Jack, thought you wanted to hide out. That's why we put you on that boat out there in the first place.

217

Where nobody was going know. Now you come here and tell me you've moved back in town."

Jack reached into his pocket and removed an envelope.

"Give this to your friend, Billy, for the use of his boat."

"You still haven't said why you left."

"Change of plans, Billy, that's all."

~~~

"How's your buddy, Jack Hunter?" Halderman asked. "Talk with him lately?"

"He was taking sailing lessons the last I heard," Gleason answered.

The two men were walking from the parking lot to the station on North Roosevelt Blvd.

"You're kidding me," Halderman said. "Fucking sailing lessons?"

Gleason laughed.

"Hunter's living on somebody's sailboat on Stock Island. He went there after his house was burned."

"Probably a smart thing," Halderman nodded. "Keep him out of trouble nosing around about those children. Not to mention somebody burning him out again. That guy's a trouble magnet."

"I doubt that it'll keep him out of trouble. He can be pretty hardheaded but since you mentioned the children, I was wondering about something myself. What the hell happened to those two doctors? I mean, they were supposed to have left town. Where did they go?"

"Who knows?" Halderman said. "Probably set up practice in another town and maybe had a family of their own to raise."

"Hunter asked both of the Ranzoas about them and got nothing. In fact, the old man was downright hostile. Wonder what that was all about?"

"Well, if you are thinking about asking them yourself, the answer is no, hell no," Halderman said. "The chief will have both of our badges."

"I'm not going to do anything rash. Just wondering, that's all. Don't suppose they have passports, do you? Be easy to check on something like that, huh?"

Halderman stopped walking and turned to Gleason.

"Are you out of your mind?"

"Guess it wouldn't be easy after all."

CHAPTER 35

"**I** want to place an ad in the entertainment section," Jack said over the phone.

He'd called the *Key West Citizen* and was speaking with a woman in their advertising department. Earlier he'd spoken to Billy about the restaurant having an open mike session at the Undrinkable Bar on Sunday. Now he was hoping to make the paper's deadline.

"Quarter page ad, right?" the voice on the other end said. "Okay, give me the details and we'll lay it out."

Jack read off the copy he'd written. And, yes, it was the Undrinkable Bar at the Inedible Restaurant.

Next, he assembled the alto saxophone he'd rented and ran though some scale exercises.

~~~

Earl Gleason was tangled up in red tape with the passport department. He'd navigated through a thicket of phone extensions to finally learn that he would need a court order for what he wanted. And even if he got one, they couldn't promise they'd find any record of the said passports ever having been issued or even say when they could get started on his request, for that matter. He thanked the person and hung up.

So much for that big idea. At least he hadn't involved the lieutenant and still had his head and his badge. No question though, concentrating on the doctors was the best option. He punched in the number.

"Hunter, this is Gleason. I was thinking about having a drink at Vino's. Want to come? I can pick you up."

"Hey, Earl, nice of you to call. Yeah, drink sounds good. I'll meet you there. I live just around the corner now."

~~~

The bar inside was packed when Jack walked up the steps to the wine bar on Duval.

"Over here, Hunter," Gleason called. He was sitting at a small table on the far side of the front porch.

"Surprised you could get a table," Jack said, pulling out a chair.

"I have friends in low places."

A couple passed by on the sidewalk below the porch, arguing in a language other than English. Two children, a boy and a girl in tow, paid them no mind and continued to enjoy their ice-cream cones.

"How's the crime business?" Jack asked.

"Booming," Gleason said. "This merlot's pretty good, too."

"Why don't we split a bottle?" Jack suggested. "I'll get the bartender."

Gleason took in the street scene while Jack was away. A bicycle draped with festoons of blue, white and red electric lights and blasting rock music from a boom box peddled past. A pick-up truck with blacked-out windows idled along in slow cruise, heavy bass notes thumping from within, three lanky kids shirtless on skateboards crisscrossing from curb to curb behind it.

Jack returned with a bottle of wine and two fresh glasses. He poured a small amount into his glass and swirled it before tasting.

"Think you'll like this," he said, pouring a glass for Gleason and then himself.

"So what's the deal with the change of address?" Gleason asked, sipping his wine and giving a nod of approval. "Didn't like Catfish Row?"

"Do you remember when I said something about flushing out the Ranzoas?"

"Yeah, I do recall. Sounded kind of stupid at the time. By the way, that exhumation in Ohio that I'd mentioned isn't going to happen."

"Why?"

Gleason grimaced.

"I talked to the lieutenant about it and also to the medical examiner in Miami. The ME's take is we should forget it. Said there's a zero chance of us finding anything. It's been too long. There's probably nothing left of the body. Bones, if even that. All we'd be doing is causing unhappiness for the family. And probably opening the department up for a lawsuit. You know how it is these days."

Jack remained silent. This was a disappointment but the detective was right. And there went their only hope for gathering real evidence, if any had ever existed.

"What about Halderman?" he asked. "Is he still with us?"

"The Lieutenant thinks we should forget it, too. But I believe I saw him wink when he said so."

"Then I guess I have to ask the next question – what about you, Earl? Think we should forget it?"

Gleason laughed and sipped his wine.

"I'm here, ain't I?"

Jack raised his glass and clinked it with his partner.

"Look Hunter, we're getting nowhere chasing after the kids. I suggest we concentrate on the two doctors. Find them and we can close the case. If they're no longer around, meaning they're fucking dead, then there's nothing more we can do."

"I agree," Jack said. "Where do we start?"

"Well, I tried to check with the passport office. Off chance they'd maybe left the country. I ran into a stone wall. Need a court order. Guy there said that even then there'd be no guarantee they'd still have the records. Besides if they went to another country it doesn't mean they'd be living there now. I don't think it's worth pursuing."

"That was a good idea anyway," Jack said. "I'm all for finding the doctors. And I believe Robert Ranzoa knows where they went."

Gleason laughed.

"Maybe we could pull a black ops." he said. "Take his ass up to the mangroves and beat it out of him."

"You know, in a way you might be on to something there," Jack smiled.

Jack told the detective about the health inspector. That they had pictures of the man planting the dead mouse and knew the name of his supervisor. He explained why he believed the Ranzoas to be involved.

"If the two yo-yos you're talking about are Jimmy Mann and Melvin Dillas, then they are indeed bad boys," Gleason said. "Jimmy has a prior for burglary. No jail time. Melvin's a little more careful but just as rotten. Could've been a career criminal if he'd put his mind to it. Arrested for robbery, assault with a deadly weapon, possession of stolen property. Thing is, none of it ever went to trial. Charges dropped. I can't figure for the life of me why those two bozos are working for the health department. Got to be a payoff somewhere."

"Jimmy was the one who came to the restaurant," Jack said. "Maybe Ranzoa is linked to it. If so, putting some pressure on Mann and Dillas might be worth a try."

"I don't see where he'd fit in," Gleason said. "These assholes are small-time crooks. Opportunists and bottom feeders. But Ranzoa is a big fish. He's more involved in political stuff. Deals. Getting in when there's money to be made. No reason for him to even know about these assholes."

"Suppose one of them found out something about Ranzoa? Mann is a burglar. Could be he got ahold of information Ranzoa wanted to keep quiet."

Gleason thought this over.

"It's possible, I guess, but I don't put much faith in it. I'll ask one of the guys in burglary what's up with Mann. Also see if Dillas has had any recent dalliances. I'll have to be careful about pulling their files. Can't do that any longer without a reason."

Jack refilled Gleason's wine glass.

"The other thing I have in mind," he said, "is what I said about getting in Ranzoa's face. He believes I've left town. I'm going to have a big open mike night at the restaurant. Got an ad running in the paper with my name featured. Just to see what shakes out. What do you think?"

"Probably get yourself killed."

Jack gave Gleason a goofy grin.

"I don't know," he said, "I kind of like the idea. I was even thinking of calling Bob Ranzoa and asking him to drop by."

"Hunter, it's not that I really dislike you. Otherwise, I'd say go right ahead and get your head blown off. But you can really be a big pain in the ass at times. This isn't some junior high school prank. I do believe that possibly a crime was committed against those kids. And if Ranzoa is even the slightest bit involved, I want to see him pay. But he's told you in plain language, to leave the family alone. What you're up to could lead to your being charged with harassment or maybe even stalking. You could have an injunction slapped on you."

The illuminated bicycle peddled past, playing Pink Floyd this time.

"Let me explain what I'm talking about," Gleason continued. "In Florida that would be called a protection order. I think in California it's a restraining order. Either way works the same. Say Ranzoa gets sick of your bullshit. He walks over to the court, pleads his case and requests an order telling you to keep the hell away. Court buddy of his approves it and sends a copy to us. Next time you're in his face, as you like to put it, he calls the police, they come and you're up shit's creek without even a pushpole."

"Okay, I won't call Bob Ranzoa," Jack said. "But I'm still running the ad and holding the open mike gig."

Gleason groaned.

Jack laughed heartily.

"C'mon, Earl," he said. "You think it hasn't gotten bad already? Now, here's another thought. Remember the guy I saw at the cemetery visiting his little sister's grave? Henry Overmeyer? I wonder if his mother is still living? He looks about my age, so she could be. Let's talk with her about the doctors."

Gleason mulled that over.

"Problem is, I'm supposed to no longer be on the case," he said. "Lieutenant will have my ass if I talk to her. But you could, Hunter."

CHAPTER 36

To Jack's good fortune, Henry Overmeyer was listed in the phone directory. He'd called the number and gotten his voicemail. Having left a message briefly explaining the nature of his call and asking him to please return it, he'd left the house on Center Street and ridden the Vespa to the builder's office, where he was now meeting with Melody Cooper.

"I thought the structure was pretty sound," Jack said. "Only a couple of joists needed replacing. Isn't that what you said?"

"It was until I crawled under the house," Melody explained. "The fire had nothing to do with what I found there. A lot of water rot and termite damage. Fortunately, it isn't as extensive as I first expected. Still, I can remove it from the estimate if you want. I mean, we don't have to have to do it now but it's not going to get better on its own."

"No, let's do it now and get it over with. Ruth probably never had the house inspected."

"Who's Ruth?"

Jack smiled.

"Ruth LaVere," he said. "She's the owner. I rent the house from her."

Melody nodded and didn't question further.

"Where do I sign and when can you start?" Jack asked.

~~~

"Davy Jones hasn't heard a peep from those people at the Vesuvius, hee-hee."

Jack was having lunch at the Inedible Café. Billy had made him a super-sized spinach salad with a special dressing he'd whipped up. He'd also included a half-dozen boiled eggs which Jack had pushed to the side.

"Next time not so many eggs, Billy. Actually, none would be even better."

"That's protein you're talking about," Billy admonished. "No protein in that rabbit food there. Man needs protein, don't you know?"

Jack forked a piece of egg into his mouth.

"Did Davy tell them that we could offer a short escrow?" he asked.

"Hell, yes. Davy's no fool. Just those Vesuvius folks seem all in a dither. Like they're wanting to sell one moment and the next don't know what they want."

Sounded to Jack that perhaps Ranzoa was calling some shots.

"Well, we'll try to nudge them into making a decision," he said. "Ask Davy to let them know that we're also looking at a couple of other places and need an answer by the end of the week."

Billy flashed a toothy smile.

"Other places, Jack?"

Jack's phone rang before he could explain to Billy that he hadn't meant they were actually looking. He checked the caller ID. It was Henry Overmeyer.

~~~

Irene Overmeyer lived in a small grey cottage on Knowles Lane. It was presently being prepped for painting and the workmen were there scraping and sanding on one side of the house as Jack pulled up on his scooter. He parked behind their truck and went to the front door and rang the bell. Henry Overmeyer answered it.

"I'm Jack Hunter. Thanks for inviting me."

"Come in," Henry said. "My mom's expecting you."

Jack stepped inside. The interior immediately put him in mind of Ruth's house. An open hallway ran the length from front to back. Wood flooring throughout. The living room was comfortably furnished, a few pieces antique. Mrs. Overmeyer was seated in an upholstered chair, a walker at its side.

"Mom, this is Jack Hunter. He's the man I told you about."

Jack came over and offered his hand.

"I'm glad to meet you," he said.

"Please sit down, Mr. Hunter. Could I offer you some tea?"

"No, thanks," Jack said taking a chair across from her. "I noticed you're having your house painted. Will it be the same color?"

"Oh, no," Irene said with a little laugh and a wave of her hand. "I want something cheery this time. It's going to be sunshine yellow. What do you think about that?"

"Sounds cheery to me," Jack said.

"My dad passed away last year," Henry said. "We're sprucing up the old place."

"I'm sorry for your loss, Mrs. Overmeyer."

"Thank you, Mr. Hunter. We had a good life together. Otis worked for the city. We'd planned to travel some when he retired but two weeks after he stopped working he had a heart attack. Then it got so it was hard for me to get around. But things have a reason for happening, I guess. Just the Lord's will."

Jack could sympathize with her in part. His dad had also died from a heart attack.

"Just listen to me carrying on," Irene laughed. "Now, Henry said you wanted to talk with me about Grace."

Oddly, Jack felt his stomach do a little flip. He cleared his throat.

"While a lot of time has passed since then," he said, "I imagine it's still a painful memory. I don't mean to cause you any grief but wonder if you could tell me about the doctors involved?"

Irene Overmeyer gave him a puzzled look.

"Well, I suppose so," she said. "First, what business is it of yours about what happened to Grace or with Doctor Ranzoa?"

"None," he said. "It's absolutely none of my business. And I'm imposing on you. But as I mentioned to Henry, I do have a reason."

After Jack had explained his involvement with the children from the beginning to the present, Irene Overmeyer surprised him with an astonishing admission.

"Ardell and I were school friends. She was a year older than me. But that didn't seem to matter. We were all young back then."

"This was while you were in school here?" Jack asked. "I mean, here in Key West you went to school together?"

"Yes, we did," Irene told him. "Up to the time when Ardell and her brother left for private school."

This was an amazing discovery for Jack. It hadn't occurred to him that somebody who might've known the Ranzoas as children would themselves still be living in Key West. Yet it should've been so obvious a possibility.

"What were they like?" Jack asked.

"Like kids," Irene laughed. "Ardell was fun, her brother was the quiet one. He used to get into fights with the boys over his sister."

"So he was protective of her," Jack said. "Were the boys flirting too much? Seems an awfully early age for that."

Now it was Irene's turn to blush.

"Actually, it was the opposite," she said. "And not very nice. But you can't blame them entirely – they were just being children. It was their parents who should've known better."

"I'm not certain I understand."

"Are you sure you wouldn't like some tea or a cold drink? Henry, would you mind getting our guest a Coke? I'd like one also."

Henry Overmeyer went to the kitchen and returned a few minutes later with the soft drinks.

"You were saying the parents should've known better," Jack prompted after everyone had settled. "About what?"

"Children are curious," Irene said. "They ask questions to learn. And while a question can be completely innocent, it often is embarrassing."

"Is this why Ardell's brother got into fights?" Jack asked. "The boys were embarrassing his sister?"

"Yes," Irene answered. "There was this little beach we would go to. Just a few of us who'd become friends. Ardell

233

and myself. Two other girls. Sometimes we didn't have a bathing suit so we'd just swim in our panties. That is, if we were the only ones. I mean no boys around. One time, we decided we'd take all of our clothes off. It was on a dare or us just being naughty, I don't know. Anyway, we were at different stages of development, the way children grow. Naturally, we all looked at each other. Poor Ardell was very different."

"How do you mean?" Jack asked.

"She was a girl and a little bit of a boy."

"You're talking about her...sex?" Jack asked.

"None of us said anything," Irene continued. "Ardell seemed to be perfectly comfortable with herself. She saw nothing at all unusual. Probably wondered what was wrong with us. But one of the other girls wasn't so nice. It didn't take very long for it to get around."

Henry Overmeyer sat slack jawed.

"That's when the fighting started between Armand and the schoolboys?" Jack asked.

"Soon afterwards," Irene said. "The taunting was just plain being hateful. That's what I meant about the adults knowing better. Perhaps if they'd explained to their children that Ardell wasn't some kind of freak, things would've been better."

"That's how people thought then and many still do," Jack said. "To them Ardell *was* a freak. Some kind of monster. The parents were probably scared that she'd somehow hurt their kids. Is this when Ardell and her brother were sent to the private school?"

"Yes, they didn't even wait till the year's end. I never heard from Ardell again until she returned."

"Hermaphrodite," Henry said suddenly. "That's what Ardell was."

Jack turned his attention to Henry.

"My dad had an identical twin," Jack said. "You couldn't tell them apart."

"Henry's a writer," Irene interjected. "Always looking for something interesting."

"It's more of a hobby," Henry said. "I haven't quit my day job yet."

"Have I read any of your books?" Jack asked. "Do you write under your name?"

"I appeal mostly to the gay market," Henry said. "I doubt if you've read any of my work."

"My guess is that market isn't as limited as you suspect," Jack smiled. "But let me ask you this, have you ever thought of investigating what we're talking about here? You know, as a writer. Could be a good story."

"To tell you the truth, Mr. Hunter, I'm not certain that there's anything here to write about, good story or not. The only facts are children's graves. Sad subject but hardly one to stop the presses over. Of course, you have rumors but everybody on the island has one about something or the other. No, thank you. Not interested in writing fiction."

Jack took all that in for a moment. It certainly wasn't how he saw things and was about to say so when Irene revealed the second startling piece of information.

"Ardell sent me a note after they'd gone," she said quietly. "It was the only time I ever heard from her."

Jack stared at her in amazement.

"So, why did she write? I didn't realize you all were close."

"I guess it had to do more with Grace. Her feeling sorry about not being able to help her. I never could understand why she had waited until after they'd moved away to write to me. You'd have thought if she was so upset she'd have written earlier or come to see me. Little Grace had been dead for nearly two years then."

Jack thought that was strange, too. Could it have been an attempt to soothe a guilty conscience?

"I don't suppose you still have that letter?" he asked.

"No, I really didn't want to keep it. You see, I had accepted our loss. I've never gotten over what happened, however. I still think of Grace every day, wonder what she might've become. Would she have had children of her own? A child never leaves your thoughts, Mr. Hunter."

"I haven't any children, Mrs. Overmeyer, but I can imagine that being so. Did Ardell say where she was living? Was there a return address?"

"No, I might've written her back had there been one. The letter just came with my name and address on the envelope, nothing else."

Jack's hopes sagged.

"Well, there was a postmark. I do remember that. It came from Miami."

Something solid at last, Jack thought. Maybe not much but a place to start. No, more than that. He was on to them now. He suddenly felt energized.

"Mrs. Overmeyer, you have really been most helpful," he said, getting to his feet.

"I know some of this must have been painful for you to recall. I do believe there is an answer somewhere to what happened to all of those children and I intend to find it. Thank you again."

Outside and before starting his scooter, he phoned Gleason.

CHAPTER 37

Robert Razona sat in his office waiting for his son to arrive so they could go for breakfast. The boy was late and Robert was getting impatient. He picked up the daily newspaper from his desk and began thumbing through it. Page three caught his attention.

"Sorry I'm late, Dad," Bob Ranzoa apologized, rushing in.

"Have you seen this?" Robert said, slapping the paper down on the desktop and jabbing at it with his finger.

Bob walked over to see what was so upsetting. A quarter-page advertisement for a jam session at the Undrinkable Bar with a picture of Jack Hunter holding a saxophone stared up at him.

"You know, I saw him the other day," Bob nodded. "He was on a red motor scooter."

Robert looked at his son incredulously.

"Goddamn, Bobby, why didn't you tell me?"

"Didn't think it mattered, I guess."

Robert slumped back in his chair.

"Didn't think it mattered," he mocked. "Sit down over there for a moment."

Bob obediently took a seat to the side of his father's desk.

"You've had a drink already, haven't you?" Robert glared. "Stink like a goddamn brewery."

"Sure, haven't you heard?" Bob chuckled. "It's the breakfast of champions."

"This Jack Hunter fellow," Robert ranted. "I don't like him, Bobby. Cocky sonofabitch from Hollywood out here poking around in our family business. What the hell gives him the right? I've explained all this to you before but apparently it didn't sink in. So let's just see if you can get one simple fact straight in your sotted brain. This man, this Jack Hunter, is no good. Got that? Easy enough for you? Fine, now let's go have a real breakfast."

Robert stood up to leave but Bobby didn't make a move. He sat and smiled at his father.

"Think I don't know what this is all about, don't you?" he grinned. "Why you're so scared shitless of Jack Hunter? Used me to set him up so he'd get the shit kicked out of him and leave us alone. That asshole I got drunk with has a big mouth, dad. Suppose Jack'd been killed?"

"Go home and sober up," Robert said. "I had nothing to do with that."

"Sure," Bob sneered. "You're so fucking upstanding. Oh by the way, I visited Aunt Ardell since I was up that way. I guess she would be my aunt, wouldn't she?"

Robert paled.

"Have a seat, dad, you're looking a little faint."

Robert eased back down into his chair, his eyes steely as a cobra.

"You've got no fucking aunt, boy!" he snapped angrily.

"I'm not stupid, dad. All the hushed whispers between you and mom when I was little and before she died? Some big secret you had to keep? Then the rumors. I've heard them, too. Jesus, they were true, weren't they?"

"What did this supposed aunt tell you?"

"She told me to come and talk to you. So here I am."

Robert remained silent, coldly appraising his son.

"There was an agreement," he said. "You wouldn't know anything about it and even if you did I doubt you'd understand."

"What kind of an agreement?" Bob asked.

"One your grandfather made with some of the town leaders concerning our family."

"Hell, if people knew half the shady fucking things this family's done, we'd be put under the jail," Bob laughed.

Robert drew a doodle on a notepad. Concentric circles.

"Look, dad, why don't we just forget this?" Bob asked. "Forget about Jack Hunter. He's going to get nowhere. Let this thing with Ardell go. It's only going to drag you down. And all this other stuff, too. We can do fine without it. We can be a real law firm."

Robert began filling in every other circle until he'd completed a bull's-eye target.

"You need to do something about your drinking, Bobby," Robert said. "I think reality has abandoned you. What you've just told me about having visited Ardell sounds like a hallucination. You were drunk. Got arrested for drunk driving even. Let's admit it, Bobby, you're out of control."

Bob snorted a little laugh.

"There are some very nice rehabs where you can get help," Robert continued. "Some are like top-notch hotels. Spend a week or two in one. I'll take care of the expense. And I'll handle things with Karen, too. She'll probably thank me for it."

Bob laughed out loud.

"I bet you'll handle thing with Karen, dad. And while you're at it why not take a moment to file for our divorce?"

"Don't be stupid, Bobby. You're not divorcing anyone. I expect a grandson from you two."

Bob cocked his head and looked sadly at his father.

"It's always all about you, isn't it?" he said. "You've never disappointed me in that respect. Well, here's a news flash. Not going to be a grandson. The fuck stops here."

Robert's face blackened.

"Want to know how I found out about Aunt Ardell?" Bob grinned. "Her address was in the safe."

"What were you doing in there? That's private! You had no business snooping around in there."

"Of course I did, dad. The safe belongs to the firm. Same as me. I had to look for an old billing record. Wasn't in the files so I checked the safe. The record wasn't there either but an envelope with the letters A and A written on it was. I was curious and since I'm not a cat, I felt confident I could open it without getting killed. And lo and behold, there it was. Speaking of felines, the cat's truly out of the bag. Aunt Ardell was very talkative. I think she was glad to finally have someone to talk to. They don't get many visitors."

Robert glared at his son.

"About my drinking," Bob continued. "I appreciate your concern but you really needn't worry. You see, I'm not hallucinating, no pink elephants, nothing like that. Not then, not now. I see things very clearly. But you are right about the DUI. Normally, that would never have happened. I'm careful when it comes to driving and drinking. I don't even have one drink if I'm going to drive. But after seeing Ardell and Armand, I couldn't help it. That's why I went to that dive bar with one of your associates. I got blasted with the creepy goon and the cops pulled me over."

"I wish you'd wrapped the goddamn car around a telephone pole," Robert said angrily.

"Well, sorry to have let you down but here's something else. You never asked about Uncle Armand? Now why is that?"

Robert gritted his teeth.

"Not curious? Not even one teeny-weeny bit? Of course not, you already know. Bet you don't know this. They both look just like you. Isn't that a riot?"

Robert got up from his chair and walked over to where his son sat and smacked him forcibly across his face.

CHAPTER 38

"What did you say, Hunter?" Gleason complained. "I can't hear a damn thing with all that banging going on."

The carpenters were in the process off ripping off the burnt siding from the house on Ashe Street. An electric saw whined at a high pitch. Inside they were pulling up the flooring. A boom box blared.

Much of the furniture – the good stuff – had been placed in storage. A few pieces and Jack's old bicycle were stashed in the small building behind the house. The same little room Jack had lived in during his first visit to Key West. During the time he'd been a fugitive.

Jack stood on the sidewalk speaking with the detective. He'd been unable to reach him since his talk with Irene Overmeyer. And he'd been anxious to bring him up to date.

"Hang on a second," Jack said. "I'll walk a couple of houses down the street to where it's quieter."

"Can you hear me now?" he asked, the racket having been reduced to a more reasonable level.

"What is this, a phone commercial?" Gleason laughed.

"Very funny. I was trying to tell you that the lady said she'd gotten a letter from Ardell. And it had come after the good doctors had blown town. That's the first real lead we've had. I'm pretty excited about it."

"Yeah, Hunter, that's good but you said there was no return address."

"It had a Miami postmark. Came a year or so after her child died. We need to start checking names and addresses in Miami from around that time."

"That's heavy resources you're talking about," Gleason said. "We don't have them. You realize how big of an area Miami takes in? And what if Ardell dropped the letter in the box on their way to Timbuktu?"

"How about we just try the telephone directories?" Jack suggested. "Easy enough to look up Ranzoa. Unusual name. Can't be all that many of them."

"Be my guest."

Jack ended the call. What a discouraging prick Gleason can be, he thought. Still, the detective had a point, maybe even a couple. The Ranzoas could've been just passing through Miami when Ardell mailed the letter. So they could be living anywhere in the country. In the world. That is, if they were even still living.

Another idea came to him. He was surprised he hadn't thought of it earlier. Well, actually, he had. But this time he'd do it differently. He decided to jump right on it.

~ ~ ~

The Key West Library occupied the northeast corner of Fleming and Elizabeth Streets. Along with containing a proverbial wealth of information, its capable air conditioners provided blessed relief from the hottest day. For either purpose the library was a popular destination.

Jack sat at one of the library's computers. He'd struck gold with the Florida Ranzoas. Two of them in Key West, one in Tallahassee. Further nosing around had revealed the Tallahassee Ranzoa to be Bob's wife, Karen. But as far as the rest of the country went – and this had been his big idea, to search state by state – he'd struck out.

He dismissed the phone directories. The library no longer carried a complete a set for the entire Miami area. He signed out on the computer and left the library.

There wasn't any real need for him to return to the house. The workers were getting along just fine without his interference. Also, it was kind of painful for him to watch. He hit the starter switch on the Vespa and, with no better place in mind, he headed for the Key West Cemetery.

Once again drawn to this peaceful little strip of land running along the fence. What did he hope to find this time? He parked the scooter and walked through the gate.

The sun was unmerciful and bounced a suffocating heat off the ground. Even the iguanas had taken refuge in their cool burrows beneath the grave slabs.

Jack slowly browsed among the tiny markers. He discovered one he'd earlier missed. A shamble of a grave, broken and unmarked, its slab covered with dirt and grown over, leaving only a single corner sticking up like the bow of a sinking ship. He knelt and placed his hand on the cracked cement. It felt hot as if warmed by fire. He concentrated, pressing his hand harder against the surface, concentrating as if he could send something from within his being, a comforting message – even love – that would pass from his hand and through this cement conduit and be received and understood by the forgotten child below.

Little Boxes

Yes, a promise that he, Jack Hunter, would not forsake this lost child nor any of the others. He got to his feet and returned to the main gate.

CHAPTER 39

Jack awoke from a tiring and fretful sleep. After leaving the cemetery and returning to his rented house on Center Street, he'd felt completely worn out. It must've been the sun, he'd figured. The past few days had been record setters, well into the nineties. He had intended to lie down for only a moment and now look, it was nearly five o'clock. He had been in bed for nearly four hours!

Yet he didn't feel rested. There'd been disturbing dreams. The wearying kind that come with the flu or some other illness. He couldn't even remember what they were about. Probably just as well. He slowly got to his feet, unsteady as an old man and taking a moment to get his bearings, then went to take a shower. Tonight was the open mike event at the Undrinkable Bar.

~~~

"Jack, been looking for you," Billy said. "People already showing up."

It was true. The bar was nearly full. Jean Thornton had her hands full tonight. Her friend Janine, who tends bar at the Pier House, was on the way over. Luckily, it was Janine's night off and she was free.

"You okay, Jack?" Billy asked. "Seem a little pale."

"I'm fine. Just the heat got to me today. Any of the guys here?"

Jack was referring to some local musicians. He'd called a few earlier. Monster drummer. Really good bass player. Another saxophonist, tenor man. He'd be on alto himself. They'd played a couple of times together before. The impromptu Jack Hunter Quartet.

"You're the first of the hep cats, hee-hee."

Jack placed his horn case behind the bar and took a seat.

"What can I get you, Jack?" Jean asked.

"You know, I'd just like some water," he said. "I'm kind of pooped."

"It's this damn hot weather," Jean complained. "Everybody's feeling it. I believe there's been a climate change. Joe says so."

Joe was Jean's husband and he knew everything about everything according to his wife, although others in his circle might share a somewhat different opinion.

Jack drank the glass of ice water and Jean refilled his glass. He emptied that one, too.

"This the place?" asked a young man carrying a instrument case that looked as if it'd been flattened by a semi. "I'm Chet Baker."

Jack laughed and said, "That's a funny-looking trumpet you've got there, Chet."

Then to Jean, "Chet Baker was a monster trumpet player. Good vocalist, too. He was *the man* during the 50's West coast jazz scene."

"Yeah, he was a killer," Chet said. "But it's always the same joke. No relation to the other Chet. No reason for the name. Just luck of the draw. I play keyboard. Okay if I set up?"

"Sure," Jack said. "We've got an amp and speakers. I'm Jack Hunter, by the way. I play alto sax. Glad you could come."

Chet went to work getting his keyboard together and Jack stepped out to the dining room to talk with Billy.

"Doing anything special on the menu?" he asked.

"Think it's going to be finger food tonight, Jack. Easy service. Especially when it's going to be a crowd. Sure you're feeling okay? Don't look none too chipper, hee-hee."

Chet began plonking a few blue notes. Jack assembled his horn and blew a couple of riffs. Janine came in and Jean made a big fuss and gave her a hug.

~~~

The bandstand was full. Through the night, a dozen or more musicians had dropped by, including a few vocalists. They finished the set with the world's fastest rendition of *Have You Met Miss Jones*. Jack announced a fifteen-minute break and stepped over to the bar.

Earl Gleason had come in earlier and had gotten a seat before the place really started filling up.

"That last number was pretty hot stuff," he said to Jack.

"Thanks, didn't know you were a jazz-bo," Jack said, wiping his brow.

Some of the band members crowded around the bar.

"Like to listen," Gleason said. "Can't play a note on anything."

"How's your work load at the office?" Jack asked. "If things ever loosen up it'd be fun for us to get back on the Ranzoas."

"The Lieutenant still has me on a short leash. Jet ski accident was pretty godawful. Well, not as bad as the two assholes from Miami whose Whaler got run over by the yacht awhile back. Don't think you were here for that – probably back in LA. Anything new on your end?"

"Just what I told you about Irene Overmeyer. I checked out Ranzoa on Google, by the way, and got nothing spectacular. Just the two in Key West and a daughter-in-law who has an address in Tallahassee. Her name's Karen."

"Yeah, I've heard she's tight with a congressman or whatever, some political hack," Gleason said. "Wonder how her hubby feels about that? This town being rumor central and all."

Jack turned toward the restaurant door and grinned.

"I don't know," he said. "Why don't you ask him?"

Bob Ranzoa had just come in and was making his way to the bar.

"Hey, Jack!" he shouted. "This is a great place you've got here!"

"Hi, Bob, good of you to stop by."

"Saw your ad in the paper," Bob said a little too loudly. "Wouldn't have missed coming for the goddamn world."

He noticed Gleason standing next to Jack.

"I'm Bob Ranzoa," he said, thrusting out a hand. "You also a friend of Jack's?"

"We've known each other for a while," Gleason smiled, ignoring the proffered hand. "I'm Earl Gleason."

"Gleason?" Bob scrunched his face. "That sounds familiar. Now where have I heard it?"

Gleason shrugged.

"Bob, what the hell happened to you?" Jack said. "That's some shiner you've got."

Bob Ranzoa placed his hand on his bruised eye.

"Could say I ran into a door," he chuckled, "but it's even more embarrassing than that. I was opening a bottle of champagne and the cork hit me. Can you believe that?"

"Guess I'll have to," Jack laughed.

"Hey, barkeep!" Bob summoned. "Give these gentleman a round on me."

The band began to gather on the stage.

"I got to get back up there," Jack said to Bob. "Why don't you stick around? Earl will keep you out of trouble."

The band had just gotten underway with the lovely ballad *Stella by Starlight* when the fight broke out.

A couple of men had come into the restaurant and jostled someone in a group sitting at a table while passing by. Words were exchanged between the parties and a shoving match ensued, which overturned the table, spilling drinks and food to the floor. Friends of the offended person jumped up and in no time fists began to fly.

The melee rapidly worked its way to the bar where Gleason was cold-cocked and sent sprawling into the keyboard. He got back on his feet, pulled out his badge and yelled POLICE! Several 911 calls had already been placed.

Bob Ranzoa slipped out through the kitchen.

~~~

The uniformed officer led a cuffed Melvin Dillas to the waiting patrol car. The restaurant had mostly emptied during the fight. Three more cops ushered the few remaining patrons out to the street. Gleason was talking with the field supervisor, a sergeant.

"Dillas started the fight," Gleason said. "I saw him when he came through the door. And he knows I'm a cop. He threw that fucking punch at me on purpose."

"We'll add assaulting an officer to the charges, Earl," the sergeant said. "You need any medical attention?"

"I'm good," Gleason said, working his jaw. "I was off balance when he hit me so he didn't really connect."

"You said there were two of them who started the fight?"

"Yeah, the other guy ran but I didn't recognize him. Only Dillas."

"Okay, take care. See you at the station."

The sergeant left and Jack, who'd been straightening up the bar area, walked over to Gleason.

"So it was Melvin Dillas from the health department," he said. "That's interesting. I mean, this whole thing is getting weirder and weirder. Now I know the Ranzoas are involved with it all – children, beating me up, burning my house, false mice."

"Anything's possible, I suppose," Gleason said. "But it's still conjecture."

"You think? Look at all the shit that's gone down since we started asking about those graves."

"Still doesn't prove the Ranzoas are involved in the cemetery part. Maybe you've just pissed them off with all the meddling and now you're getting some payback on you personally and your business."

"I'll buy that," Jack agreed. "Here's something more. Didn't I say Bob Ranzoa set me up at the Green Parrot?

Right. And now he breezes in here and all hell breaks out. Coincidence? I think not."

Gleason shrugged his shoulders.

"I'm not saying there's nothing to what you believe. It's just we have no proof, that's all. Bob Ranzoa was pretty drunk. I hope he isn't driving."

"I'm going to figure out some way to get to that little shit," Jack said. "Find out what the hell he knows."

"Again, be careful. I've got to go to the station. Want to be there when they book Dillas."

"Gimme a call when you have a chance," Jack said. "I'm going to help Billy finish cleaning up. I told Chet to have his keyboard looked at. Some ox plowed into it during the fight and probably knocked it out of tune."

CHAPTER 40

Bob Ranzoa hadn't bothered going to the office the next morning. Nor had he bothered calling Lydia the receptionist to say he'd be out.

After last night's brouhaha he'd gone straight home. Lucky to have gotten away in one piece. He should've known something was going to happen – he was surprised it'd been just a fight. His dad must be getting soft in his old age. In an earlier time he would have had the place taken apart.

Still, he knew nothing had really changed with his father. Nor would his dad's opinion of him change. He would forever be a disappointment. Never match up to the son imagined. And try as he might – and he had spent most of the night lying awake thinking about that – in the end he saw that nothing he could do would ever make things different. Ah, the love of a father. Like the man said, it is what it is. With that thought in mind, he decided he'd make today special then.

He was driving up to Bahia Honda State Park, up to mile marker 37. The park is five hundred acres of sandy beaches, foliage, clear skies and a perfect example of why people come to the keys. He intended to spend the entire day there.

If you just wanted to spend a day at the beach, Fort Zachary Taylor would do nicely. You can walk there from anywhere in Key West. But this was going to be more than just a day at the beach.

Bob stopped by Fausto's grocery store before leaving. The deli counterman put together a fabulous picnic lunch for him. Next, he picked out a chilled bottle of a good Chablis. He even bought a real wine glass. No plastic cup for him, although he would make do with the plastic eating utensils he got at the deli.

It was a great day for a picnic. Clear and sunny, a few puffy clouds keeping each other company and a balmy 82 degrees. You just can't beat that combination.

Bob swung by the post office on his way out of town and dropped a letter in the box. Now he was motoring up US 1 on the Overseas Highway. Hot damn! Traffic lightened after Boca Chica and he settled back to enjoy the ride. He turned on the radio. Someone had previously tuned it to a Hispanic station and you know what? That was okay, too.

Pretty soon he was past Sugar Loaf Key and he started thinking about how he'd spend this special day. But first things first. He spotted a convenience store up ahead and pulled into its lot.

"How'ya doing, hon?" he said to the clerk, a young girl who looked bored out of her mind. She paid him a vacant smile.

He went straight to the refrigerator section and pulled out a 12-pack of Bud. Putting that down on the counter, he got a Styrofoam cooler and a bag of ice.

"You take American Express, hon?"

The girl nodded.

He charged everything on the firm's credit card.

Back on the road he popped open a can of beer. Careful to keep it out of sight from passing motorists, he held it between his legs, sipping only occasionally. No need to invite the cops. Getting pulled over for driving with an open container wouldn't make his day. Might make the cop's, though. He chuckled at that. The rest of the cans were happily chilling in the ice chest along with the bottle of Chablis and were stowed in the trunk. It was absolutely fucking remarkable how good he felt. He couldn't remember when he'd last felt this great. Yes, sir.

The highway bent sharply at Spanish Harbor and then just two more bridges to cross and he was at Bahia Honda.

After entering the park he had to decide where to go. The road to the nude beach ran off to his left. Well, it wasn't so much that it was an officially sanctioned place for a naked romp but if no rangers were in sight, then you could. At least that's what went on, or so he'd heard. He wasn't up to taking off his clothes quite yet and drove in the other direction until he found an empty spot with a perfect view of the Atlantic Ocean.

Rather than set up on the beach he decided to remain in the car and enjoy the scenery along with another cold one or two. He got the ice chest out of the trunk and placed it on the seat next to him.

A soft breeze hardly enough to muss your hair brought in a fresh, salty taste. The car doors were standing wide open and the seat pushed all the way back. Bob reclined with one leg propped on the door windowsill. He popped open another Bud. Man, this was the life!

He should've been coming here and doing this long before now. Hell, he should've brought Karen here. She'd have loved it. They could've gone to the nude beach. Well, what the fuck? Never say never, right? He took out his cellphone.

"Bob?" his wife answered hesitantly. "What happened?"

"You won't believe where I am right now, heh-heh," he whispered. "Go ahead, try and guess."

"Are you all right?" Karen said with concern. "You sound kind of funny."

"Of course I'm fucking all right!" Bob snapped and sat up. "And what do you mean by funny?"

"Uh, Bob, I'm a little busy," she said, taken aback by his sudden change. "If this isn't important, I need to go."

"Goddamn, Karen, don't you want to know why I called? I'm sitting in my car looking at a beautiful goddamn beach and ocean and thinking of you. And how you should be here with me. And you could be if you weren't stuck in Tallahassee half the damn time. I'm so sick of this shit!"

"Bob, we've been through all this," Karen sighed. "It's what I do. My job, remember? We agreed. You have your career and I have mine. It doesn't mean that I don't miss you. Why are you so angry? Are you taking your medicine?"

Bob Ranzoa gave a sarcastic snort.

"There's a nude beach here," he said. "Now want know what I'm thinking? I'm picturing you standing on that beach right in front of me. With just the sun for clothes on that sexy body of yours. How it would feel for us to swim together naked, thighs touching, belly to belly, sleek and cool. We could maybe spawn. Have ourselves a little minnow. Think dad would be happy with a minnow for a grandkid? Oh, wow, you should see this damn water now, Karen."

"Bob, I'm worried."

"I brought us a picnic, Karen," he continued. "Had it made up special at Fausto's. Those guys there, man, they know how to treat people, huh? Trouble is now I have to eat alone. Don't you think that's sad? I do. Wait, here's an idea. We could do this, Karen. What if you just got up, went to the airport and caught a plane? Charter the fucking thing. One of those little airplanes. Fly down to Marathon. I'll meet you. How's that sound?"

"That would be fun, Bob. Which beach are you at now?"

"Ah, just a beach," Bob said, feeling he shouldn't have mentioned Marathon. Too close.

"Does the beach have a name?" Karen asked. "Tell me where you are."

Bob ended the call.

Karen would never go on a picnic, he thought to himself. Not in a million years. He must've been dreaming to think otherwise. Just stringing him along like the cunt she'd always been. If the old man asked her to go on a picnic, she would do it in a minute he'd bet. She would go to the fucking moon for him. She ought to marry the fucker. Marry his own damn dad. What an idea!. He opened another Bud.

His life was something else, wasn't it? Always trying to please everyone except his own damn self. And failing at even that, if you can imagine anything so lame. Disappointing those he so desperately wanted to please at every damn turn. Robert Ternant Ranzoa III, third-rate lawyer at a third-rate law firm. Never living up to anyone's expectations from the miserable day he was born.

A van pulled into a spot two over from him. Family with three kids. The doors had barely opened before the children were out like shots for the beach. A large, brown wooly dog with tight curls bounded after them.

"Lomax! Get back here," the mom commanded, adding, "You kids wait for your dad before going in that water, you hear me?"

No mind was paid by any one of them, including Lomax. Mom threw up her hands in desperation and proceeded to help dad unload the van.

Soon the family was settled on the beach. Bob opened another beer and sat back to enjoy the moment. The park ranger's utility vehicle halted on the road right in front of him. The officer, a blonde woman in uniform and wearing her hair pulled back and a 9mm strapped on her side, stepped out and approached the family.

Bob couldn't make out what they were talking about but after a minute or so dad walked Lomax by the collar back to the van. Apparently there'd been a violation of some rule pertaining to untethered dogs on the beach because Lomax immediately reappeared at the end of a short leash. The ranger gave Bob a long look through her mirrored sunglasses and started to approach his car. He sat up and surreptitiously slipped the top back onto the ice chest and checked the floorboard for empties.

"Hi there," she greeted him. "Welcome to Bahia Honda State Park."

Bob focused on her nametag. Anne Nilsson.

"Just wanted to remind you that this isn't an alcohol consumption area," Anne said. "You'll have to go to the picnic grounds if you're planning to drink."

"Thank you, officer, I'll certainly do that when I'm ready to eat," Bob smiled, hoping that he hadn't slurred his words.

"Have a good day, sir."

Before the ranger got in her vehicle Bob noticed her write something down. Probably his goddamn license plate. Fuck it.

One six-pack had bitten the dust and Bob thought perhaps it was time for a change-up. He fished out the wine bottle from the ice chest. Damn, wouldn't you know it? Thing had a cork stopper. He'd thought it was a screw cap. He rummaged through the glove compartment. Nothing. Maybe the new arrivals had one.

"Excuse me, folks," Bob called out, ambling toward them with the wine bottle in hand. "Nice day for the beach, huh? I was wondering if you had a corkscrew."

Lomax lunged at him.

"No, bad dog! Bad dog!" dad shouted while reining in the snarling animal. "Don't worry, mister. He's harmless. Just gets excited at times."

Bob had jumped back, the wine bottle raised and ready for a braining.

"Sorry about that," dad said. "No, we don't have a corkscrew."

Bob thanked the man, eyed Lomax and returned to his car. He sat in the driver's seat still trying to catch his breath. Of course the asshole wouldn't have a corkscrew. That ranger should've arrested the whole bunch of them for bringing along that fucking dog. What was her name? Maybe he'd report her. He couldn't remember it. He gave the glove compartment another look.

Luck this time. He found a screwdriver. After several jabs he'd managed to push the cork down into the bottle. At least he hadn't broken the neck off. He dribbled the wine into the glass. A few pieces of cork floated on the surface.

The picnic lunch consisted of a salami and cheese sandwich on rye bread and a container of cole slaw. There were also a couple of chocolate chip cookies for desert. It was all fine by him. Best picnic he'd ever had. And he'd downed the bottle of wine by the time he had finished eating.

He'd been right about switching over to wine, he thought, settling back comfortably in the car's seat. No more bloat. Drowsiness crept upon him.

When he awoke the family had gone. His mouth tasted like Lomax had taken a dump in it. He opened a Bud and swished it around before swallowing. Then he chugged the rest.

Easterly, an armada of brilliant white boats sat in the ultra marine ocean, a faint line of clouds beyond establishing the horizon. Offshore strings of pelicans swept southbound, swooping like daredevils inches above the surface.

Bob got out of the car and crossed the road to the beach. At the water's edge he threw his cellphone as far out as he could into the ocean. The park would be closing soon.

~~~

"He sounded awfully strange to me, Robert," Karen said anxiously over the phone. She'd finally been able to reach Ranzoa on the fourth call. The lawyer had had a late lunch, he'd explained.

"Well, that's nothing," Robert joked. "The boy *is* strange."

"I don't think this is funny," Karen said. "I'm worried he's going to hurt himself."

"Let me ask you this, Karen. When you said Bobby sounded strange, did you mean he sounded like he'd been drinking? If so, that's just business as usual with him. I wouldn't worry if I were you."

"He asked me to charter an airplane to Marathon, Robert. Said he wanted me to join him at a picnic on the beach. If that's not strange, I don't know what is. Maybe he *is* drunk but I think somebody should call the sheriff."

"What the hell could they do, Karen?"

"They could go look for him. In Marathon or wherever. Don't you think it's important? Suppose he does hurt himself?"

Robert rolled his eyes. The woman was verging on hysterical. Goddamn that boy!

"All right, Karen. Leave it to me. I'll take care of things."

"You'll call the sheriff?"

"Just leave it to me, all right?"

He ended the call. No sooner had he hung up than Lydia buzzed him. Robert grabbed the phone back.

"Mr. Dillas is on line two."

"Who the hell do you think you are calling here?" he snapped angrily.

"I'm your new client, motherfucker," Dillas said. "I just got a hundred-thousand dollar bail money put on me!"

This was all becoming too much, Robert thought. Well, he would provide a temporary fix until something more permanent could be arranged.

"I'll have one of my associates get in touch with you," he told Dillas. "Meanwhile, keep your mouth shut and don't call me again."

Chapter 41

The ocean had darkened almost to black and night now waited just over the horizon.

His day at the beach was coming to an end. Funny how he'd spent most of it inside his car. He stuck his hand into the ice chest and felt around. His fingers came upon a lone can of Budweiser. He fished it out and popped the top.

He started the car and drove to the road leading out. Exiting the park he turned right toward Marathon.

As he approached the Seven Mile Bridge he took the last swig of beer. He'd timed it perfectly. He was feeling better now. Yes, sir.

Seven Mile Bridge links the Lower Keys to the Middle Keys. Its length is actually 6.79 miles but who's going to argue? It crosses Moser Channel at the highest point, with an arc rising 65 feet above the water to allow for shipping clearance. The Intercoastal Waterway cut through there. The bridge had been featured in a number of films. At one time it was even among the longest bridges in the world.

Traffic, which had been light at first, slowly wound down to a crawl and then stopped completely. The bridge was right up ahead. He could see the damn thing. What the hell was going on?

~~~

"Ma'am, you say that your husband was acting strangely?"

"I said he was talking strangely," Karen replied. "I'm worried about him."

Karen had decided to call the Monroe County Sheriffs herself rather than trust Robert doing it.

"And this was on the phone," the officer said.

"That's right. He called me at my work here in Tallahassee. Said he was at a beach somewhere near Marathon. He didn't sound right. He might have been drinking, I don't know. Also, he has mood swings. It might've been his medication. I've tried to reach him but he isn't answering."

"And his name is Robert T. Ranzoa III. All right, do you know what kind of car he's driving?"

"Something blue," Karen said. "I'm really not into cars. It's a Lexus, I think. I don't know the license number."

"That's okay, we can find that out. The vehicle's registered to him?"

"I guess so but it might be in his company's name. It's a law firm in Key West. Ranzoa and Ranzoa."

"Good. And ma'am, has your husband done this before? I mean, does he have a history of, as you put it, strange behavior?"

"Nothing like this," Karen said.

"One more thing, and I have to ask this. Might there be any firearms involved?"

"Bob's never owned a gun."

"Thank you, ma'am. I'll put this out immediately to our patrols."

~~~

Bob Ranzoa got out of his car and stood on the highway. The line of stopped traffic went on forever up ahead. This was the shits. He got back inside and reached across the seat for the ice chest.

Hallelujah! One more soldier. He grabbed the last beer and popped it open. And then another miracle. The traffic began to move.

The beer had been a sign, he was certain now. He just had to keep the faith. Yes, everything was working out as smooth as silk. Like a well-oiled engine. He couldn't think of another cliché. Who needed one? Those were fine.

The Lexus passed the two cars that'd caused the delay. They'd pulled off the road. He glared over at them. Their drivers standing to the side exchanging information and angry words. The accident had been a rear ender. The trailing car had gotten the worst of it. Steam billowed from the pushed-in grill, no doubt a smashed radiator. He at last reached the beginning of the bridge.

Traffic started rolling along nicely down the lower span. Then it slowed again. Something up ahead. Dammit all to hell!

Flashing red lights sped toward him in the opposite lane, cutting in and out of traffic. An ambulance heading south in a hurry. That was the thing about US 1. Two lanes all the way. An accident or even a breakdown on either one could ruin your day whether you were involved in it or not.

Once the emergency vehicle had passed, the line of traffic on his side began shuffling forward again. The bridge started to rise in a shallow climb toward the top.

"Get a move on!" he shouted at the cars ahead and pounded on the steering wheel. He shook his head in frustration and grumbled aloud, "Fucking drivers today. How'd they even get a license."

But hold on a second, he thought to himself. What's the big rush? Why was he letting himself get in a huge uproar? Everything's on schedule, right? Stay in the moment. This was his big day. He took a large and final swig of beer, emptying the can and tossing it out the window. The car behind blew its horn at him. He looked in his rearview mirror and gave its driver the finger.

He was approaching the bridge's highest point.

Calm fully embraced him. He flicked on his emergency signal lights. The tick-ticking of the light's relay switch seemed to match his own heartbeat. Easing over to the roadside he braked the car to a full stop. He was at the very apex.

The center of the Seven Mile Bridge measures 65 feet from its bottom structure to the water's surface. Above that, give or take, is another 10 feet or so of girders and prestressed concrete. Then there's the height of the rail to take into consideration. So after adding it all up you're looking at a good 80 feet, depending on the tide from absolute top to bottom. Bottom being the water's surface.

Bob slipped quickly across the front seat and opened the passenger door. Cars behind him began blowing their horns. A few of their drivers shouted curses. A loud bang from farther down the line indicated another rear-ender.

He mounted the rail and slowly stood up, all the while maintaining a shaky balance. People in the car behind his screamed. Its driver opened his door to get out. Traffic in the opposite lane came to a halt. Bob, now having gained his balance, stood immobile for only a moment. And then, just like that, he was gone.

CHAPTER 42

Traffic on the bridge was tied up for half the night. Sheriff's investigators determined the Lexus to be registered to a Ranzoa and Ranzoa law firm in Key West. No one answered at the firm's number when an officer called the next morning. He left a message and a telephone number. Ranger Anne Nilsson had learned of the incident over her radio and, having had a bad feeling, reported the license plate number she'd earlier copied down to the Sheriffs. It matched that of the Lexus. At this point they had no idea as to the identity of the driver. They could be dealing with a stolen vehicle. The car had been towed to the impound yard.

~~~

"Jack, we had another man from the city this morning," Billy complained as soon as Jack came through the kitchen door at the restaurant.

"What was it about this time?" Jack said, pouring himself a cup of coffee. "Not another dead mouse."

"Thinking about revoking our liquor license, that's what!"

Jack leaned back against a counter. The new busboy they'd hired was busy in the dining room setting up the tables for lunch.

"That's ridiculous," he said.

"Exactly what I told the man," Billy nodded. "Said it was ridiculous, hee-hee. Then he told me it was on account of the fight. They'd had a complaint or something the other day. Hell, I said we didn't start no fight. Those fellas just came in here and went to busting up the place."

"Well, that's just more bullshit from Ranzoa," Jack said. "He has his finger in every pie in town."

"This might hurt us on the Vesuvius deal, huh? Lose our license here, gonna be hard to get one there."

"Well, we aren't there yet, are we? Have you heard anything back from Davy Jones?"

"I ain't had time to hear from nobody, Jack. Been too busy putting this restaurant back together. Maybe you should ride over to his office and see what's up?"

~~~

Searchers found Bob Ranzoa's body in 9 feet of water off Boot Key around mid-morning. The Sheriff's Department was called and the body recovered and taken to the morgue at Fisherman's Hospital on Marathon. There was no identification on the dead man.

~~~

Lydia opened the office at noon. Robert had said the day before that he wouldn't be in until the afternoon. He hadn't said that she could have the morning off but she'd decided what he didn't know wouldn't hurt him.

Last night had been awesome. She'd been at a party and had met this most fabulous woman with these striking emerald-colored eyes. And she lived on a sailboat! She'd been really attracted to her and they'd exchanged telephone numbers. She hoped Astrid would call her.

She saw the message light blinking on her phone. Oh fuck, she hoped it wasn't Robert trying to reach her. He hadn't said why he'd be out and she hadn't bothered to ask. She pushed the play button, dreading she would hear Robert Ranzoa's voice. Instead she heard a message from the Monroe County Sheriffs Office asking her to please call them. She dialed the number.

"Sheriff's Department. This is Officer Calvin Jones. How may I help you?"

"You or somebody in your department left a message with Ranzoa and Ranzoa law firm to call you. May I ask what it's about?"

Lydia at first thought it had been a joke. Maybe it still was. She'd play along.

"Yes, ma'am," Jones said. "I'd like to speak with Mr. Ranzoa."

"I'm the secretary. Mr. Ranzoa is out of the office at present."

"I see, may I have your name, ma'am?"

"Is this for real?" she asked with a laugh.

"Yes, ma'am, I assure you that you're talking with the Monroe County Sheriffs. Now may I have your name."

"Lydia Blackwell."

"Thank you, Ms. Blackwell. The reason for our call is that we've found an abandoned automobile registered to your company. It's a 2010 Lexus, blue sedan."

"That's Bob Ranzoa's car," Lydia said. "He's one of the partners."

"Is he there?"

"No, neither one of them is. Bob is Robert Ranzoa's son. It's their law firm."

"Do you expect them back any time today?"

"The senior Mr. Ranzoa said he'd be in this afternoon."

"What about his son?"

"I don't know. He was out yesterday. I haven't heard from him today."

"Well, I will need to talk with one of them. This is a matter of urgency. The car was found on the Seven Mile Bridge. Do you know if anyone reported it missing in the past few days?"

"If they did, they didn't tell me."

"All right, Ms. Blackwell, thank you. Please have Mr. Ranzoa call me at this number when he returns."

Lydia found herself in a swivet. She didn't know which way to turn or where to run first. She called Blue Heaven. Maybe they were there having breakfast. No such luck. Hadn't seen either one all morning, she was told. Next, she phoned Bob's cellphone. Dead line. That was strange. Robert didn't believe in cellphones so she called him at the house. He picked up.

"Mr. Ranzoa, I just got a telephone call from the sheriff's," she said excitedly. "Yes, they just hung up. They said that Bob's car was found on the Seven Mile Bridge. I didn't know what to say to them. He's not here."

Robert told her he'd be in the office as soon as he could get there and for her to remain calm. He asked her for the Sheriffs' number and then phoned Karen.

"Karen, have you heard back from my son?" he asked.

"No, Robert, I haven't. I tried calling him and couldn't get through. Did you phone the sheriffs like I asked? Well, I did! And they took down a report!"

"The damn sheriffs just called the office, Karen," Robert said. "Some fool thing about Bob's car being found on the bridge up in Marathon. Don't know what they expect me to do about it."

Karen gave a pitiful little cry.

"What about Bob?" she asked. "Did they say? Was there an accident? Maybe he's in the hospital."

"All they said was they'd found the damn Lexus. I don't know anything more than that. I was hoping you did."

"Robert, I think we should take this seriously. Something has obviously happened to Bob."

"I'll tell you what's happened to Bob," Robert said. "He got himself drunk and probably left his car parked on the damn bridge. Didn't you say he was talking funny? Drunk's what talking funny amounts to when it's Bob doing the talking. Lucky the cops didn't pick him up. And it wouldn't be the first time. Bet you didn't know about the DUI he recently got up in Miami? Well, that's what he did. Got himself arrested for drunk driving up there and now I've got to take care of it just like every other damn mess he's gotten into."

Karen remained silent.

"You there, Karen?"

"Yes, Robert, I'm still here. And I'm going to call the sheriff again. Somethings's wrong. Goodbye."

Robert next phoned the Sheriffs' number. Officer Jones answered.

"I'm Robert Ranzoa," he said. "You called my office. What is this about?"

"Sir, a car registered to your company was found last night abandoned on the Seven Mile Bridge. According to witnesses, its driver stopped and jumped off the bridge in an apparent suicide. This morning we recovered a body from the water near the location. A white male approximately 30 to 40 years of age. He had no identification on him. I would like to send an officer to talk with you."

Robert sat down. He didn't answer right away. Then, "Can the officer come right away?" he asked quietly.

"Someone will be there within fifteen minutes, sir."

Robert gave the officer his address and then went to the kitchen and poured himself a scotch.

~~~

The ride to Marathon didn't take very long in the Sheriffs' cruiser. They pulled around to the back of the hospital and parked.

"We can go in through here, sir," the officer said to Robert.

The Sheriffs Department required a physical identification by a family member or someone who knew the deceased. After the officer arrived at Robert Ranzoa's house and they had discussed the situation, Robert had agreed to view the body.

He was led to a small room where the corpse rested on a stainless steel table, covered with a sheet. An attendant pulled the sheet back, revealing its face.

"Sir?" the officer said to Robert Ranzoa.

"That is my son," Robert answered and turned away.

~~~

Florida law requires that an autopsy be done whenever violent deaths are involved, including suicide. Taking a dive off a high bridge qualifies.

Although no note was found in the car, the manner in which it happened and his history of depression supported the theory that Ranzoa had taken his own life.

The autopsy determined massive organ damage to be the cause of death. He'd apparently died instantly because no water was discovered in his lungs. His blood alcohol level was more than twice the legal limit.

The body was released and taken to a mortuary in Key West.

~~~

"Looks like they're gonna put Ranzoa in the ground tomorrow," Billy said, putting down the newspaper.

He and Jack were at the restaurant.

"Probably be a big thing," Billy continued. "Key West loves a funeral almost as much as a parade. You going, Jack?"

"You know, I think I will," Jack said. "Maybe not sit through the entire service. So you believe there'll be a big turnout, huh?"

"Hell, Jack, nobody's gonna miss this. Talking about a Ranzoa funeral. Let's see, you've got the mayor, all the council people, big shots, little shots. No telling who's going to show up."

"I wonder. There's not that many in the family. And I'm not so sure the Ranzoas are all that well thought-of."

"Don't matter, Jack. Then everybody will be glad to see one of them dead and buried. Besides, it's a Key West funeral. That in itself's enough to get the town out. "

Jack laughed.

"Church wouldn't take him," Billy said. "'Cause the boy killed himself. Churches can be funny. Person killing himself gets in the way of what they believe. I don't understand it myself. Man's dead, he's dead. Don't matter how he got that way. If it's suppose to be some kind of sin, then let God handle it. People putting a load on the ones left that they shouldn't. God can take care of his own business. Don't need no help from us."

"Well, I don't know how religious he was," Jack said, "so having the service and all at the cemetery is probably just as good."

~~~

Bob Ranzoa's funeral was set for ten o'clock the next morning. Rain began at nine.

The cortege made its way down Angela to the cemetery gate on Windsor Lane. Billy had been wrong – by Key West standards, it didn't even count. Two cars and the hearse. After entering, they continued on Fourth Avenue.

Another small group stood waiting at the family plot, which contained a mausoleum and several separate headstones. The cortege arrived. Robert Ternant Ranzoa II emerged from one of the cars along with a younger woman. Both were dressed in black. Six other people got out of the second car – the pallbearers it turned out.

Jack watched from beneath a Flamboyant tree, standing perhaps twenty yards away.

The rain slackened to a drizzle. Robert held an umbrella over himself and the woman. Now the rear door of the hearse was opened and the pallbearers carried the coffin to the mausoleum. A man who'd been waiting there began the sermon.

The talk lasted less than ten minutes. Next, a woman sang *Amazing Grace* in a cappella. She had a beautiful voice. Jack wondered who she was and if she were local. Then the ceremony was over.

Robert had a few words with the man who had delivered the little talk and got into the waiting car. The woman who'd ridden with him didn't follow but instead hesitated, said something to Robert that Jack couldn't hear. She then shut the door and the car drove off without her.

The woman remained at the gravesite. Jack decided to approach her.

"Mrs. Ranzoa?" he called out, chancing that she was indeed the widow.

"Yes?" Karen said, turning to face him.

"My name is Jack Hunter. I'm very sorry for your loss. I knew Bob."

Karen smiled and said, "Thank you."

"I don't mean to intrude," Jack continued. "If you'd rather be alone, we could talk later."

"Talk later?" Karen said, puzzled. "About what? Have we met before?"

"No, but Bob mentioned you often. He was helping me with a project I'm working on. I was hoping you could clear up some things for me."

"I'm afraid I'm a little lost here," Karen said. "Bob never said anything about working with anyone. What is that you are doing, Mr. Hunter?"

"Would you like to get out of this rain? There's a small Café just a couple of blocks away."

~~~

Cafe Sole hadn't yet opened for lunch when they arrived. Jack knocked on the door and asked the person setting up if they could just get a cup of coffee and sit inside until the rain stopped. He explained that they'd come from a funeral at the cemetery.

"It was nice of him to let us in," Karen said, warming her hands with the coffee cup. "You must have some influence around here."

"Not so you'd notice it," Jack laughed. "Actually, they're good people."

"How long have you known Bob? You all were working together, you said?"

"Actually, we only met three times. He thought that I was producing a movie about the Ranzoa family. I wasn't being truthful. There was no movie."

Karen considered getting up from the table but curiosity had a stronger hold.

"So what *were* you doing?" she said coolly. "Planning to blackmail the family? That movie idea sounds like so much bullshit anyway. I'm surprised Bob went along with it."

"Please bear with me," Jack said. "There is a children's section in the cemetery we were just in. Oddly, a surprisingly large number of those children died within the same year. Reportedly all were treated or seen by the same doctor. Rather, doctors. Ardell and Armond Ranzoa. There are ugly rumors about them. I wanted to find out if they were true."

This time Karen did get up from the table.

"I think you're an awfully nervy man," she said angrily. "You believe Bob's family is somehow connected to these...these rumors? How dare you suggest such a thing? Especially now!"

"Please sit down, Mrs. Ranzoa," Jack urged. "I think your husband knew something, that's all. I don't mean to cause you any grief. And I don't blame you if you want to leave. But please, try to hear me out."

Karen relented and Jack continued to tell her everything he'd found so far, including about the physical attacks on him and the health department closing the restaurant.

"And you actually believe my father-in-law was behind all this crap? You must be out of your mind. You don't have one stick of proof."

"No, but I do have reasons to be suspicious. The attempted mugging of me. The planting of the dead mouse at our restaurant. A disturbance there that now threatens our liquor license. Has to be more than coincidental, don't you think? All of this since I started asking around about the doctors. I not saying any of what happened was your husband's idea. He didn't strike me as that kind of person. My impression of Bob was that he was a nice guy but his dad bullied the hell out of him. Maybe I'm out of line here in saying that and, again, I apologize if I've offended you."

Karen sat silently.

"Do you suppose they'd let us have a glass of wine?" she asked.

Jack got up from the table and walked into the kitchen. He returned with two glasses of Chablis.

"When I first met Bob, he was a funny and considerate man. Outgoing even. He always opened the door for me. Pulled out the chair for me when we sat at a table. He was a gentleman. Of course, that was when we first met and later on when we were alone. Around his father, he was a different person. Beaten down and always trying to please him."

"He once took me to the cleaners in a pool game," Jack laughed. "Didn't realize he was a shark."

"Could've gone pro," Karen smiled. "Bob suffered from depression. As long as he took his medication he was okay. I think his dad was embarrassed about it. He could be pretty cruel."

"What will you do now?" Jack asked.

"Robert wants me to move back here. He said I could stay with him. The firm owns the house Bob and I lived in. Robert will probably sell it, which is fine with me."

"So are you? Going to come back to Key West?"

"Not in a million years. I like Tallahassee and I like my job."

"Tell me about what you do. Would you like another glass of wine?"

Karen declined.

"I work for a congressman," she said. "Kind of like being an aide. I'm an information gatherer, I guess you could say."

"The military would call that intelligence," Jack smiled. "You must hear and see some interesting things."

"Yes," Karen agreed. "But most of it is ordinary, boring even. No big secrets ever unveiled. No real dirt on anyone. Nothing earth-shattering."

"So did you commute between Key West and Tallahassee? I imagine that could get pretty tiresome."

"Bob and I had it all worked out. We have an apartment up there. I'd spend most of the weekdays in the capitol and always be here for the weekends. Sometimes he'd come up there. His dad was very keen on my staying in good graces with the congressman."

"How's that?"

Karen laughed.

"You might do well to take my father-in-law seriously," she said. "He's a pretty powerful man."

"I'm a believer," Jack said.

"Okay, here's the deal between me and Robert. He considered my job to be an information source for him. Like I said, from time to time I hear things. Mostly it's gossip. You know how it is. Talk about rumors? You should sit at my desk. Anyway, sometimes I'd pass little things on to Robert. All harmless. I'd never tell him anything that I wasn't supposed to. But if I heard about some legislation that might affect Key West, I'd give Robert a heads up on its progress. That kind of thing happens all the time. Everybody does it."

Jack questioned the legality of that kind of thing. It was unethical at best. He kept quiet, though.

"I really don't like Robert," she said bitterly. "He was terrible to Bob. I think that's why Bob killed himself. I couldn't stand to even ride back in the car with him after the funeral. I'm going back to Tallahassee tonight. "

She put her hands to her face and cried softly.

CHAPTER 43

"Might need you as a witness, Jack, if the DA decides to take this thing to trial," Gleason said. "I doubt if it'll come to that."

The detective was on the phone with Jack, who'd stopped by Ashe Street to check on the work.

"Whatever," Jack replied. "So Dillas made bail?"

"Yeah, the judge slapped him with a hundred grand bail but the lawyer made it. I was wishing he could've remained a guest of the city but no joy."

"Who's his lawyer?"

"Some sleaze from Miami. They'll probably deal. Maybe stick his ass in county for a month. I'll take that."

"Don't suppose there was any chance of getting him to rat out on Ranzoa?" Jack asked hopefully.

"Fucking guy's the sphinx. Now there's no need for him to talk."

"Hey, I'm gonna stick around here for a while," Jack said. "They're about finished with the exterior. You want to grab a bite somewhere later? I'd like to talk to you about what we do next."

"Sure, I'll let you buy me dinner. As far as what we do next, I don't think there is any next."

Jack spent all afternoon at the house. The exterior work was indeed completed and looked better than new. Melody's crew had also reinforced the foundation structure and replaced the damaged flooring. Everything was on schedule and moving along smartly.

"Earl, Jack here. They're finished for the day. Michael's is right around the corner. Want to meet there?"

Gleason said that'd be fine and he was on his way. Jack rode his scooter over to Margaret Street and parked at the curb in front of the restaurant. Gleason pulled up a couple of doors down.

"Good timing," Jack said.

Both men walked into the restaurant and sat at the bar. The place had just opened and everyone was still getting ready for the night. Nancy was tending the bar.

"Think I'll just have a beer," Jack said.

Gleason nodded.

Nancy brought their beers and left them alone.

"I was talking with the Ranzoa widow," Jack said. "She thinks the old man drove his son to commit hari-kari."

"Good as any reason, I guess," Gleason said.

"The shitty thing is, there probably went our only chance to get anything on the doctors," Jack said. "I'm sure Bob Ranzoa knew more than he admitted. And I think it bothered him."

"He was fucked up the night he came into the restaurant, that's for sure," Gleason said. "The way he gulped down that wine."

"Yeah, but I wonder if it was only the booze or was it something else. Karen, that's his wife, said that he suffered from depression."

"Lot of that going around these days," Gleason said.

"What I meant was he could've been bi-polar," Jack explained. "Maybe he was on a super high. You know, manic. Thinking the alcohol would bring him down a little."

"That's bad thinking from what I've heard. Still, I'm not sure you'd ever have gotten anything from him. His old man had the lid screwed down tight on that poor bastard. You have a feeling that the widow might know where the skeletons are buried, just as a matter of speaking?"

"Could be but I don't think so," Jack said. "She hates the old man. If she knew anything that'd burn his ass, she wouldn't keep it to herself. At least that was my impression on the day of the funeral. But here's something you should know. She's been kind of a mole for Ranzoa with her job up in the capitol. Innocent stuff, she claims. Water cooler gossip. But remember those death certificates you got from Tallahassee? Five'll get you five that she heard about it and passed it on to Ranzoa. That's why the hammer fell. So maybe she also knows more than she wants to admit about the damn family."

They picked up a couple of bar menus.

"The crab cakes are good," Jack said.

~~~

It was nearly noon the next day and Jack stood at the Southernmost Point marker straining his eyes on the horizon, as if hoping to catch sight of Cuba ninety miles beyond. It was strange, he thought, this fascination of his with Cuba. He ought to go there someday. You could do that now.

He remembered – it wasn't all that long ago but yet in another lifetime – the day he'd spent on the beach at Fort

Zachary Taylor. His eyes on the horizon and thinking about Cuba.

He'd been facing a dilemma then, as he was facing another though completely different one now.

Then he was a fugitive wanted in a murder investigation. Now he was on the other side, involved in a quasi-investigation of what was more likely merely a rumor of murder. The question then, as it was now, was what to do next? And the answer now was fast turning out to be the same as he'd concluded back then. Give up.

The depths drew an ultra marine horizon across the Straits of Florida. And as he had on that earlier day, he fantasized a Cuban sitting on an opposite beach staring across the waters to Florida, lost in thoughts of his own.

He turned away and got on his scooter.

Mid-day traffic was light on Duval Street. Jack put-putted to the Vesuvius and stopped at the curb. Not much was going on in the restaurant. He parked the Vespa and went inside.

"Lunch for one?" a girl holding a menu asked hopefully.

"Just looking," Jack said and smiled. "But may I see the menu?"

He perused the listings. Standard fare.

"Okay if I look out back?" he asked, returning the menu. "I might have some people coming to town."

The girl translated that into meaning a large group.

"Oh, sure," she said. "The patio's really nice."

Jack went outside. He already knew it was nice. It was the nicest thing about the place. But he had doubts whether that was enough to make the restaurant worth buying. He and Billy had to have a serious sit-down together.

"Thanks," he said to the girl. "I'll call you if my friends show up."

Yes, he thought, returning to his scooter. Time for him to get back to business and forget about the children at the cemetery. He was just chasing his tail. Let Ranzoa go to hell – he'll soon be finished anyway. He felt rotten.

His cellphone rang.

"Jack," Billy said urgently. "We got a letter saying they gonna cancel our liquor license!"

"Hold on," Jack said. "They can't do that without a hearing. You at the restaurant? I'll be right there."

Billy was waiting on the sidewalk out front when Jack pulled up.

"Look at this," he said, waving the letter.

Jack took it from his hand and began reading.

"Like I said, Billy, it's a notice of a hearing. We get to tell our side of the story. I don't think there'll be any problem. In fact, I'll ask Gleason to vouch for us."

"Think we're gonna be okay, huh?" Billy said. "Well, that's good to hear. Hadn't thought about getting the detective to speak for us, hee-hee. You want some lunch, Jack? Got a fresh batch of spinach."

Jack was on his second cup of coffee when Billy approached the table.

"Forgot to tell you, Jack. A letter came here for you. I was so upset by the liquor license folks that it just slipped my mind."

He handed Jack the letter and stood waiting for him to open it. Instead, Jack put it in his pocket.

"Probably nothing important," he said. "Read it later."

Billy left the table, disappointed.

~~~

It was late afternoon and Jack was taking a stroll. He wound up at the Bight and headed over to the Galleon Tiki Bar. Steve was tending the bar.

"I saved her voicemail," he said as he pointed to his cellphone. "Anytime I get stupid and think about us getting back together, I just replay her last message."

The two couples at the bar laughed. Jack pulled out a stool and sat down.

"Bud?" Steve said.

Jack nodded and a cold can was immediately placed in front of him. He reached into his pocket for his cellphone and discovered the letter he'd put there. He removed it and began reading.

Hi, old friend,

Probably a big surprise hearing from me, huh? But surprises will just keep coming. So stay tuned.

Right now a nice surprise waits for you in Lake Worth. Go to 907 Cleveland Avenue, Apt. 4. Don't delay. You're expected. Bring a Key Lime pie.

Like I said, more surprises to come.

So long,

Bob Ranzoa

Jack folded the letter and stuck it back in his pocket. He slapped a tenner on the bar and left.

He wished he'd ridden his scooter instead of walking.

~~~

Jack sat at the bar in Vino's waiting for Gleason to show up. It was early evening and the place was already half-packed.

He'd hurried straight home from the Tiki and made a couple of calls. The first was to a car rental agency, where he reserved a car for the next day. The guy there said they only had a Mustang convertible available. Jack asked if it came with a GPS unit. Yes, it did. Next he called Gleason and got his voicemail. He left a message saying to meet him later at Vino's, adding that it was important. Then he called a nearby bakery to order a Key Lime Pie.

~~~

"This better be good," Gleason said. The detective walked in an hour after Jack had phoned.

"Sit down," Jack said back. "You're going to need to be sitting."

Jack handed him the letter.

"Guy really was out of his skull, huh?" Gleason commented. "Guess I should keep this as a suicide note. Pass it on to sheriffs."

"Don't you see what he's saying?" Jack asked. "He's talking about the children, goddammit. Somebody in Lake Worth, wherever the hell that is, has information."

Gleason gave him a funny look.

"What I read is a rambling letter from a man verging on killing himself," he said. "Key Lime pie? And bring it to a mysterious address? Here's the kicker. Waiting to give you a nice surprise? Better watch out for that one. For your information, Lake Worth is north of Miami."

"I can't believe this," Jack huffed. "You must be blind."

Gleason held up a finger to get the bartender's attention.

"Listen," Jack continued. "I think Bob Ranzoa was talking about the doctors. I've always thought he knew what happened to them, remember when I said that?"

"I remember you saying that he knew more than he was telling you," Gleason answered. "But that could've been about anything. Jack, you're hunting for straws. There is no reason to believe the doctors are alive and well in Lake Worth. Ranzoa flipped his lid and bellyflopped off the bridge. End of story."

Gleason picked up his glass of wine and sipped it.

"You could be right, Earl, but I'm going to check it out anyway. I've rented a car. Want to drive up with me tomorrow? It's a convertible."

Gleason solemnly shook his head.

"No can do. The lieutenant's all over me with this whole monkey business. Next somebody's going to play the bleeding heart card. 'Ranzoa's boy jumped off the fucking bridge. Left behind a grieving widow and a poor old dad.' People with much higher pay grades have already brought down heat on the department. The brass will eat my lunch if I start nosing around again. I'm sorry, man. Would if I could but I can't. I've got to butt out of this thing now."

Jack nodded slowly and clapped Gleason on his shoulder.

"Okay, I can appreciate your situation," he said. "But *I* can't let it go. Funny, earlier today I'd considered dropping the whole thing. Getting out of the detective business and back to minding my own business. Now that this letter has come the hunt's on again. I've got to follow the fox to the end."

"It would've been my act three," Gleason muttered under his breath.

"What was that?" Jack asked.

"I said be careful where you step."

CHAPTER 44

Daybreak came so quietly even the birds missed their cue. The whole island seemed to have taken on an ethereal quality. The moment was to be short-lived. Streets suddenly awoke with a clamor, whoops and whistles arose on the harbor, roosters got the birds up and soon Key West was welcoming the start of a new day with all of its heart.

Jack put the top down on the Mustang. He'd picked up the car the night before. Grabber blue with a black interior. It was both cool and hot. He had chosen to wear a pair of jeans and a subtle Hawaiian shirt for the trip. The drive to Miami should take about four hours, he'd figured. With luck he should be there around mid-morning. Then, if all went well, he'd be back in Key West for dinner. Two big ifs. Actually, he had no idea of what he was in for or how long it would take.

The car came with a dashboard-mounted GPS. How to work the thing was more or less intuitive, which was good because the guy at the rental agency had been clueless. Jack punched in the Lake Worth address. The little unit accepted the information and a directional arrow appeared on the map. He was in business.

He had to make one stop before leaving the island. Naturally, it was in the opposite direction from where he was going. The GPS immediately began to complain.

Fifteen minutes later he was back on course with a boxed key lime pie sitting on the passenger seat. US 1 lay ahead.

He'd forgotten to get a cup of coffee at the bakery for the drive. He spotted a convenience store and pulled into its lot. The coffee was self-served from a couple of pots. He filled a 12-ounce paper cup and paid the girl at the counter. She seemed to be still asleep or else on another planet. Must be the early hour, he thought.

With the sun to his right and the wind in his hair he motored up the Lower Keys. Cudjoe. Summerland. Big Pine. Ramrod. Little Torch. He crossed the bridges at Spanish Harbor and Bahia Honda. Up ahead stood the Seven Mile Bridge.

Traffic flowed along at a steady rate and, as the Mustang passed over the bridge's highest point, Jack couldn't help but give a sideways glance at the railing where Bob Ranzoa departed from the world.

He continued on US1 to the mainland and began picking up heavier traffic. The sun was becoming unbearable. He pulled into a gas station and put up the convertible top. He also took the opportunity to check on the key lime pie. Looked a little flushed. He turned the air conditioning on high.

US 1 can put you on the Florida Turnpike at Florida City. Or you can continue on it to Interstate 95 and take that north. Or just plain stay on US1. All three highways would eventually get you to Lake Worth. Jack opted for the US 1 scenic coastal route and soon joined the remnants of the morning rush hour in stop-and-go traffic through beautiful downtown Miami. He was falling behind his loose schedule so he cut over to the interstate. Traffic there was only somewhat better.

A sudden rain shower slowed everything to a creep. Then a fender-bender stopped it completely. Finally the cars began to move again and the rain fizzled out. Bright sun now commanded the clear blue sky while the GPS led the way to Lake Worth.

LAKE WORTH

Finding the address turned out to be a hassle even with the GPS. A couple of streets were closed for repairs and Jack had to detour several times. But he'd at last come to 907 Cleveland Avenue.

The apartment building looked 1970s. A quadrangular affair influenced by the Tiki school of architecture and featuring a swimming pool set in its paved center court. There was no security gate, which was surprising.

Jack gathered up the key lime pie and walked to the entrance, where he saw a row of mailboxes fixed on one wall. He examined them and found that apartment number 4 belonged to a Mr. and Mrs. Andrew Tabor.

The apartment was on the ground floor at the back of the building. He rang the bell.

"Yes, who is it?" a woman's voice inquired from behind the door.

"My name is Jack Hunter, ma'am."

A pause and then, "We aren't religious. You might as well leave."

"Bob Ranzoa said you were expecting me," Jack said. "I have your key lime pie."

"Just a minute."

Two lock-bolts rattled back and a chain-lock dropped and then the door cracked open to reveal an elderly woman's face, which reminded him immediately of Robert Ranzoa.

"Come in," she invited, opening the door wider.

"Thank you," he said and entered.

The door opened right into a small living room furnished with a rattan sofa and chairs that'd seen better days. Bookcases stood against one wall and a desk piled with papers occupied a space by the window.

"Have a seat," the woman said, while taking the pie box from Jack and peering inside. "My, this has been out of the refrigerator for some time. I'll have to put it in the freezer."

She left Jack standing there and went to a tiny kitchen. Jack sat in one of the rattan chairs. He looked around the room. There seemed to be only one bedroom. Its door was closed but he could hear a television station playing from inside.

"My name is Mrs. Ashley Tabor," the woman said, returning and taking a seat on the sofa. "How may I help you?"

Jack didn't answer immediately. Stunned by her resemblance to Robert, he was momentarily lost for words.

"I'm sorry," he finally said, "I didn't mean to be rude. It's just that you remind me of someone. You wouldn't have any relatives in Key West, would you?"

Mrs. Tabor smiled.

"The Ranzoas?" Jack offered.

"My name is Tabor."

"Well, you have a twin down there," Jack laughed.

"Interesting you should say that," Mrs. Tabor said. "Twins are a subject I've studied."

Jack sat up and took note.

"I do notice you have a lot of medical books," he said, pointing to the bookcase. "Did you study medicine?"

"One of my fascinations."

Laughter came from the bedroom.

"Andrew is watching television," Mrs. Tabor said. "I'll ask him to turn down the volume."

"Oh, no, don't get up," Jack said. "It doesn't bother me. You mentioned twins. My father was a twin."

Now it was Mrs. Tabor who leaned forward with interest.

"Are you a twin also?" she asked.

"No, I'm an only child."

"Brothers and sisters can be nice. You must have been lonely growing up."

"Not at all. I had lots of playmates. My uncle was close by, too."

Mrs. Tabor widened her eyes at this.

"Were they identical twins, your father and your uncle, or just fraternal?" she asked.

"You couldn't have told them apart," Jack smiled. "They used to share the girls they dated. Thought it was a big joke. Most times the girls really didn't know."

Mrs. Tabor got up and walked over to the desk and picked out a few sheets from a stack of paper.

"There have been many studies on the subject of twins," she said, returning to the sofa and sitting. "People think identical twins are clones but they're not. The correct term for identical twinning is monozygotic. The fertilized egg splits into two parts after conception. Dizygotic twins, those are fraternal, result from two eggs fertilized by two separate sperm from the same man. With me so far?"

"Yes," Jack said, "but what's the point?"

"Ah, that's the rub," she said gleefully. "Then there's a third option. Semi-identical twins. Sound interesting? *I* think so."

Jack was beginning to feel uneasy. He couldn't figure out where all this was heading. Mrs. Tabor continued.

"Semi-identical twins," she repeated. "Both twins have identical DNA from the mother, since they shared the same egg, but not from the father. That DNA came from two sperm from two *different* men. Not everyone believes that this is possible but it is.

"I don't understand how that could happen," Jack said.

"Don't you? Think about it. How could the mother have had different sperm fertilize her egg? Let's see, did the father have two penises? Not likely. Well, then the answer must be there were two different fathers."

Mrs. Tabor sat back in her seat and smiled at Jack.

"Still not getting it, huh?" she said. "Okay, what happens is the mother conceives with one sperm. Then, almost immediately, another sperm from a different donor is introduced. That one also fertilizes the egg. Egg divides. Two little souls. Amazing but true."

"I guess that's possible," Jack said. "Maybe in an orgy or something. Still, sounds pretty farfetched."

"Possibilities always abound in science," Mrs. Tabor explained. "In one case, one of the twins is normal. The other has sexually ambiguous genitalia. A little bit of both, in other words."

Jack could only look at her.

"Nobody wants to talk about what it means to that ambiguous individual," she added, suddenly angry. "Which means nobody can help you understand yourself. Can you imagine how painful that can be? Having to live a life hiding a part of who you are? Feeling ashamed of your existence? The embarrassment you've caused?"

"I imagine the family would talk about it," Jack said. "They'd understand and be supportive."

"Understand? Supportive?" Mrs. Tabor scoffed. "Of what? They would consider it an unfair burden on them. Having a freak in the family. The exception of course would be the other twin. Twins often share a special bond. I believe they can actually feel the other's pain. And children in large are very accepting of differences. Up to the point when they begin to grow older. Then they become cruel."

Jack suddenly realized they'd crossed from the hypothetical to this woman's painful reality. More muffled laughter came from the bedroom. Cartoon voices.

"I'm going to take Andrew some key lime pie," she announced.

Mrs. Tabor got up from the sofa and went to the kitchen.

"This is his favorite," she said, slicing a narrow wedge and placing it in a bowl. "This will only take a minute."

Mrs. Tabor tapped lightly on the bedroom door and then entered the room. Jack got up to take a look for himself. He saw a man sitting in a chair watching television. Jack stared. He looked exactly like Robert Ranzoa.

The man smiled and Mrs. Tabor patted him on the shoulder before giving him the bowl. He greedily ate the pie and she took back the bowl and returned to the living room leaving Andrew watching the cartoon channel.

"How long has he been like that?" Jack asked, sparring for time. The realization of who he was facing blew full-blown into his mind.

"The dementia began nearly ten years ago. Slowly at first. But then progressive. Now he's pretty much confined to the house."

"Is it Alzheimer's?"

"Yes, our personal physician diagnosed it. Are you surprised that doctors see doctors? We all have our illnesses."

"You and Andrew are actually Ardell and Armand Ranzoa," Jack said, almost in disbelief that suddenly he was sitting across from one of the quarry he'd been searching for for so long.

"I think Ashley and Andrew are prettier names, don't you? Tabor was our mother's maiden name. We decided to take that after we moved. The first names belonged to long-dead relatives on her side."

Jack was still in shock from his initial encounter with her brother.

"Robert and Andrew could almost have been taken for twins," Mrs. Tabor explained, noticing Jack's expression. "Their resemblance to one another is striking. But that's not as rare as you might think. Family members often share physical characteristics. They certainly did in ours. Strong genes."

"So the three of you are brothers and sisters?" he said.

"Andrew and I are semi-identical twins. Robert would be one of our half-brothers."

"I don't understand."

"As I explained earlier, we're identical on our mother's side but share only half of our genes on our father's side. Remember, two daddies? Robert's father was also one of ours. He and our mother apparently had an affair. Amazingly, we were all conceived within...well, minutes between the initial conception or at least in a very short time period. Claude and Victoria were the parents who raised, however."

"What happened that caused you both to end up here?"

"That's such a long story. Are you sure you want to hear it?"

Jack nodded.

"Well, now you know how we came to be who we are," she began, "you might as well know the rest. Our childhood was actually quite nice during the early years. I was more of a tomboy. My brother was less outgoing, a gentle little boy. That changed with school. Having a hermaphrodite for a sister wasn't easy for him. My little brother became my defender. Even after we left for private school. Notes were constantly being sent home about his fighting classmates. Which was hard for him because of his gentle nature, but he did it to stand up for me."

"You both went on to become doctors," Jack stated.

"Yes, and we returned to Key West to join our father's practice."

"You treated children," Jack said. "But an extraordinarily large number seemed to have died under your care."

"What an awful thing to say! What are you suggesting? Bobby told me that you were an impertinent man. Perhaps I shouldn't have agreed to see you but he was most insistent that it was time that someone hear our story. I do have to say I was surprised when he showed up at our door. However, he was family after all. So anyway here you are and we'll just get on with it, shall we?"

Jack looked her in the eye.

"I am here for those children buried in the Key West Cemetery, Dr. Ranzoa. I want to know what really happened to them. Bobby told me that I would find the answer here. You still haven't answered my question. Why you and your brother were forced to leave a place where your relatives had lived for generations?"

"Certain family conditions made it impossible for us to continue our practice there. It was agreed by all that we should leave. We went to Miami. To a lovely place in Coconut Grove. Later we moved here to Lake Worth. It's a nice little community."

"Do you and your brother still practice medicine? Rather do you still practice?"

She shifted uncomfortably.

"No, we gave that up when we left Key West. That was part of – how should I say – the agreement? We saw no patients, neither my brother nor myself. However I still have my medical license, although I haven't met with the Board of Exams for years. But I do keep abreast of my field so I don't believe there would be any question about my competency."

This last remark came with a gesture at the bookcase followed by a proud smile.

Jack wondered if she knew about Bob Ranzoa. Would the incident have been carried here on the news? Was the television set ever tuned to anything other than cartoons?

"Your nephew, Bob Ranzoa, is dead," he stated as a matter of fact. "He committed suicide."

She tilted her head slightly, a puzzled expression on her face.

"Why, that can't be. He was just here. He didn't appear suicidal. Are you sure?"

"He jumped off a bridge, Doctor."

Her expression turned to nonplused. She remained silent.

"I think I'll make a cup of tea," she said abruptly.

Jack remained seated while she busied herself in the kitchen.

"Now where were we?" she asked, returning with a single cup for herself.

"I was talking about your nephew, Bob Ranzoa," Jack said.

"Oh, yes, as I said, he dropped in unexpectedly. One would have thought he would've shown better manners."

"The two of you had never met before?"

"We didn't keep in touch with the family once Andrew and I had left."

"How did he know who you were, then? And where to find you?"

"I thought it odd, too," she laughed. "But then he explained how he had come across our address at his work. He's also a lawyer with his father, as you probably know. While we were no longer close to Robert, there were communications regarding the financial terms of the agreement. After all, if Andrew and I were no longer practicing, then we had to have some form of income. Robert's side of the family was more than able to afford that."

Jack leaned forward.

"Those conditions you mentioned," he said, "the ones responsible for your having to leave Key West. Did you and Bob talk about them?"

"Bob seemed very eager to know. Said it was time that the truth be told. I thought that was funny. Actually, he already knew quite a bit. Children aren't as innocent as we like to believe. They hear more than we think. Apparently, Andrew and myself were frequent subjects between Robert and his wife."

"And what is the truth, Doctor? And by the way, can we skip the charade? You *are* Ardell and Armand Ranzoa, are you not?"

She bridled at the remark, paused, then finally agreed.

"The truth? Something that my nephew obviously couldn't handle. Can you, Mr. Hunter?"

Jack took in this woman seated before him. How inhumanly cold she must be. And how ironic that it was only Bob Ranzoa who felt the guilt of this family, suffered a culpability so reprehensible that it drove him to end his life.

"Yes, Doctor, I can handle whatever you wish to say."

"Robert will soon be the last of the Ranzoas," she began. "I have Stage 4 cancer. The prognoses is not favorable. I have painkillers so I'm comfortable, but I shouldn't be long. You've seen my brother. He could go at any time. Sooner than later, I imagine. So there's really no reason for us to pretend any longer, is there? That was Bobby's contention."

Jack's mind numbed at his next thoughts. They would escape any justice that might have been served. He had learned the truth too late. And who would believe him by himself? He wished Gleason had been able to come. Finally, what of the children? Had he now failed them? No, his resolve to continue to advocate on their fate had only hardened. Somehow he would find a way.

"These children you are so concerned with," the doctor continued off-handedly. "My brother could better answer your questions. Why don't you go ask him?"

She gave a cruel laugh.

"Forgive my joke," she said. "Of course you can't talk to him so I'll talk for him. My brother is an interesting study. He had a psychopathic personality and was obsessed with death. Absolutely terrified of his own mortality yet fascinated with the clinical aspect of dying. It never left his mind. Now his mind has left him."

Another heartless little chuckle.

"And there was another reason, perhaps the stronger one. My beloved brother told me many years later that he hated normal children because they would never have to suffer the misery of abuse that I've endured, that they might even grow up inflicting the same sort of abuse on other unfortunates like me."

The woman paused. A proud look came over her face.

"You see, he loved me. He took revenge on those little darlings for me."

Jack shuddered and drew in his breath. Silence lay heavy on the room. He couldn't believe she was finally going to admit to what they'd done. He asked, "How and when did you become aware of what was going on?"

"It wasn't until after the third child who had been brought to us suddenly died of a heart attack that I began to suspect something was wrong," she said. "I noticed a bottle of succinylcholine was missing. That's a muscle relaxant. I'd recently ordered it so it should have been there. We didn't use the drug that often. Then a new bottle appeared."

"Did you confront your brother about it?" Jack asked.

"Not then. After all, he was my brother. But another child we were treating for pneumonia suffered a spontaneous hemorrhaging. I couldn't save her. But I discovered a small mark on her. Later I found that a vial of heparin was gone. Heparin is an anticoagulant. We saw our patients together. That way we could compare diagnoses."

"Surely you could have said something to him then?" Jack insisted.

"The rumors had already done their harm. The agreement was that we leave and not return."

"Then what about your oath?" Jack asked bitterly. "'Do no harm.' Isn't that the Hippocratic oath? How do you square with that?"

"In my brother's mind, he was doing no harm. To him he was merely standing up for me, as he'd always done.

Correcting the massive wrong that had been done to his beloved sister."

Jack let out a long breath. He looked up at the ceiling, then returned his attention to Ardell. This amoral fraud of a doctor. Willing to overlook the willful murder of a child to protect her homicidal brother. He thought of all of those little graves in the Key West cemetery. He couldn't even remember how many now.

The room seemed to close in. The air had grown stale, as if he were in the bottom of a fathomless pit. He felt something deep within him under threat. His very soul, his own sanity in danger by attempting to comprehend the enormity of the unspeakable acts committed by these two people and their apparent lack of remorse.

There was nothing more for him here. He needed to get away, out into some clean, clear air. But first he had a final question. He stood.

"Why did you never tell someone, Doctor?"

"Because no one ever asked me."

Thank you for reading.
Please review this book. Reviews help others find
Absolutely Amazing eBooks and inspire us to keep
providing these marvelous tales.

If you would like to be put on our email list to receive
updates on new releases, contests, and promotions, please
go to AbsolutelyAmazingEbooks.com and sign up.

About the Author

Robert Coburn is originally from Norfolk, Virginia. After high school in Norfolk, he spent three years in the US Army as a helicopter crew chief stationed in Berlin, Germany. He returned home to attend college at Richmond Professional Institute (Now VCU) in Richmond, Virginia, where he earned a Bachelor of Science degree in Advertising. He also met his wife in Richmond while a student there.

Coburn has worked at major advertising agencies in New York and Los Angeles. His ads have won top awards both nationally and internationally. He is an instrument rated commercial pilot and plays saxophone. He and his wife now live in Carmel, California.

The New
Atlantian Library

NewAtlantianLibrary.com
or AbsolutelyAmazingEbooks.com
or AA-eBooks.com

www.ingramcontent.com/pod-product-compliance
Lightning Source LLC
Chambersburg PA
CBHW060947030726
47503CB00003B/771